No Substitute for Maturity

Carolyn J. Rose

No Substitute for Maturity

Carolyn J. Rose

2014

Thanks to my long-suffering husband.
This book wouldn't exist without his patience and support.

Chapter 1

Baggage.

It's not just for vacations or business trips.

We lug it with us every day.

I'm talking about emotional and psychological cargo like attitudes, opinions, expectations, preconceptions, preferences, and prejudices.

You may not realize you're carrying a backpack loaded with beliefs or a tote bag crammed with foregone conclusions, until your baggage collides with that of another.

And mine was slamming into Dave Martin's as he moved into the condo now known as "ours."

Dave, despite being a trained investigator, apparently had yet to notice the impact, or consider the effect on our relationship

So, on the morning of Memorial Day, he came through the door whistling as he lugged another bloated cardboard box to contribute to the merger of our households. Even from my position—bent over the dishwasher loading the far-less-than-clean bowls and mugs he'd jammed into the previous box—I spotted a crusty sock and the mud-caked leg of a pair of sweatpants.

"Don't even think about taking that upstairs," I said in a voice tight as piano wire.

"It's my running gear, Barb. I'll stick it in the bedroom closet."

Dave shot me a smile and cruised toward the staircase. (For the record, Dave's smile is part six-year-old boy with a hand in the cookie jar and part wise-to-the-world police officer. On an average day it would turn my insides to mush. This, as you probably gathered, was no average day.)

I hit him with a withering, laser-like glare, one I honed daily as a substitute teacher. "Dirty clothes don't go in the closet."

He halted with a foot on the first step, lowered his head, and sniffed. Apparently grime, slime, and dried sweat didn't exist unless accompanied by an odor pungent enough to attract a male musk ox. "I guess it wouldn't hurt to run some of this through the wash."

Wouldn't hurt?

He turned and headed across the combined living-dining room. "I'll dump it the corner and get to it later."

I waved a coffee-stained mug with the Reckless River logo—a traffic jam on the bridge across the Columbia River—and a bowl splotched with dried oatmeal. "Is 'later' the same time you intended to wash the dishes in the last box?"

"Whoa." He ducked and executed a sideways jig. "Allison's job. I told you."

"Yes, you did, but—correct me if I'm wrong—aren't you Allison's father? Aren't you the man in charge of seeing that she washed these dishes before you stuck them in the box?"

Dave adopted the wary look of game-show contestant who suspects any answer he comes up with will result in a penalty. "Um . . . I'm sorry?"

I slipped the oatmeal bowl into the sink to soak in hot water and rubbed the small of my back. We both were well aware that Allison was an unguided missile carrying a megaton payload of teenage angst and drama. "Put the clothes in the washer. Set the shoes on the deck to air out."

As if there was enough air in all of Southwest Washington to do that.

"Okay. I gotta tape up the toes anyway." Dave dropped the box by the washer. "We knew living together would be rough at the beginning, but once Allison and I get all moved in and we put a few systems in place, it'll work."

Ah. He *had* noticed the impact.

"Come here and give me a hug." He turned and opened his arms, revealing a reddish brown stain on the front of his sweatshirt.

My breath caught in my throat. "Is that blood?"

"Huh?" He glanced at the shirt, then yanked down the collar and peeked inside. "No stab wounds." He released the collar. "At least not recent ones."

He laughed.

I didn't.

Dave's occupation—drug cop—put him in regular contact with people who bend, break, and trash the laws of Reckless River and the state of Washington, not to mention federal rules and regulations. These same people seldom comply peacefully when Dave orders them to put down their weapons and raise their hands. So, even though Dave is a plan-ahead kind of guy who brings a gun to a knife fight, light-hearted remarks about stab wounds don't leave me convulsed in laughter.

He opened his arms again. "Come on, how about that hug?"

I put the door of the dishwasher between us. "Not while you're wearing that revolting sweatshirt."

"Good point." He yanked the shirt off over his head and used it to wipe sweat and more of the brownish substance from his chest.

(For the record, Dave has a great chest—not so layered with muscle that it's like steel, but not too soft, either.)

"Want to take a little break and show me how much you love me? And vice versa?"

Under other conditions, the answer to that would have been not only "Yes," but "Hell yes." But my brain was occupied with the source of that stain. "If it's not blood, then what *is* it?"

He sniffed at the sweatshirt. "Barbecue sauce?"

"You don't know?"

He shrugged and sniffed the shirt again. "Could be salad dressing or teriyaki sauce. Maybe a lid came off, or a bottle broke. Seems like the box was soggy when I picked it up."

Gritting my teeth, I did a mental three-count. "Where's the box now?"

"In my car."

"Please tell me it's in the trunk."

That losing game-show contestant expression reappeared. "Back seat."

I groaned.

"Or maybe the front."

See what I mean about baggage? Mine contained standards for sanitation, as well as the notion that anyone with an ounce of common sense wouldn't pick up a soggy box in the first place, let alone put it on a car seat. Dave wasn't burdened with those concepts.

I wasn't about to let go of this particular piece of baggage, but for the sake of getting on with the move, I swallowed the lecture and went with stress relief instead. Emitting a series of shrieking laughs, I pounded the counter with my fists.

"What?" Dave opened the washer and tossed in the sweatshirt. "What's so funny?"

"Nothing," I gasped, meaning exactly that. I found no amusement value in a puddle of who-knows-what on a seat where I might place my backside. Men and women weren't from different planets; they were from different galaxies. At least this particular man and woman were.

"I'll never understand women." Dave grabbed a dripping sponge from the sink, swabbed the smear on his bare chest,

4

then tossed the sponge on the counter where it landed with a squishy plop. "Now how about that hug?"

"How about you take your mind off sex?" a voice boomed from the hallway. "And put your clothes on!"

Chapter 2

I knew that voice well. I heard it for the first time mere hours after birth when my mother placed me in the arms of my sister. In those days she was known as Jeannine Reed. But woe betide the person foolish enough to call her that since she became a feminist force and named herself Indigo Zephyr. Iz for short.

Dave curled his fists, brought them up against his shoulders, and flexed his muscles. "I'll put a shirt on *after* you admit you're wild about my pecs."

Iz snorted. "I'm as wild about your pecs as I am about racism or sexism or small-minded political—"

"Got it." Dave plucked a crumpled T-shirt from the box of running gear, then hustled to help her wrestle a box spring along the hallway and up the stairs to Allison's new bedroom. Penelope, Iz's romantic interest, followed, bearing pieces of the metal bed frame, a hammer, and a pair of pliers. She shot me a smile and a wink as she passed.

While Iz was what you'd call robust—if you put a positive spin on it—Penelope was slender. While Iz owned her space and got in your face, Penelope tended to stand at the outer rim of a conversational circle and speak in a quiet tone. While Iz's wardrobe ran to cargo pants and T-shirts with inflammatory anti-male, anti-establishment messages, Penelope, when not on the job, wore colorful silky blouses and slacks with crisp creases. While Iz made her mark in the world by writing and lecturing about interpretations of the feminine in myth, mainstream, and marketplace, Penelope worked as an electrician and volunteered for a charitable home-building project in her spare time. Despite their differences, they'd been a couple since March when they joined the throng to rescue my dog from a drug dealer.

Penelope paused on the stairs. "Where's Cheese Puff?"

"Next door with Mrs. Ballantine. Lola's there too."

Lola, a drug-sniffing Golden Retriever, is a member of the Reckless River Police Department and Dave's partner. Cheese Puff, a ten-pound orange mutt I found shivering in the rain a year ago, is the darling of the older residents of my condo complex. In spite of his less attractive characteristics—he's stubborn, picky about his food, and prone to shed on their best outfits—they adore him. To see that he was walked and entertained while I subbed and took graduate classes, Muriel Ballantine formed the Cheese Puff Care and Comfort Committee. As a result, Cheese Puff led a far more interesting life than I did.

"Are they all watching *The Godfather*?" Penelope asked with a grin.

That's Mrs. B's favorite movie. Her late husband was reputed to have been an accountant for the mob, but Dave claimed Marco Ballantine manufactured that rumor to appear dangerous and more fascinating. The aura of danger gave him an edge over others courting her in the days when she reigned as queen of Las Vegas showgirls. If Mrs. B knew it was a myth, she never let on. And I never asked.

"She's blocking out a dance routine for the TV show," I told Penelope. The show in question being *Still Got That Strut*, a reality-style program featuring former showgirls.

"Oh." Penelope got a better grip on the frame and tossed her head to clear aside blond hair falling across one eye. "Gonna have to get hair clips. Or give up on the dream of a long do. Did they set a date for taping the show?"

"Not yet, probably at the end of summer. She's been working with a personal trainer since she signed the contract. And she hired a band to write a signature song."

"Hired a band? A whole band?"

Not that Mrs. B couldn't afford to do that. Or almost anything else. Marco started with a pot of inherited money and investments earned him a ton more. "The band consists of Josh and four of his buddies—all high school students. She probably pays them in pizza, gas money, and new guitar strings."

Penelope smiled. "Sounds like she wants to outshine the other competitors."

"Well, legend has it she did back in the day." When she appeared on *Still Got That Strut* she wanted to flow across the stage without a hitch or hesitation, even wearing four-inch heels, a feathered headdress, and sixty plus years.

"I hope they let her bring an entourage for the taping. Iz and I—"

"Can't set this bed up until we have the frame," Iz bellowed.

Penelope got a better grip on her load and headed up. "Duty calls."

"And in a voice that could shatter glass," I muttered when she'd climbed out of earshot. What Iz saw in Penelope was obvious, but what attracted Penelope to my sister remained a mystery to me.

Dave thudded down the steps. "Going for the mattress."

"Don't forget to put the new bed skirt on over the box spring."

"Bed skirt?" He said the words as if they were in a foreign language.

"That ruffled thing that hides the box spring and the frame. It came with the comforter and sheets we bought."

"Oh. Right." He rubbed his knuckles against the stubble on his chin. "Where *are* those sheets?"

We had a deal. He and Allison would pack up their apartment and I would cull and sort and make room for what they hauled over. Most of that belonged to Allison. A teenage girl "had to have" enough stuff to fill the average industrial warehouse. Even with Dave vetoing 90% of her demands, Allison had a massive collection of clothes, shoes, and accessories for her room, including that new set of dazzling blue sheets and a comforter featuring a flock of flamingos in a lagoon.

The birds glowed like neon pink bubblegum; the lagoon resembled a toxic spill. Allison had announced plans to paint her room to match but, wise to the fleeting nature of her whims, Dave and I had yet to pick up paint samples.

When she emerged from a Goth phase last fall, Allison went to opposite extremes. Eventually—or so I hoped—she'd settle somewhere in the middle. And even if she chose a hideous color for the walls, posters would obscure it. And mounds of clothing would soon hide the comforter.

Meanwhile, the issue of where that comforter and sheets were at the moment came under the heading of "Not My Problem." I smiled and spoke in a sugary voice. "I imagine the bedding is where you put it."

"In a box in the stacks in the office." His tone implied that saying this might make it true.

"Did you label the box?" I bet myself a buck the answer would be "No."

"Uh, maybe."

Meaning he hadn't. I put an imaginary dollar into a kitty growing exponentially. "Guess you'll have to open boxes until you find the sheets. Or leave that job for Allison."

His expression brightened. "They *are* her sheets. And she weaseled out of helping today because of the emergency rehearsal."

Allison had landed role in the Captain Meriwether High School production of *The Importance of Being Earnest*. I suspected the practice session today had less to do with last-

9

minute preparations than with her attempts to "improve" on her lines, embellish her gestures, and remodel her costume.

While begging Dave to make every effort to rein her in, drama teacher Clive Mason confided that he put up with her antics only because her understudy had proven to be more of a disaster. To his credit, Dave exhibited great patience when he explained the time period of the play, the language of the day, the manner of dress of that age, and the function of a director who saw the big picture while some actors tended to focus only on their parts or themselves. Allison, of course, denied she was one of those self-centered players.

"Let *her* find the sheets." Dave wiped his hands on his jeans. "She can make up the bed when she gets home."

"It's your call. But practice is likely to run late, tomorrow's a school day, and she has math homework she hasn't started."

"Math? You're sure it's math?" Dave asked in a hopeful voice.

I nodded. I handled helping with research and checking assignments for English and history; he got science and math. My skills with numbers maxed out at balancing my checkbook to within ten dollars and computing gas mileage for the rolling collection of low-budget replacement parts and stopgap repairs I referred to as a car. "Math. Definitely math."

"Crud."

"And we have to assemble something for dinner."

He brightened. "No problem. I'll order pizza."

Normally I would have seconded that motion but, as evidenced by the snug fit of my jeans, we'd scarfed pizza far too often lately. And, although I knew I could count on her to devour at least four slices, before she stuffed them down her gullet, Iz would complain that so much fat, salt, cheese, and white flour wasn't healthy. Listening to Iz carping didn't rank as the ideal way to end *any* day. "We're feeding Iz and Penelope, so no pizza."

"Not even with salad on the side?"

"Not even."

"Chinese?"

Iz would find fault with that as well. But then, Iz always found fault. "Maybe. If you order dishes with lots of vegetables. See what they want."

Dave recoiled as if I'd asked him to saw off his own arm without benefit of anesthetic. I didn't blame him. Even a simple question could open the floodgates for a multi-topic lecture from Iz. "Get Penelope alone and see what she thinks."

He trudged off to unload the mattress from Penelope's truck and then search for the sheets. To the sound of a hammer striking metal up in Allison's room, I fished another bowl crusted with dried milk and sugary cereal from a box and slipped it into the sink.

Logically, this was far from the most opportune time for Dave, Allison, and Lola to move in. Exhausted from finishing up my graduate work and subbing every day, I was also anxious about the state of my finances and about finding a summer job and interviewing for positions for the coming school year. The possibility that there might not *be* any positions compounded that anxiety.

Tossing a chipped mug into the trash, I told myself that logic had seldom played a huge part in my decision-making processes, but I was still standing. Well, okay, I wobbled a lot, but I was on my feet. When we had unpacked, sorted, and stowed everything, order would emerge. Then anxiety would diminish.

Or not.

"Did someone call for Paulette to the rescue?" a voice trilled.

My hyper little heart pounded with joy. "No, but I should have."

"Never fear, I am here." An enormous basket in each hand, Paulette staggered along the hallway. "Wine, cheese, ham, bread, crackers, salads—all on ice so you don't have to find

11

room in the fridge—and enough cookies and tarts and chocolate-cashew brownies to make my fat cells cry out in ecstasy."

As if. Paulette's fat cells seldom cry out for anything but mercy. She's the poster girl for looking fabulous at 50. Thanks to her, I was hooked on water aerobics and knew feng shui wasn't a type of mushroom. And thanks to her, Iz met Penelope and got hooked on volunteering for Paulette's pet project, building homes for abused women starting new lives.

"Let me clear the table." I jammed another mug in the dishwasher and hustled to scrape sandwich wrappers and soda cans left from lunch into a trash bag, wiping at smudges with used napkins as I went. Paulette, with her immaculate makeup, casually impeccable hairstyle, and flawless manicure, would never allow her house to look like mine, even if an entire battalion bivouacked in the living room. In spite of that, she took me as I was, and we'd become friends.

"That's clean enough." She hoisted the baskets to the table. "Now tell me what needs to be done."

The floor shook and Dave swore. "Lost my grip on the damn mattress. Messed up the bulletin board."

"You better help him," Paulette counseled.

"Okay. Can you find Allison's new sheets and her flamingo comforter and bed skirt? They're somewhere in the office—or so we hope. Dave isn't big on the concept of labeling."

The way my luck ran, I would have discovered the bedding in the last boxes in the bottom row. But Paulette got it on the first try. By the time Dave and I staggered into Allison's room with the mattress bent like a taco shell between us, she came right behind with the bed skirt and a mattress pad. "I'll bring the sheets and comforter while you put these on," she instructed.

Iz scowled—she hated anyone else giving orders—but Penelope shook out the blazing pink bed skirt and smoothed it. "This will brighten the room."

"Like a nuclear blast," Dave muttered as we set the mattress in place and stepped aside to let Penelope fit the elastic corners of the pad.

Paulette returned with the sheets, a puffy comforter, and a frown. "I think the bed should go slantwise. In the corner."

"The corner?" Iz shook her head. "That's—"

"Interesting." Penelope slid the bed at an angle. "It opens up more space in the center."

"There's a little triangular table in the office," Paulette said, "that will fit behind it."

"And the lamp from Barb's desk will be exactly right," Penelope said.

Paulette patted my shoulder and went to work with the sheets. "The lamp is all wrong for that room and you need better light on your desk anyway."

"I knew that," Dave muttered.

"I'll get the table." Iz headed for the stairs mumbling comments about interior decorating I can't repeat in a book designed for the family audience.

I went for the lamp, determined to put my opinions aside and allow Paulette to do her thing. The only danger in letting her rearrange was that she'd run afoul of Mrs. Ballantine who had placed the living room furniture when I moved in after Christmas. If Mrs. B had a proprietary interest in seeing things stay as they were, it would be less stressful to watch two tornadoes collide. Two very polite tornadoes. Tornadoes using question marks like rapiers.

For the next hour I kept my head down—after making it clear to Paulette that my cabinet and drawer arrangements were "only temporary," in case fault was to be found. I cleaned and put away kitchen-related items that came to light as she and Penelope dug through boxes in the office. After that I washed, folded, or hung up articles of clothing they tossed at me. Dave unloaded his car with Iz supervising and occasionally lending a hand. When the offending soggy box and its contents

13

CAROLYN J. ROSE

landed in a trash bin, and Dave had done something to the seat involving an entire roll of paper towels and two different spray cleaners, they took Penelope's truck for the last load. Later they broke apart cardboard boxes, scooped up a welter of newspaper packing, and carted the whole mess to the recycling bin. That gave them room in the office to stack things that had no "official" placements elsewhere in the condo.

Penelope and Paulette moved on to the living area where Penelope leveled a painting in the dining room while Paulette, with an expression of dissatisfaction, contemplated Cheese Puff's favorite chair. Before I could utter "That's off limits," her phone rang.

Her eyes widened and her fingers tightened on the jeweled turquoise cover as she listened to the caller, then, mouth crimped into a tight line and eyes blazing, she disconnected. "Someone threw a firebomb into one of our project houses."

14

Chapter 3

"A firebomb?" Penelope gripped the metal level like a baseball bat. "Which house?"

"The one we just finished. Denise Ryder's."

"The woman with the twin girls?" Iz thundered from the office. "The one I built the raised garden beds for?"

"Did they get out?" Penelope asked.

"The kids are fine. But Denise has burns on her legs." Paulette's eyes filled with tears and her voice quavered. "She ran back in. She tried to save the house."

Penelope and I wrapped our arms around Paulette and I stroked her feathery bronze hair and whispered words I wasn't at all sure of—that Denise would be okay.

Iz kicked an empty box against the wall and leveled a finger at Dave. "Ex-husband. I bet you a hundred dollars."

"No bet," he said. "He's my first choice."

"He got away with beating her," Iz said. "Will he get away with this?"

"Not if there's proof."

"And a prosecutor who gives a damn about crime against women." Iz's tone implied she doubted such a person existed. In her defense, she could cite plenty of cases where prosecution fell short. But, extremist to the core, she never mentioned cases where zealous prosecutors pushed for conviction.

"I'll see what we can salvage and when we can start repairs." Penelope broke from the group hug and headed for the door. Iz fell in behind.

"I'll go with you," Paulette said. "It's not just the house. That poor woman needs our support. And we need to show everyone that she's not alone, so this doesn't get swept under the rug."

"You should go along," I told Dave. "You'll know the guys on the scene and you can get the whole story." I lowered my voice. "And see that Iz doesn't punch someone out."

"Right." Dave jogged to catch up with the women. "Hold on. I'll drive."

"Your car has toxic spill residue on the seat," I yelled.

He waved a hand in acknowledgement and trotted off, leaving me alone with a dishwasher to unload, clothes to fold, and a teenage drama queen due to make an entrance and launch homework avoidance maneuvers.

On the plus side, I had two picnic baskets filled with goodies.

An hour later, having finished wiping the kitchen counters and sweeping up shreds of newspaper in the hall, I was salivating over a colossal cashew-laden brownie when I heard footsteps on the deck.

Muriel Ballantine appeared with Cheese Puff and Lola in a swirl of orange and blond dog hair and wagging tails. She pointed to the brownie. "Having dessert first?"

"I deserve it." I took a huge bite. The rich taste of dark chocolate unfurled in my mouth. An involuntary moan issued from low in my throat.

Cheese Puff circled at my feet, hoping I'd drop a few crumbs. Lola, far less driven by the urge to snack, sniffed her way around the living area. Mrs. B pushed up the sleeves of her apricot linen blouse, brushed a puff of silvery hair from her forehead, and cataloged the contents of the baskets. "Sliced

Swiss and cheddar, blue cheese spread, cherry tomatoes, two kinds of olives, sliced onions, salads, bread, four kinds of crackers, ham, and pepper-crusted salami. And the tarts and brownies look scrumptious. Whoever brought those is a true friend."

"Paulette brought them. Heck, she probably *made* them." While standing on one foot mastering a yoga position and carrying on a conference call. Her husband flew for a commercial airline and Paulette packed the many hours he was away with her job for a marketing and research firm as well as a range of activities and projects. If you looked up "perpetual motion" in the dictionary, you might see her picture.

Mrs. B tipped her head toward the staircase. "Where is she? Where is everyone?"

Guilt made the brownie taste like dust—old dust. Here I was, enjoying a treat, while Denise Ryder suffered. I swallowed and set the remainder on a napkin. "Someone firebombed one of the houses their group built."

Flashing rings with enough diamonds to pay off my mortgage, Mrs. B brought her hands to her cheeks. "How awful. Was anyone hurt?"

"A woman named Denise Ryder. She pulled her kids clear, but burned her legs trying to put out the fire."

"How bad?"

"I don't know." I glanced at the clock. "They should be back soon."

"That poor woman. She'll need a place to stay when she gets out of the hospital. And help with the children." Mrs. B headed for the door. "And a fund for what insurance won't cover. I'll get my purse."

Have I mentioned that Mrs. B is loaded?

She returned with a cream-colored leather purse about the size of a paperback book. I smiled, thinking of those pictures of Queen Elizabeth with her purse and speculation about its contents. Mrs. B, I bet, carried a heck of a lot of cash, not to mention a platinum credit card. She set the purse on the table and plucked a cherry tomato from one of the baskets. "Who threw the firebomb? The ex?"

"That was my first thought."

"He should be slapped in jail for the rest of his life."

"And then some."

Her sapphire eyes clouded and she rolled the tomato in her fingers. "Speaking of jail, dear, there's something you should know."

I gripped the edge of the table, recalling the drug dealer who used my car as a drop point and who kidnapped Cheese Puff to trade for the stash of meth Dave confiscated. "Tony Montgomery? Is he getting out?"

Cheese Puff yelped. Lola came on the run and licked the top of his head as if to assure him she saved him once and could do it again.

"That nasty man will stay behind bars as long as I have breath in my body and political arms left to twist." Mrs. B popped the tomato in her mouth and patted her fluffy hair. "I've been promised the words 'plea bargain' won't be mentioned and the prosecutor will demand the stiffest sentence allowed."

She twisted one of her rings. The diamond caught a beam of sunlight slicing through the deck door and scattered tiny rainbows on the wall. "This is about Jake."

My blood pressure spiked. "Jake? As in my ex-husband? The man whose steroid-pushing girlfriend shoved me in the river and tried to kill me?"

Mrs. B nodded.

"He didn't make a deal, did he?"

"Not yet. And not from lack of trying. But the jail is at capacity, he's considered low risk, and he's employed. They'll release him this week."

"Release! That's not right! And if Jake has a job, I bet it's not legitimate." Yanking at my hair, I walked in tight circles. "You have to stop this!"

"I called in a lot of markers over that nasty drug dealer." Mrs. B stepped into my path, gripped my arms, narrowed her eyes, and pursed her lips in her trademark get-with-reality expression. "I can't ask for favors right now."

I hauled in a deep breath. "Okay . . . well . . . okay. As long as Jake is far away from here. As long as I don't see him."

Mrs. B shook her head and her eyes softened.

"What? What?"

"Maybe you better sit down, dear."

My fists clenched and blood pounded in my head. I don't know about you, but being told to sit down makes me come out of my corner swinging.

I pulled free and spoke from between gritted teeth. "I'm not sitting. Tell me the rest of it. Now."

Chapter 4

"All right." Mrs. B sighed. "Jake will be working here."

"Here? Here at the condo complex? Here, as in the place I live?"

My voice rose to a shriek. Cheese Puff sat on his haunches and yowled. Lola barked and raced around him.

"Here, as in the place I can't afford to move out of to escape him?"

Mrs. B winced and nodded.

"Why am I being punished? What have I done?" I glanced around for something to throw, saw nothing I wouldn't regret breaking, seized the remainder of the brownie, and stuffed it in my mouth.

Mrs. B calmed the dogs and offered a baby carrot to Cheese Puff. He snubbed it; Lola slid out her tongue and reeled it in. "I'm sorry, dear. I heard about it a little bit ago from Jim. He heard it from Verna who got it straight from the horse's mouth."

"That horse being Bernina Burke?" I mumbled around the gooey mass of brownie stuck to the roof of my mouth. "The woman who hates my guts?"

"I don't think she actively hates you, dear. You two simply have a personality conflict."

"We might, if she *had* a personality."

Mrs. B ignored that and rinsed her hands at the sink. "The landscaping service wants to do less and charge more and the

20

plumber and electrician aren't always available on short notice, so the condo board gave Bernina the okay to hire a handyman to live on the premises. By the time Verna found out Bernina intended to hire Jake, the wheels were in motion."

Bernina, the condo manager, thought Jake hung the moon. Further, she believed the steroid-dealing charges against him were the result of a series of misunderstandings, misinterpretations, and misrepresentations created by those jealous of his handsome face, muscular body, and relentless charm.

I swallowed and sucked chocolate from my teeth. Jake was fastidious about his appearance and about who he appeared with. Not as tall and lean as others, I showed up as a significant aberration on his entanglement chart, the result of his need for cash coinciding with my need for comfort after Albert plunged to his death from a cliff. Bernina, who outweighed Jake and had all the charm of cholera, would be charted as an aberration the size of New Jersey. "Where will he live? With Bernina?"

"I'm sure she'd like that, but no." Mrs. B rummaged in the basket, brought out a jar of Greek olives, and twisted the lid loose. "For the time being he'll live in that little unit at the far end and fix it up to serve as a short-term guest quarters for residents."

I eyeballed a second brownie. "There's nothing you can do?"

"I'm afraid that if the Committee opposes Bernina on this, she could very well ramp up that pet-limit campaign again."

That was something to be avoided. Bernina dropped her efforts to set the limit at one pet per unit after I offered to promote her as a character witness for Jake's defense. She tolerated Cheese Puff and Lola, but made it clear they rated only a step above an infestation of poisonous snakes.

"How about presenting a few harsh facts to the condo board? For one thing, Jake's no handyman. When we were married he tried to replace a faucet washer and destroyed the sink. There's no way he can rehab that unit."

Mrs. B nibbled on an olive. "Well, he probably can't make it worse."

After the bank foreclosed on the unit in question, the owners made a statement on the way out—punching holes in the walls, shattering the ceiling light fixtures, and shredding the carpet. That allowed the condo association to purchase the place at a fire-sale price. "I wouldn't bet on him not making things worse. But he's so lazy he probably won't do anything— good *or* bad. Didn't the board check his resume?"

"They left the hiring to Bernina. Verna says never again!" Mrs. B selected another olive. "There will be so much oversight next time it will make airport security seem like a supermarket check-out stand."

"Well they better start that oversight now. If they don't account for every nail, he'll siphon off the repair fund."

"Don't worry. I'll see to that." She screwed the lid tight. "On the positive side, dear, Jake will be where we can keep an eye on him. The Committee will put the word out, and if he dangles even his little toe off the straight and narrow path, we'll jump all over him. And all over Bernina. Her contract is up at the end of the summer and there are plenty of people searching for jobs with a decent salary and a place to live thrown in."

Mrs. B put the olives in the refrigerator. "Verna made it clear to Bernina that Jake is not to get anywhere near you. If he sees you, he's to walk away. But if you want, she and Jim will help you get a restraining order."

"Thanks, but that seems a little extreme. I'm not afraid of Jake. I don't think he would ever hurt me—at least not on purpose. He's more of an annoyance, like a stone in my shoe." I moved the baskets to the counter and snagged a sponge to wipe the table. "A really big stone. What was I thinking when I married him? Why did I believe his smooth talk, and let him wipe out my savings?"

"You were in a bad place, dear, and he took advantage. Jake was certainly a lesson, but he's a lesson learned, and one that made you smarter and stronger." She opened the silverware drawer. "And perhaps he's learned a few lessons himself."

Fat chance. People who think they're above everyone else aren't inclined to recognize mistakes, and Jake has an ego that a world-class megalomaniac would envy. But if Mrs. B wanted to delude herself, I wouldn't argue. As Dave often said, she was a force of nature. Once she set a course you'd better get out of the way.

"How many are we?" Mrs. B held up a handful of knives and forks.

I counted on my fingers. "You and me and Paulette and Iz and Penelope and Dave and—"

"I'm back." Flip-flops smacked the floor in the hall.

"And Allison," I finished.

"What's for dinner?" Dave's daughter appeared wearing an orange halter top and denim shorts cut high and fraying at the hem. "Can Josh stay?"

"Sure." We had plenty of food and he'd been nice enough to deliver her to rehearsal and pick her up. Plus—so far—he seemed like a darn good kid, smart and polite and kind. I raised another finger for Mrs. B's count. "But he has to leave right after because you have homework to finish. Math homework."

Allison emitted a sigh that emptied her lungs. "I hate math."

I bit my tongue so I wouldn't say, "And your grades show it." Since she got a role in the play, Allison let everything else slide. When Dave brought that up in their weekly counseling session, she acknowledged it and promised she'd buckle down after opening night on Friday. Call me a pessimist, but I had my doubts about said buckling down. I feared Allison would continue at an elevated level of drama-queenism long after the run of the play.

23

"And I really, really, really hate geometry. It's stupid." Allison appealed to Mrs. B. "No way will I need math when I'm a famous actress."

"You'd be surprised, dear." Her tone light and chatty, Mrs. B carried silverware to the table. "You'll need to know the difference between gross and net and how to figure percentages so producers and agents don't cheat you and so you don't leave skimpy tips when you dine out. It pays not to have angry waiters telling tales to the tabloids."

Allison tugged at her shorts, considering. "Okay, maybe. But I bet *you* never used geometry after you left school."

"Only whenever I rehearsed on a new stage." Mrs. B headed to the cabinet for plates. "Oh, and later when I started designing sets. You can't take a chance on exceeding the space allotted or not having room to maneuver. And then—"

"I get it." Allison pouted and kicked the table leg, making the silverware rattle. "Dad and Barbara got to you. You're on their side. You don't care about anything *I* have to say."

Mrs. B set the stack of plates on the table with a clatter, squared her shoulders and straightened her spine. She didn't say a word, didn't make even a single tongue click of disapproval. While I stood by, envying her power and control and wondering if she'd give me lessons, Allison withered under the blue heat of her gaze. In ten seconds it was all over.

"Sorry," Allison whispered. "I'm being a brat. But I'm soooo sick of school."

"Who isn't," I said.

"Nineteen more days," Allison moaned.

And then a summer without paychecks. Such was the plight of a substitute teacher. No school meant no opportunity to fill in. I'd kept an eye out for "help wanted" ads and signs, but so far the only one I spotted leaned in the fly-specked window of a downtown pawn shop. The sign was printed on a torn piece of cardboard and held upright by a moth-eaten stuffed creature. The taxidermy job was so shoddy I couldn't tell if it was a large bat or a small badger. I was desperate, but after a quick survey of the dusty contents of the display window, my sinuses informed me I wasn't *that* desperate—at least not yet.

As if she'd read my mind, Mrs. B patted my arm. "It will all work out."

But which way? In my favor? Or—

"We're back," Dave called. "Found Josh hanging around the door waiting to be asked in."

"Sorry, sorry, sorry." Allison raced to collect her boyfriend. "Barb says you can stay for dinner, but I don't know what we're having."

"It's always good." Josh came into view, Allison tugging on his arm. "Hey, Mrs. B. We're working on that song but rhyming something with 'ostrich feathers' is tough. I mean, if we want to keep it clean."

My busy brain churned up possible lascivious word combinations. Josh interrupted the flow. "Thank you for inviting me."

I shook my head to clear my thoughts. "And thank you for thanking me."

Allison rolled her eyes. "Suck up," she hissed.

Josh hung his head so his long hair hid flaming cheeks and dug at the carpet with the toe of his sneaker.

"Kid's seventeen and he knows more about how to charm women than I do," Dave groused.

"Who doesn't?" Iz pushed past him and headed for the baskets. "What's to eat?"

"Nothing until we all wash up," Paulette called out.

I rinsed the sponge, hiding a snicker. It amused me to hear Iz getting orders. It amused me more to see her slink off to the powder room tucked under the stairs.

Allison led Josh upstairs to her bathroom, burbling about her new comforter and how we were going to paint the walls as soon as she picked out a color.

Her eyes bright with interest, Paulette watched them go. I had a feeling that before the evening ended, she'd be in the decorating loop and I'd be out of it. Yesss!

"The damage isn't as bad as I expected," Penelope told me. "There are no rooms above the living room and Denise closed the double doors to the dining area and held back the fire. There's only smoke damage to the rest of the rooms and not much of that."

"With any luck," Paulette said, "we can rebuild just the living room."

"And how's Denise doing?" Mrs. B asked. "And how are her children?"

Paulette pumped soap into her palm and lathered up at the kitchen sink. "Also better than we expected. She should be out of the hospital in no time. The girls are with her sister. They'll have a thrilling story to tell their kindergarten class."

Dave bumped me with his hip. "Who knew that rearranging furniture could save someone's life?"

Chapter 5

I blinked. "Moving furniture saved her life?"

"When we carted her things in, Denise placed the sofa under the windows," Paulette said. "But that created a glare on the TV screen. And it made her nervous to sit with her back to the street."

"Turns out she had good reason for that." Iz emerged from the powder room wiping her hands on one of the tiny pink towels a member of the Committee gave me as a housewarming present in January. I'd loathed pink all my life and I *really* loathed the fuchsia cats on the trim of those towels. I wasn't alone. Dave refused to use them, drying his hands on his shirt so he wouldn't be stricken with "the creeping cuties." If I ever had a few extra dollars, I planned to replace them and put the word out that Cheese Puff felt upstaged and displaced by the felines. Never mind how ridiculous that sounds, Committee members who doted on my dog would swallow it.

"If she'd been sitting on the sofa," Iz continued, "she might be dead."

"But she'd pulled it forward and turned it to one side." Penelope took her turn at the sink. "The windows were wide open and the screens haven't arrived yet, so the firebomb came right through. It hit the arm of the sofa and bounced against the wall."

"Denise pushed the sofa on top of the flames." Paulette took up the story. "That bought her time to get the kids out and

27

call for help. If she hadn't gone back in, she wouldn't be hurt at all."

"The guy who made the bomb was an amateur," Dave added. "But when it comes to fire, even an amateur can do a lot of harm."

Later, lying in bed with Dave sprawled beside me and Lola and Cheese Puff tangled at our feet, I thought about Denise and her girls and the firebomb. If her ex-husband threw it, how had their relationship spun so far out of control? What happened to corrupt a wedding-day pledge to love and honor? What made him abuse her? Loss of power and control? Betrayal? Had he cheated on her, expected her to accept it, and exploded when she didn't? Or had Denise cheated on him?

Thinking about cheating led to thinking about Jake.

I sat up in bed. In the bustle of dinner and prodding Allison to finish her homework, I hadn't told Dave.

I stretched out a hand to shake him awake. But before my fingers touched bare skin, he flopped onto his side, snorted, sucked air, and settled into a trough of pillows.

The issue of Jake could wait. Dave needed his rest. He wasn't—at least so far—the jealous type. He'd probably be amused by the idea of my ex as a handyman.

Or would he?

I glanced over at Dave again. How well did I know him? Was there more to the story of his first marriage than the few snippets I'd gleaned? All the tiny adjustments and compromises and conflicts of living together created friction. And friction created heat. Not only the heat of passion, but also the heat of anger.

What happened *before* his wife claimed she needed more personal space, plugged another man into that space, and ran off to Miami leaving Dave with Allison and a drawer full of unpaid bills?

28

What kind of baggage had Dave acquired that I had yet to see? And how would it clash with all the crap I carried?

Mentally unpacking and repacking emotional cargo, I thrashed and tossed most of the night.

The sun streaming through young leaves on the trees around Captain Meriwether High School spangled the asphalt in my usual spot at the far end of the faculty lot. Although I filled in at CMHS every day, I was still a sub. That, plus self-esteem that usually ran at least a quart low, made me hesitant to take a more convenient parking spot. There were those who felt subs weren't "real" teachers and shouldn't presume to park in the faculty lot at all, let alone in a prime position.

"There are lots of spaces up close," Allison said. "Why do we have to walk so far?"

"Teachers have their favorite spots. Besides, you're closer to the cafeteria here than if you rode the bus."

She scuffed her flip-flops on the worn rug in the footwell. "I guess."

Was "I guess" a step up from "whatever"? Did it carry a shade of actual agreement?

In my never-ending search for enlightenment about the workings of the teenage brain, I made a mental note to run the question by the gang in the teachers' room during lunch.

Allison got out, hoisted her backpack, and waved at a boy cruising by on a skateboard. His gaze swept over my car—a vehicle too old to be cool, but not old enough to be classic—and he raised one corner of his top lip in a sneer.

"I wish we could take Mrs. Ballantine's car," Allison said. "It's awesome."

"That it is." Not to mention newer, more expensive, and a bright metallic red. Mine, bleached by summer sun and pummeled by winter wind and rain, was a color that defied description—except for the ever-expanding patches of rust on the fenders. They were, well, rusty.

29

"Maybe she'd swap you." Allison fluffed her hair as another skateboarder rolled past.

I laughed and pulled my briefcase from the back seat. "Would you?"

"No way." Allison studied my wheels with an expression of loathing I reserve for fennel and slimy things discovered crawling out of the bathtub drain. Then she brightened. "Maybe she'll let me learn to drive in her car."

At the risk of sounding like a stuck record, I trotted out that two-word question again. "Would you?"

"I guess not. At least not on the first day." Shoulders slumping, she made her sigh into a full-body experience. "Tomorrow, drop me around back so no one sees us, okay?"

I mimicked her sigh. "Whatever."

Allison frowned. I shot her a broad and innocent smile and topped it off with a cliché. "Have a nice day."

"Seriously?"

She shrugged her backpack onto her shoulders and cut across the lawn to the front door. I followed at a more leisurely pace, waving to one of the security guards, and threading my way at an angle through a pack of teens texting as they shuffled toward the cafeteria.

At a few minutes before 7:00, the office was as noisy and chaotic as usual. Teachers rushed to get their mail and make copies and subs lined up to pay homage to Wilhelmina Frost, secretary to Principal Jerome Morrow and the woman in charge of payroll, personnel, and placing substitute teachers. A hardy few had earned the right to exchange sarcastic remarks with Big Chill, but I never heard anyone question either her authority or the administrative orders she passed along—until this morning.

"It's a load of crap, there's no reason for it, and I won't do it." Aston Marsden's shouts blasted from the open door.

"What's going on?" I whispered to the attendance clerk who was peering from her office and chewing on a knuckle.

"The board is up and nobody's happy."

30

"Ah."

I'd heard rumblings about the board. It was, in reality, several large poster boards marked off with squares and rectangles in which administrators noted room assignments and specific classes for the coming year. For the past few weeks, speculation had run rampant—speculation that someone high up in the educational food chain thought full-bore change would be good. That high-upster, rumor had it, planned to change things around, shake things up, and generally jar everyone out of their ruts.

Big Chill must have answered Aston in a low voice because the next thing I heard was another shout from him. "That's another load of crap. If anyone could change this, it's you."

The attendance clerk nodded in agreement. Big Chill had worked at CMHS for decades. She'd seen them come and she'd seen them go. She knew where all the bodies were buried and who had shoveled dirt onto the coffins. I had no doubt that she could bend policy if she wanted to apply a little gentle pressure. I also had no doubt she wouldn't do that for Aston, especially not after this morning's outburst.

"You haven't heard the end of this." The history teacher backed through the doorway punching his fist in the air. "I'll go to the board. I'll go to the union. I'll go to the media."

The subs in front of me cringed and scuttled away from Big Chill's door. I didn't blame them. Big Chill in a good mood was the queen of caustic comments. Big Chill in a bad mood . . .

My fingers turned to ice.

The sub behind me, a short man with darting eyes and trembling lips, pushed me forward. "She likes you," he whimpered. "You go first."

Other subs clustered behind him, forming a human wall. Retreat blocked, I sucked in a breath—possibly my last—and stepped into Big Chill's lair.

To my surprise, she wasn't foaming at the mouth, shredding her blotter with her fingernails, or stabbing pins into a doll-size replica of Aston. Instead she raised a cup of coffee to lips curved into a smile.

A smile?

What was that about?

She nodded at the pile of sub forms on the corner of the desk. "Dig yours out of the heap. You're in technology."

That meant freshmen.

Freshmen and computers.

Two elements that, in my experience, didn't mix well.

Freshmen classes were generally large and filled with kids who—to put it kindly—weren't exactly eager to settle down and tackle an assignment. Computers created opportunities for kids to play games and surf to sites not considered appropriate. Most of those sites were blocked, but a few kids found ways around the virtual walls built to keep them out.

While I admired their inventiveness and determination, I dreaded the hours I'd spend trying to spot games that by no stretch of the imagination could pass as educational, or sites where I might see things I didn't want to know about.

But I stifled a groan and accepted my fate. After being the recipient of Aston's high-decibel wrath, Big Chill wasn't likely to give a damn about my preferences. If the lesson plans called for me to hang by my thumbs from the ceiling or scrape paint with my toenails, she'd tell me to suck it up or step aside for another sub.

With stony silence weighing on me, I riffled through the pile of forms. Normally I'd ask Big Chill about her weekend or she'd tip me to a subbing opportunity coming up or mention a sale or let me know she'd restocked the chocolates stashed in a cabinet behind her desk. But that smile on her face frightened me more than any scowl, so I said nothing, slid my form from the stack, and jotted my name.

Big Chill held her silence until I reached the door. "Tell those other subs to get in here," she said in a voice as harsh as a serrated knife sawing at a soup can. "I don't have all day."

When lunchtime finally rolled around I got the story behind the confrontation. As he hacked at a chunk of petrified salami with something that looked a lot like a mini machete, Aston unloaded. "Not only are they forcing me to change classrooms, but they have me teaching CWP."

CWP was shorthand for Contemporary World Problems. Contemporary to Aston meant the Civil War. He spent his spare time recreating decisive battles or dressing as a mountain man for living history events. He knew the world had moved on, but he wasn't interested. For him to get up to speed on events of the past 140 years would require a full summer of study.

And then there was Aston's classroom. It was packed with shelves and cabinets scavenged from yard sales and thrift stores and crammed with miniature stockades and forts built from ice cream sticks, chunks of beaver-gnawed trees, birds' nests, plaster casts of animal tracks, dried ears of corn, plastic cows, pigs, chickens, and horses, and tiny teepees constructed from twigs and bits of fabric. The walls were covered with photographs of determined men and dazed women standing by ox-drawn wagons, and portraits of soldiers in blue and gray uniforms.

The most memorable thing about Aston's classroom, however, was the odor. It was earthy and overripe and gamy and—

Lest I ruin my appetite for pasta salad and other leftovers, I abandoned my quest for the right adjective and laid out my lunch while Aston finished his rant.

"—since my first day at this school. Fourteen years." Aston glared at each of us in turn as if he expected someone to argue with his addition. "No one ever gave a hoot that my classroom isn't on the same hallway with the rest of the department. And no one ever suggested I teach anything but Washington history. That's what I know best. That's what I'm good at. And I'll tell you one damn thing." He leveled the machete at Gertrude Suttle. "If Susan was still here, this wouldn't be happening."

All heads turned to the empty chair where Susan Mitchell, history department chair until last December, sat until the day she confessed to the murder of Henry Stoddard. Almost as one we sighed. Then silence ballooned over the table. Gertrude broke it by unzipping her insulated lunch sack and popping the lid from a plastic container of salad. In a few seconds Doug Whitman, one eye on the machete wavering two feet from his head, peeled the wrapping from a burrito and took a huge bite. I stabbed at bowtie pasta and stuffed my mouth.

There were two reasons to get to the business of eating quickly. First, the lunch period was a measly 25 minutes. Second, the dishes Brenda Waring brought had a lot in common with that smell in Aston's classroom. As she reached into the paper sack in front of her, Doug swallowed a lump of burrito the size of my fist and took another bite. Brenda pulled out a glass container filled with a brownish yellow substance crowded with black specks.

Everyone pretended disinterest but our gazes bounced back and forth between Brenda and Aston. They'd had an on-again, off-again relationship since March. How he reacted to what she brought for lunch, and how she reacted to his reaction, would clue us to the current state of that relationship.

Brenda stirred the contents of the container, releasing the scent of dill and something that reminded me of briny debris washed up on a beach and left to bake in the summer sun. Aston frowned and swung the machete to point at her. "What the hell is that?"

Brenda's nostrils dilated and she wrapped her hands around the container as if to protect it. "It's a puree of lima beans, turnips, shrimp, and dill pickles, with flax seeds and a dab of caviar."

I slapped the lid on my pasta. Doug grunted and swallowed, massaging his throat to help the process. Gertrude, who had been eating lunch with Brenda a lot longer than we had, shrugged and went on with her salad.

"Not that my lunch is any of your business, Aston," Brenda said. "And as far as the board is concerned, we'll all be affected by the changes. About half the teachers are swapping rooms and everyone will have at least one new class in the fall. I have to say that for once I'm on the side of the administration. Change can be a tool to help find new perspectives and sharpen skills."

She raised the dripping spoon and aimed it at him. "Your problem is that you don't want to change. You're stuck. Your teaching is as stale as those biscuits you eat on your stupid campouts. And your room is a health hazard."

Aston's lips pursed, making his beard and mustache ripple. "Your lunch isn't?"

Doug, Gertrude, and I slid our chairs a few inches away from the table.

"I wouldn't bring up lunch if I were you, not while you're eating meat that came from a half-rotted mastodon carcass deposited by a retreating glacier."

Aston picked at the green rind on his salami with his thumbnail. "And I wouldn't use the expression 'bring up lunch' if I were you. Regurgitation might improve the slop in that bowl."

Doug, never comfortable with conflict, bolted to his feet and snatched his burrito. "I'm outta here. Grading to do." He nodded at me. "Want to help?"

Normally the answer to that question would have been a resounding "No." But today I seized my pasta salad and water bottle and trucked along behind him.

"I've been wanting to talk with you." Doug unlocked his classroom door and ushered me inside. "About a business proposition."

Chapter 6

"If it involves making money over the summer and it's more than 30% legal and not too fattening, then I'm all ears."

I set my lunch on a table near the door and pulled out a chair, noticed a crack in the plastic seat, and pulled out another. In September the classroom chairs were in good condition, but by the end of the school year, not so much. Sitting without checking could deliver a painful lesson in what the expression "catch your tail in a crack" meant.

Doug checked a chair of his own and sat across from me. "Larry plans to reopen the auto repair shop in June."

"Tony Montgomery's shop?"

"Yeah. Larry's buying it. Tony needs funds for his defense."

I didn't see how a person who confessed to drug dealing and dognapping could *have* a defense, but that's the way the justice system rolls. I also didn't see how Larry, barely out of his teens and with relatively little experience as a mechanic, could persuade a bank to give him a loan. "Where's Larry getting the money?"

"He has an investor."

I forked up pasta. "Your sister?"

"No. Every dime she makes at the coffee shop goes into their wedding fund." Doug rolled his eyes. "And I'll be glad when *that's* in my rearview mirror and she and my mother can talk about something besides veils and flowers and bellyaching bridesmaids. Which I'd be one of, if I had to wear a lime green dress with puffy sleeves."

I laughed, remembering fashion failures—one with feathers *and* sequins—I'd wedged myself into in the spirit of friendship and supporting the bride on her big day. That might explain why my own weddings were bargain-basement affairs. I married Albert at a courthouse on our way to a birding vacation on the Gulf Coast. We wore jeans and T-shirts. Iz, who stood up for me, wore spiked hair, a nose ring, and a scowl. When I married Jake at another courthouse, Iz refused to attend. I would have saved a lot of money and heartache if I had done the same.

"This investor is a friend of yours," Doug said. "Muriel Ballantine. She called Larry out of the blue and suggested it."

I was surprised, yet not. Mrs. B met Larry at the party she threw to celebrate Cheese Puff's rescue. She seemed taken with his scrubbed appearance and aw-shucks attitude and thought it unfair that he lost his job when the repair shop that fronted Tony's drug ring closed.

"Tony rented the building," Doug went on. "And Larry can assume the lease at a sweet rate. The investment is for the inventory, and setting up a fund for payroll and insurance. Stuff like that."

"And I would figure in this enterprise how?" I wagged a finger. "And don't say 'doing the books' because I know next to nothing about accounting."

"But you know a lot about people." Doug unwrapped his burrito. "Larry knows a bunch of guys who need work or want to move from the shops they're at, so he's got mechanics. And he figures he can manage the shop and his mother will do the books at the start. But he needs someone to hold the fort at the front desk."

"I can answer a phone without strangling myself." I popped the lid on my pasta. "But I know more about the interior of Jupiter than I do about cars."

37

"That's okay. Most people know even less." Doug nibbled at his burrito. "Larry says they're mostly freaked out because their cars are wrecked or make weird noises or won't start. All you have to do is calm them down and—"

"Easier said than done."

"You manage it with 150 kids every day you sub."

"Wrong. I manage it with about 140 of those kids." I forked up pasta. "The rest kind of bounce around the classroom until the bell rings or I send them to security."

"I can guarantee you long lunches," Doug wheedled. "Time off to run errands. Opportunities to write creative radio ads, make fliers, and come up with ideas for special events to attract customers. A comfortable chair and a parking spot in the shade. Pretty much anything except a huge salary."

"Yeah, Larry has that investor to account to." I smiled and chewed pasta, imagining Mrs. B going over his accounts while wearing a green eyeshade.

Doug laughed. "The same investor who gave him a loan with an interest rate that's all to the right of the decimal point?"

"That's her. The same investor who probably suggested he hire me."

I'd finally discouraged Mrs. B from laying funds on me outright, but she found ways of subsidizing without cash— meals brought over because she'd "cooked too much," and discount coupons for restaurants and movies.

I sighed and, for the second time that day, gave in to my fate. "I need a summer job. And there isn't much out there."

"And consider this." Doug tapped his chest. "You'll be working with me."

"I didn't know you were a mechanic."

"I'm not. But I know how to make parts runs and take checks to the bank and shuttle customers to their jobs. Besides, it's in my best interest to help Larry get the business off the ground. If he doesn't make a go of it quick, they'll put off the wedding and I'll have to suffer through more endless Sunday-dinner discussions about flowers and candles and catering."

He mimed strangling himself. "Save me. Please."

I laughed, poked my fork into my pasta, and thought about my finances (grim), my options (few), my desire for summer employment (strong), and the lobbying campaign (relentless) Mrs. B would launch if I declined.

To be honest, the part about writing radio ads and planning special events piqued my interest. Thanks to Tony Montgomery's drug dealing, almost everyone in Reckless River knew about Start 'er Up Auto Repair. Maybe I could capitalize on that name recognition.

I stuck out my hand. "Deal."

When I got home I traded my slacks and blouse for ratty jeans and a T-shirt, scooped up Cheese Puff, snagged his harness and leash, and went out the sliding door onto the deck. When she arranged for me to buy the condo next door to hers, Muriel Ballantine removed the privacy panel separating our decks. That provided a larger area for outdoor living; she was using most of it at the moment. Dressed in a baggy gray sweatshirt, bright pink leggings, and shiny black leather tap shoes with thick heels, she clicked out a rhythm on the boards.

I dropped into a patio chair, settled Cheese Puff on my lap with a finger hooked in his collar to prevent escape, and raised my eyebrows. "Auto repair?"

Smiling, she went on tapping, swinging her arms from side to side and moving backward.

"Is there no length you won't go to when it comes to rearranging my life?"

She brushed a wisp of silvery hair from her forehead and executed a jump to the right.

"Isn't it bad enough that Paulette and Penelope rearranged almost every stick of furniture in my condo?"

Her smile didn't falter.

"And that you and the Committee have alienated the affections of my dog to such a degree that he barely tolerates me."

"You're exaggerating, dear," she said, panting a little.

"But not by much. Watch." I straightened my finger and raised my hands, releasing Cheese Puff. Without a backward glance, he raced for Mrs. B, twining himself between her ankles and bringing her dance to a stumbling halt. "See. He'd rather risk being trampled by you, than sit on my lap."

Mrs. B picked him up and rubbed her nose against his. "Well, the little prince hasn't seen me all day. Jim had to go to the DMV and the Social Security office and you know how long those lines can be, so Cheese Puff went along to keep him company. Then they had lunch with one of Jim's lady friends."

Somewhere in his 70s, Jim didn't let age slow him down. He had more lady friends than I had excuses for needing a handful of crunchy cheesy snacks at the end of a day of subbing.

Mrs. B set Cheese Puff on a chair and blotted her face on the hem of her sweatshirt. Not that there was even a tiny drop of moisture to blot. Mrs. B glowed instead of perspiring. "I don't remember her name, but she's the one who lives in that high rise. She has a parrot—Cheese Puff doesn't much like him—and an artificial leg."

A parrot and an artificial leg? "Does she have an eye patch? Does she say 'Arr' and threaten to make Jim walk the plank if he doesn't clean his plate or do other things to her satisfaction?"

"What other things?" Mrs. B gave me a puzzled frown. "And why would she do that?"

"Because that's what you do when you're pretending to be a pirate?"

"Pretending to be a pirate?" Her frown deepened. "What are you talking about?"

I felt my cheeks scorch. "You weren't joking? About the parrot. And the artificial leg."

"A parrot is a perfectly acceptable pet. And an artificial leg is no joke, dear."

Embarrassment morphed to guilt. "Of course not. I didn't mean that it was. I thought she and Jim were . . . oh, never mind."

"The parrot belonged to her uncle. They are long-lived birds, you know."

I did now. Time to change the subject. "How's the routine coming?"

"Slowly. And painfully." Mrs. B sat in the glider and fanned herself with her hands. "Dancing didn't seem like this much work all those years ago." Cheese Puff leaped up beside her. "I watched the first-season shows and I know I can do better, but I haven't yet." She gestured at the scuff marks on the deck. "I thought tap might be the way to go because I love the sound and I could wear a top hat and tails. But that's all been done."

"Maybe something more Fred and Ginger? Dario says you were the goddess of grace."

Mrs. B's eyes sparkled at the mention of Dario O'Brien, the old friend from her days in Vegas, who now held a position as chief assistant to the assistant producer in charge of research for *Still Got That Strut*. His job involved locating talent for the show, but tracking and signing former showgirls didn't seem to get in the way of visiting Reckless River every two weeks.

"That's a good point, dear. Tap is fun, but it's not exactly elegant. And it's exhausting."

"Could you use it as a transition? Show that you know the moves and you've still got the stuff, then ease into something else."

She studied her shoes, clicking the heels together like Dorothy. "I can design costumes that tear away, but getting in and out of shoes is more difficult. I need more support than I had all those years ago. My ankles are a little wobbly."

"When I'm your age, I hope that's all that's wobbly." I stood and nodded to Cheese Puff. "Ready for a walk?"

41

He turned to Mrs. B as if seeking her approval. See what I mean about alienation of affection? Sometimes I wonder why I continue to refer to him as "my" dog.

"Go on. You need to exercise off lunch." Mrs. B patted his head. "Jim's lady friend loves to cook."

Cheese Puff licked his lips and belched.

"Where are your manners?" she asked him.

"A creature that's idolized doesn't need manners." I stuffed him into his harness. "And I don't want to know what kind of a gourmet meal he had."

"It was only pot roast and gravy," Mrs. B said. "With potatoes and baby carrots. And maybe just a smidge of lemon cheesecake with whipped cream."

Cheese Puff belched again and jumped from the glider. "Only kibble for dinner," I warned him. "And damn little of that. Lola won't love you if you get fat and flabby."

With another burp and a longing gaze at Mrs. B, Cheese Puff let me lead him across the deck and through the tiny rose garden to the trail at the top of the riverbank. "Upstream or down?"

Lifting his knob of a nose into the breeze, he sniffed, then headed upstream.

When we returned, Dave sprawled in the patio chair I'd vacated, a beer in his hand. I ruffled his hair. "You're home early. Make a big bust?"

A big bust meant a rush of adrenaline and energy that carried over into the bedroom. Energy had been in short supply last night and I'd had to settle for a few quick kisses. But Allison would be at rehearsal for at least another hour. Sixty minutes of romantic possibilities.

Dave scowled, tipped the bottle to his lips, and drained it. "Yeah. I busted my career."

"How?" I sank to the glider beside Mrs. B. Cheese Puff leaped up between us. "What happened?"

Visions of Dave busted to rookie status bloomed in my mind. Visions of the impact on Dave's paycheck followed. Close behind came visions of life as I'd hoped it might be sinking into the sunset.

"It sounds worse than it is," Mrs. B assured us. "These things always do."

"What sounds worse?"

"I shot off my mouth." Dave set the empty bottle on the deck. "When I should have kept it shut."

Since that was one of *my* prime failings, I made a mental note not to fault him for it. At least not until I knew more.

"You can't be penalized for having opinions," Mrs. B insisted.

"In theory." Dave picked up the empty bottle, tilted it, and set it down again.

"I'll get another." Mrs. B shot to her feet. "You tell Barbara what's going on."

Dave rubbed the stubble on his jaw. That whispery sound usually gives me a tingle on the back of my neck, but my nerve endings were busy ordering my stomach to tie itself in knots and couldn't handle other tasks.

"The chief resigned effective in September. Going to Kansas. Bigger city, better opportunity, blah, blah, blah." Dave held up his hands. "I have no problem with him—Marv was always fair and he went to bat for the department and all of us in the trenches. And I have no problem with him leaving. But I *do* have a problem with *what* is in line for his job."

I didn't need the italics to realize that Dave said "what" instead of "the person." I do, after all, have a degree in English—although my grammar, sentence construction, and punctuation might make you wonder.

"Can you talk to the chief? If you're not the only one who's worried, maybe . . ."

"Doubtful. He made it clear he would remain neutral and impartial about decisions that were not in his domain—

meaning we should just suck it up. Then he went off to catch a plane to somewhere north of the back of beyond to fish for salmon."

Mrs. B tapped from her unit, handed Dave a beer, and slipped a tall frosty glass into my hand. "Perhaps this person you're concerned about won't get the position," she said in a soothing tone.

"Oh, he'll get it all right. Dick McBain has been kissing city council butts—especially Ron Weador's—for so long his lips are locked in a permanent pucker. They'll appoint him acting chief, then dance around a bit until anyone who objects gets tired, then make it official. The dance will go faster if Weador is elected mayor."

Dave took a slug of his beer and wiped his mouth with the back of his hand. "On paper Dick looks good—lots of years on the job, worked his way up the ranks, serves on a bunch of civic committees, born in Reckless River, two adorable kids, and one blond wife in great shape and behind him all the way."

I took a huge swallow of my frothy drink. "What about *off* paper?"

"Let's say he leads from behind and builds himself up by sniping at everyone else. He cross-indexes grudges so he never loses track, and he takes malicious pleasure in the mistakes and failures of others."

"Ah." I'd had bosses like that. "But you're not in the line of fire, are you? I mean, aren't there a couple of ranks between you and the chief? Wouldn't your lieutenant take heat before you?"

Dave laughed in sharp and bitter way that conveyed no amusement. "He would if he stuck around. But the minute he got word of Marv's 'defection,' he grabbed his phone and started networking." He took a long pull at his beer. "He'll be gone in no time. But even if he stayed I'd be screwed. Dick's had it in for me since our training days."

I had trouble imagining anyone having it in for Dave. He was dedicated and hard-working, but also flexible and easy-going. "Why?"

"He's the kind of guy who never thinks outside the box or colors outside the lines. Never cuts a corner. Never liked being on the streets and never got results out there. Which is why he's been pushing paper for the last few years. He's good at organization and number crunching, I'll give him that, but graphs and charts alone don't make a dent in crime."

"Maybe a more attractive candidate will appear," Mrs. B said.

"All the candidates in the world can appear," Dave said, "but Ron Weador will shoot them down. He and Dick are buddies."

Mrs. B twitched her nose. "If the chief's not leaving until September . . ."

A hopeful expression flitted across Dave's face, then he shook his head. "You have great powers of persuasion, Muriel, but Dick McBain wants the job so bad he'll take it for less than anyone else. In this economy, that alone should get him hired."

I took another slug of my drink to give myself the courage to ask about Dave shooting off his mouth—but Mrs. B got there ahead of me. "I assume from what you said earlier that you made a mess in the nest."

"I did a lot more than make a mess. But yeah, if Dick gets in, I'll be out—one way or another. That's what you get when you sound off in the locker room before checking to see if the toilet stalls are empty."

Having done stuff like that myself—and far too often—I refrained from saying anything negative. "Maybe he didn't hear."

"Oh, he heard. I used my Allison-get-in-here-and-explain-this-right-now voice. People on the street probably heard. Pilots of low-flying planes, too."

45

I groaned and swallowed the rest of my drink so fast I got a brain freeze.

"Well, we have a few months before the chief leaves," Mrs. B said.

"A few months for me to find a job," Dave mourned.

I rubbed my forehead. "Where? With the county?"

"They're not hiring."

"Portland?"

"They're cutting staff."

"The state patrol?"

"Maybe. But the way things are going, I'd probably be assigned to work nights out of Spokane or Bellingham and my days off would be Tuesday and Wednesday."

Not a viable situation for a man with sole custody of a teenage daughter—a man embarking on a live-in relationship.

"That won't happen." Mrs. B snatched my empty glass, stood with a clack of tap shoes, and headed inside. "This situation will be dealt with."

Whenever Mrs. B said something would be "dealt with" I wondered if maybe there were grains of truth to the Marco-and-the-mob story. Lately I also wondered about Dario O'Brien. Was he just posing as a gangster, or was he a thug to the bone?

Dave, staring into his beer bottle, didn't seem concerned by her statement. Seeing as how he had a badge, I decided to let him do the worrying—if there was legitimate worrying to be done. Besides, as Mrs. B slipped a fresh drink into my hand, I spotted a looming crisis of my own—Jake Stranahan, strolling our way along the river trail.

Chapter 7

From the appearance of my ex-husband, jail had been nothing like a fitness spa. Jake, who took great pride in his appearance, must wince every time he peered into the mirror. He sported a ragged haircut that made even the worst mullet look good, and he was pale and stringy where he wasn't doughy. His T-shirt couldn't conceal a roll of flab, and his jeans were too tight in the waist and saggy in the butt.

By Jake's side marched Bernina Burke who appeared to have trimmed off at least a dozen pounds in the past few weeks. Holding a clipboard, she pointed a pen at weeds sprouting along the base of the low rock wall at the edge of the steep drop to the river.

The looming crisis mushroomed when Cheese Puff whined and my sister Iz emerged from my condo.

Iz hated Jake. But Iz *really* hated Bernina.

Dave glanced toward the river, squinted, and shaded his eyes. "Hey, isn't that—?"

"Jake Stranahan." Iz roared and galloped across the deck to the gate and the steps leading to the trail. "You sorry excuse for a human being. Why the hell are you out of jail?"

Jake, displaying all the backbone of a jellyfish, ducked behind Bernina and used her as a shield.

The condo manager, having fought Iz to a draw in a war of words two months ago, planted her fists on her hips. "The jail is at capacity. And Jake isn't a criminal."

47

"He is so. He belongs in jail, not here at the scene of his crimes. I don't care if the cells are so full that they have to chain him in a broom closet."

"He is NOT a criminal," Bernina repeated through clenched teeth. "He hasn't gone to trial yet. And—not that it's any of your business since you're not a resident—he's here because he's working for the condo association."

"Working?" Iz pounded the railing, making the deck shimmy on its pilings. "He's never done a lick of real work in his life. He doesn't know the definition of the word." She glared at Jake who faced away and hung his head.

While Iz and Bernina traded disparaging remarks, Dave raised one eyebrow. "The condo association hired Jake? To do what, help elderly widows invest their savings in offshore accounts in his name?"

"Rehab work on the foreclosed unit on the end," Mrs. B said. "Bernina slipped it past the condo board. But if anyone on the Committee finds he's even *thinking* of working a scam, we'll drag him back to jail so fast he'll have scorch marks on his heels."

Dave raised the other eyebrow. "Can you live with this, Barbara?"

"As long as I don't have to live with *him*. And as long as the Committee watches him like a hawk. Like a whole herd of hawks."

"I don't think that's what you call a group of hawks, dear." Mrs. B wrinkled her nose. "They're not a flock or a gaggle or—"

"I'll look it up. Later." Dave hoisted himself from his chair and headed for Iz. "Right now I have to separate those two. Or else charge admission to the fight."

I peered along the line of condos. Iz and Bernina were drawing a crowd, a crowd that released a smattering of groans and protests as Dave wedged himself in front of Iz. "Show's over," he said.

Iz turned her glower on him, then flung her last words at Bernina. "Don't expect sympathy when he siphons off the petty cash. *If* you have the intelligence to notice it's gone!"

Mrs. B sighed. "And I thought Penelope was having such a positive effect on your sister."

"She is. But only when she's in the immediate vicinity." I took a gulp of my drink. "The rest of the time Iz is—"

"Mad?" Iz rounded on Dave as he herded her our way. "You're damn right I'm mad. I'm beyond mad. I drive all the way over here because no one answers their damn phones and I find a jailbird on the loose and you all sitting around sipping pretty drinks."

Her face the color of a stop sign, she jabbed a finger at Dave's chest. "What's with this 'jail is at capacity' crap?"

Dave shrugged. "Budget cuts. Staff cuts. I'm surprised Jake wasn't released before this."

The finger jabbed at me, coming close enough to my eyes to make me flinch and be glad I wore glasses. "And you! You're sitting here being a victim like usual? You're not objecting to this . . . this . . . sham of employment?"

Cheese Puff growled and lunged for Iz's stabbing digit.

"Barbara and I have discussed all of this." Mrs. B reached out and batted Iz's finger aside. "Jake may find working here tougher and more tedious than being in jail. The Committee intends to make sure he doesn't approach Barbara, that he doesn't mingle with others unless invited, that he works a full eight hours every day, and that his work isn't shoddy."

"Shoddy is Jake's middle name." Iz grabbed my glass, tilted it to her lips, and guzzled the contents. Wheezing, she pounded her chest with her fist. "What the hell was that?"

"Rum," Mrs. B said. "And fruit juice."

Iz coughed again.

"Not *very much* fruit juice," Mrs. B added in a whisper directed at me.

"Why can't you remember that I don't drink spirits?"

Mrs. B drew herself up, eyes flashing blue fire. "Why can't *you* remember that it's a display of extremely bad manners to grab someone's drink and swill it without asking permission?"

Iz slammed the glass on a wooden table beside the glider and turned to watch Bernina and Jake pass from sight around a curve in the trail at the end of the condo complex.

I made a mental note to ask Mrs. B how she got her eyes to spark like that.

"They arrested her ex-husband," Iz mumbled.

It took me a few seconds to dredge up context for that comment. "Denise Ryder's ex-husband?"

"And his girlfriend." Iz dropped into Dave's former chair. "Well, she kind of arrested herself. She threw a fit when detectives came to question him and went after a cop with a broken beer bottle. Ryder got in the way of the cop who tried to pull her off and they took them both in."

She craned her neck to scowl at Dave who stood behind her. "How come you didn't know? I thought you were dialed in."

"Not today," Dave said, his gaze fixed on a motorboat zigzagging on the far side of the river. "Today the phone is off the hook."

The corner of Iz's mouth twitched and her eyes narrowed, but Dave said nothing more and she turned her attention to me. "I don't understand these women who believe the jerks they get involved with are worth fighting for."

That statement—in case any of you haven't figured it out—was partly about Ryder's girlfriend and partly about me marrying Jake and sticking with him for more than a few hours.

Before I could say anything, Mrs. B patted my wrist and took charge. "Those women don't have your perspective, Iz. And many of them are afraid."

Iz, who would never admit she feared anything, even if she was rigid with fright, short of breath, suffering heart palpitations, and wetting her pants, sat straighter in her chair. "But, they—"

"That's all we need to say about it," Mrs. B said in a sharp voice. "It was good of you to bring us the news."

Iz gaped for a few seconds, then closed her mouth and pressed her lips into a tight line.

I gazed at Mrs. B with adoration. Yesterday she shut down Allison and today she shot down Iz. How did she do that? And, more to the point, would she give me lessons? Her powers were clearly miles beyond the stink eye techniques I used at school. Techniques that had made exactly no impression on the freshmen in today's technology classes.

She patted my wrist again. "Don't you and Dave need to pick up Allison?"

Without a glance at his watch, Dave took off for my condo—now our condo—leaving me to collect Cheese Puff and follow.

By mutual consent, we edited the politics of the police force from any discussion that might reach Allison's ears. Being abandoned by her mother had left her vulnerable; the last thing she needed was uncertainty about the future. The next-to-last thing she needed was to discover her father had acted the way he counseled her not to.

I did my best to keep things normal—considering that our living arrangement constituted strange territory for all of us and the definition of normal had yet to be hammered out. Although Allison claimed to be happy to occupy what had previously been the guest room, it was apparent the move had also created stress. And that, in turn, provided the basis for more drama than usual.

"But Dad's shoes are in the middle of the living room," she complained when I asked her to collect her flip-flops from the hallway. "Why do I always have to do everything and he does nothing?"

51

I hauled in a deep breath and, knowing ten wouldn't be enough, counted to twenty. Since we finished devouring leftovers in the name of having dinner, Dave had been lying on the sofa, staring at the ceiling and muttering. So much for not telegraphing signals to make his daughter apprehensive. Even the dogs were on edge. Lola had taken up a position on the floor beside Dave and Cheese Puff sat on the arm of the sofa leaning forward like a buzzard perched on a limb. I'd been keeping up a semblance of life going on by chipping away at the remaining boxes in the office.

"No one is asking you to do *everything.*" I kept my tone neutral—or as neutral as a tone can be when a woman is gnawing the inside of her cheek in frustration. "I only asked if you could take a minute to pick up your shoes before someone trips over them."

"But I need to call Josh."

"Pick up your shoes." Dave raised himself to one elbow. "Please."

"You pick up yours!"

"I will when I go up to bed."

Allison flounced toward the open door to the deck, texting as she went. "Then that's when I'll pick up mine."

Gosh, this was going well. All those hours spent in counseling were really paying off with clear goals, open communication, and calm discussions.

"Pick them up now," Dave ordered.

Allison turned, hands on hips, and stomped a bare foot.

They glared. Lola whimpered. Cheese Puff leaped to the security of his favorite chair and burrowed between the cushion and the arm rest.

"Or what?" Allison taunted.

Not having the benefit of family counseling to control it, my annoyance level shot into the red zone. "Or I'll ground you both."

Allison turned on me with an expression of amazed defiance. Dave sat up and scowled. "You can't ground me," they said simultaneously.

"I wish I could."

I plucked leashes and Cheese Puff's harness from the hooks in the hallway and whistled for the dogs. "Come on. Let's go."

Lola raced to my side and sat. Cheese Puff practically shot into his harness. I opened the screen door to the deck. "When the great shoe issue is resolved and you two are finished acting like preschoolers, hang one of those kitty towels on the gate. When I see it—if I see it—I'll think about whether I want to return."

Silence was the only response to my ultimatum.

Was that good?

Or bad?

I'd tromped half a mile along the trail before I started to wonder what I'd do if no towel hung on the gate when I returned. Mrs. B would take me in and comfort me with a frothy drink and jumbo cashews, but that would mean sharing more of my ever-growing heap of dirty laundry and, worse, having her think I couldn't handle conflicts on my own.

And I could. Only not anywhere near as effectively as she did.

Dejected, I pulled the dogs away from a particularly intriguing scent at the base of a tree and headed home, head hanging, feet dragging. Was this how it would be every day? Was having Dave and Allison move in the dumbest thing I ever did? Next to marrying Jake, of course. Was Iz right? Was I so desperately in need of a man that I had no vestige of self-esteem or common sense?

Lola barked and pulled at the leash.

I glanced up to see Dave and Allison trotting toward me. Each of them waved a kitty towel like a flag of truce.

The next morning Dave shook me awake a few minutes before the alarm went off at 5:30 and pointed to a cup of steaming coffee on the nightstand. "I'm making banana pancakes. They should be ready when you come down."

Wary that accepting guilt-trip coffee might signal complete forgiveness, I lifted the cup and sipped. It was strong, with the right amount of milk.

Within seconds my internal engine revved up. Apparently it had no problem with the reason behind the coffee, all it wanted was fuel. "Ummm."

Dave grinned. "Did I get it right?"

"It's terrific."

But what about those pancakes? What kind of a mess would he create in the kitchen? And would he clean it up? Or would I get stuck scraping the griddle and wiping spatters off the stove?

My fat cells voted unanimously to indulge in the pancakes now and consider grease splatters and batter drips later.

Dave leaned over, brushed hair from my forehead, and planted a quick kiss between my brows and a lingering one on my lips. My nerve endings tingled and pointed out that a little mess in the kitchen seemed like a fair trade for activities in the bedroom.

"I'll clean up before I go to work." Dave straightened and squared his shoulders. "And I *am* going to work. I won't pretend that nothing happened, won't defend or explain, won't ask anyone to take my side. I'm good at my job. That should transcend politics or prejudice."

The operative word being "should." "You'll be a shining example."

"Yeah. An example of stupidity." He kissed me again. "But I'm trying to learn from my many mistakes. See you downstairs."

Ninety minutes later, fueled by a short stack of pecan-studded banana pancakes and encouraged by the enthusiasm Dave demonstrated while scrubbing the sink, I dropped Allison at the door beside the gym and drove to the faculty lot. Billowing clouds above the trees promised heat, humidity, and an excellent chance of showers. I was hustling toward the main entrance and working an arm out of my sweater when someone yanked at the back of it.

"You ratted me out, Ms. Reed," a deep male voice said. "I went to jail on accounta you."

Chapter 8

Eddie!

Yikes!

In March he claimed to be selling odds and ends to help his family. He was actually part of a shoplifting ring run by Mitch, an older boy with a flashy car and a knack for manipulation. To the joy of Detective Charles Atwell, I passed along my suspicions, and he broke up the ring.

If Eddie decided to even the score with a punch or two, I had no illusions about the outcome. I'm not in the worst physical condition, but Eddie is taller, heavier, and stronger—not to mention younger. So I stuck to two of the rules of subbing—remain calm and show no fear. My vocal cords, however, had other ideas, and my voice squeaked when I ordered, "Let go of my sweater, Eddie."

To my surprise, Eddie released it immediately.

I swallowed, turned, and stepped to my right. That put me in a better position to pivot and run, and it gave teachers entering the lot a good view of us. "I'm not sorry about telling the police about Mitch and the shoplifting, but I *am* sorry you had to go to jail. That must have been pretty bad."

Eddie shrugged and brushed dirty blond hair from his eyes. "It was only a couple of weeks. And the food didn't half suck." He shuffled his feet. "I didn't steal any of that stuff, Ms. Reed. I just sold it. I knew it wasn't right, but whenever Mitch paid me, I didn't think about that, I just spent the money."

I nodded. Money had a way of clouding the brain—especially a teenage brain in the process of rewiring.

"Anyway, my dad was kinda pissed, but my mom said he got some of the blame because he shoulda been spending more time with me." Eddie raised his chin and squared his shoulders. "And she said he should be proud that I manned up and didn't argue about what I did or about going to jail."

"Manning up is tough. Lots of people never manage to do it." Jake, for example. "*Is* your dad proud? *Is* he spending more time with you?"

"Oh yeah!" He grinned. "We're buying a junker car and we're gonna fix it up together." He raised his fist for a bump. "Bonus."

I tapped my knuckles on his.

"So, thanks, Ms. Reed. Gotta go."

"Me, too."

I watched for a few seconds as he hustled away, then swung about and jogged to the front door. Being a few minutes late wasn't a crisis if Big Chill was in a good mood, but if more teachers were angry about the coming changes, and if they were teeing off on her, I'd be lucky to suffer only scowls, growls, and a bottom-of-the-barrel assignment.

Bracing myself, I peered into her office.

"About time. Were you waiting for me to roll out the red carpet?"

Ah. The creepy serene smile was gone. Sarcasm reigned. All was right with my little world.

Until Big Chill uttered her next words.

"History. You're filling in for Aston. He says the lesson plans are on his desk."

Eeek.

Having recently seen the state of Aston's truck and his grade book, I suspected that deciphering his lesson plans would be about as easy as translating Sumerian into Swahili by way of Mandarin. And there could well be blotches and smears of who-knows-what on the paper. Aston's ideas about hygiene were rooted in the 1860s and his concept of sanitizing was to spit on something and wipe it on the seat of his pants.

I shuddered. My breakfast flipped in my stomach. "Is Aston sick?"

"Only in the head." Big Chill shoved the sub form my way. "My guess is he's 'punishing' me for refusing to step in and let him keep his empire of trash intact." She tapped pearly fingernails on the desk. "I respect his commitment to giving students a window into the past, but something has to be done about that room. The custodians are about to lodge a formal complaint with the district office. Besides the clutter and the bugs from that moss he uses to make miniature trees, the smell is worse every day. Plus there are so many blobs of glue and gum stuck to the carpet that it needs to be torn up and replaced. And that can't happen unless he moves those bookshelves and boxes and what all."

I filled in the sub form and kept my lips zipped. Silence was often a stronger prompt for conversation than questions or give-no-ground statements about hot-button topics.

"And I'm not going to buck the superintendent on this. He wants to improve school standings and he thinks sweeping change and a complete shake-up is the way to do it."

Big Chill's tone implied that she wasn't in complete agreement with that strategy, but *was* resigned to not obstructing it as long as she wasn't affected.

"And if Aston thinks I feel punished because he's not in the building, he can grow up and think again." She drew in a long breath. "If you talk to him, tell him the air I breathe is fresher and cleaner because he's not here."

Hoping that Aston wouldn't call—and that if he did I could successfully play dumb about Big Chill's stance—I took my copy of the sub form and trotted to his room. It was exactly as I remembered it. And more.

The odor within the walls—earthy, woody, and musty—seemed to stalk me as I found the light switches and wove my way through a maze of tables and chairs to Aston's desk. There, atop a stack of papers leaning like that famous Italian tower, I found a note scribbled on a scrap of paper about the size of my hand. "Show the movie," it read.

A tiny sigh of relief leaked through my lips. Showing a movie meant I wouldn't have to skim through material and prepare a presentation, wouldn't have to copy packets in a mad rush. But showing a movie was not without difficulties. The configuration of wires run among power sources, projectors, computers, DVD players, speakers, and document cameras at Captain Meriwether High School wasn't consistent from classroom to classroom.

Sometimes the computer had to be on and the video played through it. Sometimes the document camera had to be unplugged. Sometimes speakers worked and sometimes they didn't. Teachers who remained in one classroom and worked with the same equipment every day, tended not to realize their systems might have quirks. Consequently, they never left notes or diagrams for subs to consult.

Configuration issues didn't faze me. They could usually be resolved by connecting and disconnecting until the system worked. What worried me was the movie mentioned in Aston's note. It wasn't *with* the note.

I opened the DVD player drawer, hoping to find a disc.

No luck.

I checked the computer.

Nothing.

I scouted around the desk and peered into the drawers.

Clutter, junk, and grit.

I spotted more of that when I peered at the aging TV and video player on a built-in shelf in the corner. Coffee and soft-drink cups ranged in front of the player and stacks of rolled-up poster projects were stuffed on top of it—signs that even Aston now projected videos onto a screen or the white board.

Maybe he intended that I borrow a movie from the library or show one from the archive service. I flipped the note over, hoping to see further instructions or, at the very least, some clue to the title of the movie.

That side was blank.

Okay, so maybe Aston wrote the title in his lesson plans.

I scouted again, searching for the planning book.

Nothing.

Taking a deep breath, I made a more intensive search of the desk drawers. They were crammed with things I'll leave to your imagination, but not one of those items bore any resemblance to a movie or planning book. Remembering what Big Chill said about bugs, I stayed well clear of the shelves as I scanned them.

Not a trace of a video or the book.

Moving at a trot, I headed for the teachers' room and Aston's second desk. Chaos reigned there as well—chaos accompanied by wadded paper bags and crusted tin pans. Whimpering, I scrabbled through the debris.

"Looking for something?" Doug Whitman asked.

"Subbing for Aston." I yanked out a drawer to reveal a tangle of string and rubber bands. "Can't find the movie."

Doug stashed his insulated red lunch sack in the refrigerator and brushed invisible specks from the sleeves of his spotless green-and-blue checked shirt. "What's the title? Maybe you can borrow a copy from another history teacher."

I whimpered again. "His note said 'Show the movie.' That's all."

"Typical. Maybe he wrote the title in his lesson plan book."

"I can't find that, either."

"Did you search the classroom?"

"Yes. Well, I mean I searched—"

"As much as you could without getting your fingers caught in a muskrat trap?"

"Aston said he took the traps home."

Doug laughed. "And you believed him?"

I slumped into my usual chair at the table. "I'll have to call him."

Doug pulled a cell phone from his pocket. "I'm on it." He checked a list posted beside the door, punched in a string of numbers, and put the phone to his ear. It took a full minute for his usual chipper smile to sag. "Not answering."

I hadn't expected he would. Aston was sending a message, and using me as the carrier pigeon. Emphasis on pigeon. Or should I make that sitting duck? Or cooked goose?

If Susan Mitchell was here, she'd calmly pull a video out of a well-organized cabinet in her classroom and instruct me to run it and not worry about fallout from Aston. But Susan was in jail awaiting trial for murdering a history teacher who made Aston look like the poster boy for flexibility and cooperation.

"Let's call Tremaine," Doug suggested.

I sagged lower in the chair. Taking this problem to Assistant Principal Tremaine Scott amounted to ratting out Aston. I doubted he'd take that as well as Eddie had.

Doug patted my shoulder while he dialed, explained, listened, and disconnected. "Study day. Tremaine says they can make up back work or do projects for other classes or go to the library. He'll deal with Aston later."

I winced. That would give Aston yet another reason to dislike the administration and escalate his campaign, a campaign that wasn't likely to end in triumph and might result in collateral damage to innocent bystanders—namely me.

When I got home I noticed a knot of condo residents clustered by the hedge that ran along the downriver end of the complex and separated condo property from a string of restaurants and small businesses. I seldom gave that long green rectangle more than a second glance. It was just a block of shrubbery. Occasionally it was a block of shrubbery festooned with wind-blown scraps of paper or plastic. Nothing about the hedge held my interest.

Until today.

Today the hedge was fascinating—fascinating in a morbid way, like a car wreck or a bridge collapse or a candidate backed by big money taking a shellacking.

Where once it had been straight lines and sharp edges, it now had the appearance of jagged green mountains. Clumps of hacked foliage lay in a tangled mass around the trash bins. An orange power cord laced through the heap and around the side of the bins. The chattering of a hedge trimmer blended with a string of curses.

Jake's voice.

A dozen residents headed in that direction, two of them carrying video cameras, several with their cell phones out. Unable to resist a close-up view of unfolding disaster, I followed. Easing around the trash bins, I peered over the shoulder of the man in front of me.

And there stood my ex, wearing a red tank top that did nothing for his pasty skin and a pair of brown shorts about to split in the seat. Unaware of his audience—possibly because of a set of scratched plastic goggles and the headphones clamped over his ears—he swung the hedge trimmer like a tennis racquet, narrowly missing his own knees.

The crowd gasped as one.

The trimmer bound up on a thick branch. Jake muscled it free, raised it like a golf club, and brought it around again.

The trimmer stuttered and hung up on another branch.

The crowd groaned.

Jake cursed and jerked the trimmer from side to side, working it free in a shower of bark and twigs and tattered leaves.

The crowd called out encouragement. "Don't take any bull from that bush." "Show that shrubbery who's in charge."

Jake ripped the trimmer loose once more, raised it like an axe, widened his stance, and swung with all he had.

Chapter 9

The blade sent up a spray of shredded leaf confetti and rebounded from a beer can wedged in the shrubbery.

Chattering and spitting bits of twig, it came right at Jake's face.

A woman behind me screamed.

Jake torqued his arms to the right.

The blade missed his nose by inches.

It came around in a wide arc.

And sliced the power cord.

The crowd applauded.

Demonstrating that time behind bars had increased his vocabulary, Jake unleashed another volley of profanity. He tore off the scratched goggles, pulled the headphones from his ears, and turned. "What's everybody looking at?"

"The best show in town." A man to my left pointed at the damage. "When Bernina sees that disaster she's gonna tear you apart."

Jake glanced at the hedge. His eyes widened with horror. "Don't tell her, please don't tell her. I couldn't see with those goggles she made me wear. It'll grow back. Please don't tell her."

"Won't have to say a word," a man behind me said. "She's headed this way right now."

The crowd scattered.

Jake, like the cheese in that children's song, stood alone.

64

Laughing, I headed for my condo, waving to Bernina along the way. Jake's stint as a handyman promised to provide way more entertainment than summer-season TV comedies or reality shows. Granted, the plot might be episodic and predictable—Jake messing up one assignment after another— but there were the additional elements of resident outrage, the efforts of the Committee to oust him, and Bernina's attempts to defend and/or clean up after him.

Inside, I found a message from Allison reminding me that Josh was driving her home and she was really, really excited because her fifteen-and-a-half birthday was coming up and she could get her learner's permit. "I already know all about how to drive, but Megan says there's a stupid test with lame questions, so you and Dad have to get me that book so I can learn all the dumb rules that Tiffany says you never need to know again after you pass the test. Oh, yeah, and I need $20 or $25 or something for that and a dumb form Dad has to sign. Anyway, get the little book thing from the driving place *right now.*"

"Wrong," I told the answering machine as I headed for the deck. "Right now I plan to air out my head."

Only the screen was closed, so I knew Cheese Puff would be with Mrs. Ballantine. And he was, ensconced in the glider. He gave me a quick glance and a two-centimeter wag of his tail, and returned to watching her hit a series of chalk marks as she wove her way through a phalanx of chairs.

"Imagine the chairs are dancers," she told me, "young male dancers with bare chests. Imagine they're wearing tight pants."

"How about you imagine a man with pasty skin wreaking havoc on the hedge by the trash bins?"

She stopped in mid twirl, balancing on heels high enough to give me a nosebleed. "Jake?"

"Right in one."

She danced over to the glider, sat beside Cheese Puff, and gestured for me to tell all.

I did.

When I finished, Mrs. B sighed. "Well, I never cared much for that hedge, but if a man can't trim shrubbery then there's not much hope for any other project he tackles. I confess that I didn't take your concerns about his competence as seriously as perhaps I should have. No offense, dear, but you do have a tendency to exaggerate."

I opened my mouth to object, recalled some recent hyperbole, conceded that point, and changed the subject. "Allison is about ready to get a learner's permit. She left a message ordering me to pick up the rules-of-the-road booklet."

"Seems like only yesterday that I learned to drive." Mrs. B shook her head. "How time rolls along."

"Speaking of rolling along, she doesn't want to be seen in my car. She's hoping she can train in yours."

Mrs. B winced. "Is she taking a driver's education course?"

"That would be ideal, and Dave is more than willing to pay for it, but Allison claims she already knows everything about driving. And get this, her friend Tiffany told her she could forget the rules after she passes the knowledge test."

Mrs. B fanned herself with her hand.

"I know. That's frightening. But look at Iz. She never had a lesson, she ignores most of the rules and limits, and she gets around."

"Only because other drivers have the good sense to get out of her way." Mrs. B paled. "You don't think Iz would—"

"Volunteer to teach Allison to drive? You bet. There's nothing she likes better than passing along her wealth of knowledge."

Mrs. B pressed her folded arms against her stomach and rocked for half a minute. Then her nose twitched. "This is a job for the Committee."

Not exactly an improvement over Iz. A few members of the Committee no longer drove and others should have had their licenses yanked years ago. Two could barely see over the steering wheels of gigantic cars they'd owned since the 80s, one could barely see the steering wheel itself, and several parked their cars diagonally across two spaces.

But these were the same people who adored my dog and helped me keep my life on track, so I said nothing. Silence, however, often speaks volumes.

Mrs. B's brow furrowed. "You may have a point, dear." She scratched Cheese Puff's ears and gazed off into the distance. "Some Committee members are a shade past their driving prime. And overall their nerves are not what they used to be. How about Dario?"

Dario was big, burly, and had displayed nerves of titanium in the face of danger. But were those nerves any match for a teenager flaunting the rules of the road while courting collisions? "Do you think he'd do it?"

Mrs. B fluttered her lashes. "If I ask him nicely."

"Stupid question." I smacked my forehead. "He'd walk through fire for you."

"He *is* smitten." Mrs. B fluffed her hair.

"Smitten? He's poleaxed."

She blushed and fluffed again. I felt happy for her, but worried too—for her *and* for Dario. Never mind that her departed husband's legend had—probably—been built on a lie, Marco had been the great love of her life. He'd been intelligent, witty, urbane, and classy. Dario, on the other hand, was . . . well . . . pretty much none of those things.

I bit my tongue and didn't ask where their relationship was going, mostly because that question could be tossed right back at me. Dave referred to moving in together as taking our relationship to the next level. But he hadn't mentioned what his expectations were for that particular level, or how he envisioned any levels beyond. And, after two less-than-successful marriages, the idea of doing the aisle walk again made me queasy.

A wedding wasn't a finish line for the obstacle course of a relationship. It was a new starting line. And Dave and I had a lot of baggage to sort out before we got on our marks.

"He'll need a car for the training sessions," Mrs. B mused.

True. Dario occasionally rented a car, but generally Mrs. B picked him up at the airport.

"The best plan might be to use mine," I offered. "It's already a wreck."

"It is. I've been thinking we should get you a new car."

Note the pronouns in that sentence. I = Mrs. B. We = Mrs. B + ?

As far as I could remember, I'd taken part in no discussions about replacing my car. In fact, I recalled saying I intended to drive it until it was nothing but four wheels and a windshield, or until I got a teaching job and held it long enough to build a savings account to a pre-Jake level. Having Mrs. B for a friend was a special and wonderful experience, but because of her interventions I seemed to be making less progress toward becoming a genuine grown-up.

(For the record, I define that as being able to make smart decisions most of the time, picking out clothes that don't make too many people roll their eyes, and not having to beg for an emergency loan more than once a year.)

"At the very least, I think we should get you a new set of tires." Mrs. B stroked Cheese Puff's head. "I wouldn't want you to have a blowout with the little prince in the car."

Never mind that I'd be in the car too.

Cheese Puff shot me a smug glance as if to remind me that he was the center of Mrs. B's universe and I was a mere outlying planet spinning around a distant star. "Maybe I'll qualify for an employee discount when I start that new job someone 'found' for me."

"Employee discounts. That's a good idea. I'll talk to Larry a—" She frowned. "Ah, you were being sarcastic. That's not your best quality, dear. In fact, it can drive people away."

"Really?" I feigned shock. "It hasn't worked with Iz or Jake or Bernina."

Mrs. B flipped her fingers and opened her mouth to speak. The phone in my condo rang. "Probably Allison." I stood and headed for the door. "Asking if I got the instruction booklet yet."

"Don't answer," Mrs. B advised. "The longer you delay, the more time we have to get Dario on board. If Dave approves, of course."

The message machine clicked in and I heard my voice and then Iz's, tight with fury. "He's out. Brendon Ryder is out of jail."

Chapter 10

I raced inside and dove for the phone as Iz concluded. "His girlfriend took the blame for making and throwing the firebomb. Apparently you don't care, or you'd answer your phone."

When I snatched up the receiver I heard only the dial tone. Just as well, considering the edge to her voice.

I called Paulette and got confirmation, tipping the phone away from my ear so that Mrs. B could hear. "The girlfriend claims she did it and the police don't have any proof she's lying. Plus, Ryder doesn't have a record. Denise was too scared to have him arrested whenever he beat her up."

"Is that poor woman all right?" Mrs. B asked. "Denise, I mean. Not the girlfriend."

"She's angry," Paulette said. "And worried. And scared."

"Someone needs to stay with her," I said. "In case he—"

"That's covered. Several men and women who worked on her house have volunteered—your sister is organizing them."

"Then we don't have to worry about her safety."

Mrs. B nodded with satisfaction and I had to agree. When Iz got her teeth into something, she was a pit bull.

"I wish I knew whether the girlfriend is covering for him or telling the truth," Paulette said. "And that opens another door. Did she do it on her own or because he manipulated or forced her to? I'll let you know if I hear more."

Paulette disconnected, Mrs. B stroked Cheese Puff's ears, and I gripped the phone. Possibly the girlfriend was in so deep that she threw the firebomb to prove love and loyalty, believing she did it of her own free will. Or possibly she was sick and possessive and wanted Denise and the children gone, so no one else would have a claim on Brendon Ryder.

I shuddered, wishing I could wash that thought from my mind.

"Let's hope the police sort this out soon. If that man did it, or made her do it, I want him off the streets." Mrs. B set Cheese Puff on the sofa, wandered into the kitchen area, and opened the freezer. She poked around, then surveyed the contents of the refrigerator. "What are you making for dinner?"

I blinked and set the phone in its cradle. "Dinner?"

"Dinner is important, dear. That's the meal where family members reconnect after individual adventures, and share their hopes and dreams over plates of nutritious food."

Uh-oh. Not only "food" but "nutritious food" with emphasis on the adjective. Clearly that meant no leftovers, no pizza, no sandwiches, and no suggesting that Dave and Allison fend for themselves.

"What you serve is only part of it." Mrs. B opened a cabinet, took out a sack of rice with about ten grains left, and tossed it in the trash. "Allison needs more structure and a firm schedule. And you and Dave need to take time every day to make sure the channels of communication are open. You need to listen to Allison's concerns and share your own."

While Dave and I had concerns related to drugs, pregnancy, and dropping out of school, Allison's concerns were mostly of the everyone-else-is-doing-it-and-I'm-not variety or the you're-mean-and-don't-want-me-to-have-any-fun ilk. But I knew Mrs. B. An attempt to make light of the situation wouldn't fly.

"It's kind of hard to set a firm schedule when Allison has play rehearsals and study dates and Dave could be off on a drug

71

bust or undercover. And what about my water aerobics classes?"

Another thought careened into my mind, one so horrible that my legs quivered, my knees knocked, and I slumped into a chair at the table where the alleged dinners would take place. Who would prepare those meals?

My culinary skills were rudimentary at best given the fact that Iz raised me after my parents checked out emotionally following my brother's death. If you needed a PB&J sandwich or someone to gussy up salad from a sack or slice cheese to top a few crackers, I was your girl. If you wanted homemade artisan bread, a soufflé, special sauces on your meat, and berry tarts for dessert, you were out of luck.

To my knowledge, I'd never exchanged a recipe with a friend, never torn one from a magazine in a waiting room, and never went on-line to find new and exciting ways to cook broccoli. Neither of my marriages had been measured in hours spent braising, grilling, simmering, coddling, steeping, poaching, or deglazing. Before Albert died on a birding expedition, he was fond of items labeled with the words "heat and eat" or "dinner in a box." As for Jake, he was fond of eating out, mostly with other women—a fact I discovered when his credit card maxed out and he appropriated mine.

And what about shopping for groceries? When I started at the auto repair shop, I'd be working 40 hours a week. Was Mrs. B expecting I'd put in another 40 stocking provisions and preparing nutritious meals? And what did a nutritious meal consist of? How many specific elements?

I groaned.

Cheese Puff scampered over, sat at my feet, and cocked his head.

"You'll divide up the tasks, of course," Mrs. B said.

"Of course," I echoed, envisioning Allison's reaction if I asked her to peel potatoes. I wondered if she'd ever seen a potato before it was sliced into shoestrings and fried in a vat of bubbling oil. Had there been a time, before her mother departed, that she climbed on a chair and helped stir the batter for a cake or chopped carrots for a salad?

"But *you'll* need to be in charge," Mrs. B added.

"Why me?" For a second I almost channeled Iz and played the card labeled: Because-I'm-a-woman? "Why can't Dave be in charge?"

"His schedule is more erratic, he's in a crisis situation at work, and he has the main responsibility for Allison. Besides, you have a good . . . a *better* grasp of what a healthy diet is all about than he does."

Talk about faint praise. At least Mrs. B had the grace to blush before plunging on to the next platitude. "I know it will be a little difficult at first."

"Yeah, like climbing Mount Everest wearing flip-flops, handcuffs, and a blindfold."

"You're exaggerating again, dear."

But not by much.

Mrs. B dusted her hands. "Well, there's no time like the present to get started. I set the frozen chicken breasts out for you to season. If you roast the broccoli with olive oil and sea salt you'll hardly notice it's not quite fresh. Then make a pasta salad with the odds and ends in the vegetable crisper and toss it with what's left in that bottle of raspberry vinaigrette dressing. For dessert you can scoop out sorbet and decorate the bowls with orange slices."

She made it sound as if she believed I could do all that successfully *and* in one afternoon.

"You'll want to get started soon so you can put dinner on the table between 5:30 and 6:00. That way you'll have time to eat and talk and clear away before you leave for water aerobics."

"You're not going to stick around? In case I need help?"

She rolled her eyes as if to say this was dinner, not splitting the atom. "I have things to do, dear. Tomorrow I'll make a list of staples you'll need to have on hand. And I'll poll the Committee for recipe and meal suggestions."

With a little finger flutter, she left.

My lower lip pushed out into a major-league pout and I kicked at the carpet.

Cheese Puff raced for the safety of his favorite chair and burrowed between the arm and the seat cushion.

I wondered what I'd been thinking when Dave suggested he and Allison move in. Scratch that. I knew exactly what I'd been thinking—that Dave and I would have more time for activities involving bare flesh and whispered suggestions. I hadn't thought beyond that. Certainly not about nutritious dinners—or about me being in charge of seeing that they got on the table. Never mind that Mrs. B had a point about why Dave wasn't the prime candidate for the job. Why did I have to be the grown-up?

A few more kicks at the long-suffering carpet and I stood, took a deep breath, and marched off to launch the culinary battle with an attack on the layers of plastic wrap around the ice-encrusted chicken.

The phone rang.

I lunged for it.

Even talking with a telemarketer seemed preferable to a glimpse of frost-burned chicken skin.

"Rehearsal's gonna go another hour and Josh can't drive me," Allison whined. "Dad's not answering and I'm tired, so park real close to the drama room when you come to get me."

Saved by the belle!

My favorite Mexican restaurant was on the way. They had a drive-up window. *And* they took call-in orders.

I tossed the chicken back in the freezer.

Good nutrition could wait another day.

So could growing up and taking responsibility.

"Aston's out again," Big Chill told me the next morning. "Carrying on his campaign to change things for his convenience. Acting like a child."

I thought of myself, kicking the carpet and snatching even the weakest excuse to shirk a task. Until I womanned up, I couldn't criticize Aston.

I signed the sub form. "Did he e-mail in lesson plans?"

Big Chill snorted. "No. And he doesn't answer his phone. Tremaine's rounding something up."

She leveled a finger at me. "If you or any of your cohorts talk to Aston or send him a smoke signal or carve a sign in a tree, tell him he's got one more day to get his act together. He's not the only teacher who ever had to move to another classroom or teach different subjects. In fact, he's the only one who hasn't had to change a thing in the past ten years. So if he thinks he'll get support for this sit-out, he's 110% wrong."

A few hours later I heard that exact percentage once again. This time, to my amazement, it was coupled with the word "right" and used in reference to Iz.

Chapter 11

"Your sister is 110% right." Mrs. B's message on my cell phone proclaimed. "The justice system is broken. She's calling for a sit-in at the courthouse starting at 4:00. I'll pack lawn chairs and a picnic supper. Be ready at 3:30."

"Bad news?" Doug Whitman asked.

"No." I tucked the phone in my pocket and took my steaming lunch from the microwave. "Just another day filled with avalanching events over which I have no control—events that might sweep me over a precipice and into a crevasse so deep sunlight will be little more than a memory."

"Nice image. A little over-the-top, but nice. What's up?"

"My sister's mad as hell at the justice system. She's organizing a sit-in at the courthouse. 4:00 PM if any of you are interested."

"I might be," Gertrude said. "If it's to protest that wife-beating firebomber getting out of jail."

I bit into the remains of a veggie burrito. The wrapping was soggy and the vegetables inside were gummy, but I reminded myself I hadn't had to cook it and chowed onward. "*Alleged* wife-beating firebomber," I mumbled. "They don't have a witness and his girlfriend's taking the blame."

"I'd give him the benefit of the doubt if he didn't look like such a smirking pretty boy in that picture in the paper."

"I hate smug. Especially in a man." Brenda shot a glare at Aston's vacant chair. "How long will it last?"

"I have no idea. Mrs. Ballantine is packing lawn chairs and a picnic supper."

Brenda opened a plastic container, unleashing the scent of gin and garlic. "Some of those sit-ins go on for days."

True. But surely Mrs. B wasn't planning on that. Surely her intention was that we listen to a few speeches and chant a few protest slogans along the lines of "No bail. Keep him in jail." Maybe we'd stick around until dusk and light candles, then leave the rest to hardier souls who didn't have to work in the morning.

"You better bring blankets." Brenda stirred the contents of her container. "And a tarp in case it rains."

Doug eyed the container and wrinkled his nose. "I wonder if Iz ordered trash cans and portable toilets."

"Don't think I don't know what you mean by that remark." Brenda drove a fork into the container and brought up a mass of wilted spinach and red cabbage. "If you want to insult my lunch, Doug, then come out and do it."

Doug raised his hands, fingers spread. "I meant a crowd makes waste. Plus they'll lock the courthouse at the close of the day, and the nearest public facilities are in the park several blocks away. Sooner or later, someone will make use of the shrubbery around the courthouse."

Scowling, Brenda stuffed salad into her mouth.

"I bet Iz thought of that," Gertrude said. "She's organized lots of protests."

"I don't know how much 'organizing' she does," I said. "She sees herself as a catalyst. She makes incendiary remarks. She incites people to action."

"Kind of a professional lightning rod," Doug mused.

"Nice image."

He grinned. "Not on a scale with your avalanche."

"I've had more practice embellishing." Too much, according to Mrs. B.

"And more practice getting caught in the avalanches of life. I hope you don't get tear gassed."

"Me, too. I don't have time to buy a gas mask between now and 3:30."

A bright thought blazed across my brain. If I went to the protest, I wouldn't be expected to make dinner. And if I got gassed, I'd need a few days to recover.

Doug glanced at the empty chair next to his. "Has anyone heard from Aston?"

Gertrude shook her head. Brenda stabbed at her salad, sending another whiff of gin and garlic my way. Talk about aromatherapy. "I wouldn't answer if he *did* call. That man—no, that overgrown boy—never thinks about anything but dressing up in stinky old clothes and eating disgusting food."

All gazes shifted to the container that held her lunch. In the silence that followed I decided that being a grown-up meant not only knowing when to keep my lips zipped, but also doing it.

"Wow," Allison exclaimed, "you can hear Iz from here."

"Here" was the slice of street in front of a jewelry shop two blocks from the courthouse. A sign labeled that slice a loading zone, but Mrs. B was having none of that.

"There isn't another spot within miles, and it's hot enough to scorch the polish on my toenails." She fluttered diamond-laden fingers and headed for the door. "I spend a lot of money in this shop."

In less than a minute she returned with a balding man who bowed after every sentence, insisted she take his personal space in the alley behind the store, and mentioned a shipment of rubies due in at the end of next week.

"Money talks," I whispered to Allison.

"But not as loud as Iz."

I had been surprised when Allison invited herself along—until she asked if we'd get arrested or be on the news. Then I realized she hoped to attract attention and perhaps make her friends envious.

I was also surprised when Dave agreed she could come, saying, "It's okay, if she doesn't have homework. I know you'll keep an eye on her."

I hadn't brought up the difficulty of keeping an eye on someone while being chased by mounted police officers. Dave would have laughed at the idea of a protest in Reckless River growing large and rowdy enough to merit police intervention on that level. But Dave had never seen Iz's scrapbook.

"Besides," he'd said, "Mrs. Ballantine will be with you."

And we all knew she was a shining example of taking the rational route. Two months ago she pooh-poohed the idea of waiting for the police to get a team together, and led the charge to rescue Cheese Puff from a drug dealer.

The jewelry store owner bowed once more, Mrs. B handed over a spare key to her car, and we headed off, sweating like stevedores as we marched along in the wake of dozens of women of all ages. Some were in groups, others in pairs or alone or with children in tow. They wore jeans and shorts, message T-shirts and office attire, ball caps and big-brimmed straw hats with bright ribbons like Mrs. B's.

Hundreds of women and a few men—some looking cornered and others committed—had already staked out places on the lawn. I spotted Penelope, her blond hair in a stubby ponytail, and Paulette, a pair of sparkly earrings catching the sunlight. Dressed like dozens of others in white blouses with black armbands and wearing white ball caps with the words "justice now," they were handing out leaflets, answering questions, and urging protesters to fill in empty areas.

Several uniformed police officers stood on the sidewalks on either side of the four-story brick courthouse. More were in the street, signaling for gawking drivers to move along and directing a huge police department van into a no-parking area. Two golf-cart-sized parking patrol units cruised the meters, ready to write tickets. I wondered if Dave was on call to help with crowd control.

Allison pointed to woman pacing at the foot of the courthouse steps. Dressed in a flowing robe, she carried a plastic sword and a set of scales. "Shouldn't she have a blindfold?"

"Perhaps she's making the point that justice isn't blind as it should be," Mrs. B answered.

"Or maybe her insurance doesn't include protesting with her eyes covered," I suggested.

Telling myself I shouldn't be so cynical, I lugged lawn chairs, a golf umbrella, a jug of ice water, a blanket, and a plastic tarp. Mrs. B and Allison staggered ahead, each holding a handle of a wicker picnic basket large enough to provision an expedition to the Bering Sea.

(Okay, so that's an embellishment, but the point is that Mrs. B tends to do—or overdo—things in a big way.)

Wearing an enormous white shirt that gave her the appearance of a pregnant polar bear, Iz balanced on a folding table in the center of the wide lawn. "Stay out of the flower gardens," she bellowed. "Do not block the road. Do not drive stakes into the lawn."

"She doesn't have a microphone or anything," Allison marveled.

My sister, the human bullhorn.

"Do not litter. Do not use profanity or display lewd signs. Do not engage or antagonize police officers assigned to monitor this event."

"That's almost more rules than at school," Allison groused.

I laughed, lost my grip on the umbrella, gathered it up again, and dropped the rolled-up tarp in the process. I kicked it forward a dozen feet, caught up with it, and kicked it again, ignoring the stares of people I passed. The contents of that picnic basket had better be worth all this.

Mrs. B and Allison zigged right and then zagged left in search of a piece of level ground among the roots of a spreading maple tree. Toe poised for the next round of kick-the-tarp, I listened to my sister.

"We have no permit for this rally and no approval from Reckless River officials. But I believe our First Amendment right to assemble far outweighs petty rules and bureaucracy. And our First Amendment right to free speech, in my mind, means we should not have to pay for a piece of paper giving us permission to talk about what's wrong with the justice system in this city, this county, and this nation."

The gathering crowd roared its approval.

Mrs. B settled on a spot and they lowered the picnic basket to the grass, rubbed their arms, and flexed their shoulders.

I kicked the tarp and caught up, wondering what the heck Mrs. B had in that basket. A whole turkey? Two watermelons? Gold ingots?

"And why, when we're here for justice, justice for women, should we be required to have insurance?" Iz asked in a voice loud enough to disrupt salmon runs heading up the Columbia. "Did those who signed the Declaration of Independence have insurance?"

She raised her fist in the air and pumped it. "Today we answer to a higher law!"

The crowd roared once more. Allison joined in.

Iz pumped her fist again. "Today we don't answer to the man."

Another roar.

"Today we stick it to the man!"

A louder roar.

"Who's the man she's talking about?" Allison asked. "The judge? The one that let that guy out?"

"No, 'the man' refers to anyone in authority." I dropped the lawn chairs, umbrella and blanket, released the jug with a greater degree of care, and arched my aching back.

81

"It means to oppose those in power, generally through acts of civil disobedience." Mrs. B shook out the tarp, detailed the legal logic behind Brendon Ryder's release, and explained that Iz focused on this case to make broader points about abuse and prosecution and attitudes toward women. From there she went on to give Allison an overview of the history of bucking authority, tossing about names like Thoreau, Gandhi, and King.

After about a minute and a half—a good 45 seconds beyond my personal best attempt at keeping her focused—Allison's gaze slid toward the far side of the courthouse. "There's Jennifer. And Lisa. Her brother Sam's a senior. He's hot!" Waving to her friends with both hands, she took off across the lawn.

"Hot trumps all." I pulled a canvas chair from its fabric sheath and unfolded it.

"I suppose it did in my day as well." Mrs. B dropped into the chair and fanned herself with her hat. "Iz certainly knows how to stir up a crowd."

"One of her many talents."

"I confess I did a little searching on the Internet. Does she *always* get arrested?"

"That's pretty much how she knows the protest is a success."

Mrs. B opened the picnic basket, dug out a plastic cup, filled it from the water jug, and passed it to me. "How long does it usually take? For her to get arrested?"

I sipped, then splashed a little into my hand and rubbed it on the back of my neck. "It all depends on the cause, the crowd, and the city. Her record is 89 minutes. Sometimes it takes days. Once she was at it for a week."

Mrs. B filled a cup for herself and wedged it into the holder built into her chair. "I'm glad I brought plenty of provisions."

Uh-oh.

"You're planning to stay for the whole thing?"

"I want to show solidarity." She fitted the hat on her head and cocked it to one side. "And I don't want to be a party pooper."

Perish the thought.

"Think how educational this is for Allison."

Yeah, right. Allison, who was giggling with her pals as they ambled around the perimeter of the swelling protest. Probably getting an education about Sam's favorite foods and whether he slept in gym shorts or briefs.

I splashed more water on my neck. Iz jumped from the table and a woman in a blue blazer and tan slacks took her place and accepted a bullhorn handed up from one of Iz's minions. She introduced herself as a candidate for the legislature and said she'd fight for tougher laws dealing with violence against women.

"Fight!?! Why must they always use that word?" Mrs. B asked. "I'm in favor of tougher laws, but I'd rather vote for someone who promised to convince the other side by remaining calm and using superior logic."

I snorted. "Superior logic seldom has a place in politics."

"It should."

I snorted again, checked to see where Allison was, and watched another two dozen women stream onto the lawn. One pushed a walker. Another maneuvered a wheelchair. A third carted a bottle of oxygen. A pang of guilt jabbed my brain. I needed to adjust my attitude.

I started by adjusting my chair, wiggling it to a more level spot and slumping to ease my back. If Mrs. B intended to stay for the duration, so would I. If I didn't make it to Captain Meriwether High to cover Aston's classes tomorrow, too bad.

"You ladies got any spare water for a thirsty man and his dog?"

I turned to see Dave and Lola trudging our way. Lola's tongue hung from the corner of her mouth. Dave wore jeans and a black, sweat-stained T-shirt with white letters spelling out "I Brake for Potholes."

"I wondered if you'd get called in," I said. "Is Lola sniffing for drugs?"

"Not unless my orders change. The lieutenant told me to wander around, blend in with the crowd, ignore anything involving drugs unless it's major league, be prepared to step in if I'm needed, and," he made quote marks in the air, "stay as far away from Dick McBain as possible."

Dave accepted a cup of water and drank while Lola sniffed Mrs. B's enormous straw purse—a purse that, naturally, matched her hat.

"The little prince isn't in there," Mrs. B told her. "He's at home. I worried he'd get stepped on or eat something that would make him sick."

"Like a common everyday dog biscuit?" Dave asked. "The kind regular mutts eat?"

"Cheese Puff has a highly developed palate. And he's not a mutt. He's simply a breed that hasn't been recognized yet."

Dave rolled his eyes, held the cup out for a refill, and lowered it. Lola sniffed, then lapped, splashing water up his arm. "Hey, I don't need a bath."

Mrs. B patted Lola's rump. "Neatness doesn't count when you're thirsty. Would you like a roast beef sandwich, girl? I'll scrape off the horseradish."

Lola wagged her tail.

"She'll get gas. I'll eat the sandwich later so it won't go to waste. It will be a huge sacrifice." Dave grinned and glanced around. "Where's Allison? Didn't she come with you?"

I pointed to the trio of girls on the courthouse steps taking pictures of each other with the Lady Justice impersonator. "Iz announced that she didn't get a permit for this shindig. Or insurance. Is that reason enough to shut the rally down?"

"Technically, yes, but I doubt anyone wants to risk negative publicity by tossing a bunch of women off the courthouse lawn."

"Even Ron Weador wouldn't be that dumb," Mrs. B said. "More's the pity. What's the law enforcement plan?"

"I wouldn't know. I'm so far out of the loop I might as well be in Indiana." Dave opened the picnic basket and surveyed its contents. "Pudding cups," he said with a sigh of contentment. "Chocolate pudding cups."

"I heard Iz on the radio this morning promoting this rally," Mrs. B said. "And I heard Mr. McBain talking about security. Wasn't there a strategy meeting?"

"You bet. Dick McBain led it. He had pictures of Iz's previous rallies. He had diagrams and logistical charts. He had bullet points." Dave tore the lid off a pudding cup and dug in with a plastic spoon. "Anybody who is anybody attended."

"Ah. I see." Mrs. B nodded. "You've been ostracized."

Dave swelled out his chest. "You're looking at the pariah of the police force."

I studied the proud smile on his face. "You're an awfully happy pariah. Why is that?"

He ruffled my hair with his free hand. "Because Dick McBain is in charge of police response while the chief is away. He thinks this will be his chance to show Reckless River he has the right stuff."

"And you think he has the *wrong* stuff," Mrs. B mused. "And that might be revealed before the evening is over."

Dave scraped out the last of the pudding and licked the spoon. "Right after world peace, that's my fondest wish."

I glanced around and noted more police officers than before. "This won't be like Chicago in 1968 will it? Will we be gassed or clubbed?"

Chapter 12

"Odds are you'll be fine as long as there's TV coverage." Dave crumpled the pudding cup and stashed it in the basket. "It's in poor taste to appear on the news gassing or clubbing a woman."

"If that's a joke, I'm not laughing."

"Lighten up, Barb. We get confrontation training and we learn the steps to this kind of a dance helping out in other jurisdictions." Dave scratched his chin and frowned. "Well, except for Dick McBain. He's never been in a situation like this, and I'm living proof he isn't known for letting insults roll off his back."

Leaning closer, Dave lowered his voice. "He called in everyone who isn't on vacation. He's got an army. And when you've got an army—"

"You're tempted to use it." Mrs. B finished the sentence.

"If nothing else," I added, "to justify the cost."

"McBain is in that police van right now watching the feeds from the cameras on the roof and monitoring communications. If your sister lights his fuse and nobody tries too hard to snuff it out . . ."

"The result could be less than politically correct?" Mrs. B guessed.

"That's my opinion," Dave said. "But what do I know? I'm a pariah."

He ruffled my hair again and shot Mrs. B a victory sign. "Don't give away that sandwich."

Mrs. B promised it was his and settled deeper into her chair.

The woman who wanted to be a legislator wrapped up and Iz took the table again and reminded everyone to be respectful of others.

"It's a good thing she doesn't have to *demonstrate* being respectful of others," I groused. "They'd have to call in a stunt double."

Mrs. B didn't laugh, but her eyes twinkled and she didn't urge me—as usual—to be more charitable toward my sister. I chalked up my snide comment as a success, but didn't push my luck with another.

Allison wandered over as Iz wound up a diatribe against men who skip child support payments and suffer few penalties, then introduced the next speaker and helped her up on the table. One side of the woman's head was shaved and a row of stitches ran through the bare spot. Her right arm was in a sling. She spoke in a soft and hesitant voice, saying she feared her boyfriend for years, but took the beatings until she realized she wasn't at fault. Now she intended to speak up to help herself and others.

Mouth agape, Allison sat on the folded blanket beside Mrs. Ballantine's chair. "Her boyfriend beat her up? Why?"

Mrs. B twined her fingers in Allison's hair—auburn this week—and in a low and patient voice talked about fear and control and dependency and possession and the cycle of beatings and apologies. Her gaze fixed on the injured woman, Allison chewed at her lip, nodding occasionally. When Mrs. B wrapped up, Allison went on chewing for a few seconds, then frowned. "Josh would never do stuff like that. Would he?"

Mrs. B and I exchanged wary glances. Josh was a great kid and seemed kind and mellow and respectful, but how well did we really know him?

I nodded at Mrs. B to field the question, but Allison spoke first. "He better not." She jabbed air with her fists. "I'll punch him right back and then I'll leave so fast he'll think I went invisible."

"And then you'll tell your father," Mrs. B said.

Allison mulled that. "What if Dad thinks it's my fault?"

"He won't."

"Are you sure? I can be kind of annoying."

Kind of?

I bit back that comment. This was a serious conversation. "Annoying is no excuse for abuse."

"Abusers get away with what they do because their victims keep quiet," Mrs. B said. "So tell the adults you know. Tell your friends. The more people who know, the less likely that guy will hurt you again. Or hurt someone else."

Allison nodded and watched Iz help the battered woman to the ground. The sheen of tears on her eyes told me she got the message. But messages had a way of being misplaced or forgotten, so I made a mental note to raise this topic again in casual conversations.

Iz vaulted to the table, shaded her eyes, and gazed out over the crowd. Women—and a few men—were still streaming in. Some carried only purses and light jackets; others had bulging packs and determined expressions that said, "I'm prepared for anything and I intend to stay until it happens."

Cars rolled by, pausing to drop off more protesters even as police officers directing traffic gestured for them to move on. At least half the license plates were from Oregon.

"There's a TV truck." Allison pointed off to the west.

"And there's another coming the other way," Mrs. B said.

Iz turned toward the first TV truck and I guessed her day was now complete—protesters from two states *and* live TV coverage. She ran her fingers through her cropped hair. No more Mohawk. No more dye in astounding colors.

88

Mrs. B pulled a phone from her pocket. "I'll get the Committee to record the news reports."

Allison fluffed her hair. "Will we be on TV?"

"Not sitting way over here we won't," Mrs. B said.

Wrong response.

I shot her a warning glance, but it was too late. Allison jumped to her feet and announced, "I'm gonna go up by Iz. Maybe I'll get interviewed."

Wouldn't Iz love that! But how would Dave feel?

I did a mental scramble and came up with, "I don't think they can interview you unless you're over 18. If you're not, you have to have permission from a parent."

Mrs. B raised her eyebrows, but Allison didn't question me. "Why is there always some lame law getting in the way of what kids want to do?"

Because what kids want to do usually leans toward ridiculous, rebellious, risky, or rude?

"Beats me," I said.

Allison whipped out her phone and punched Dave's number. In a moment she blurted out her demand that he come to the courthouse and help her get on TV—after going by the condo and picking up her turquoise top and the earrings with the silver feathers. She pouted as she listened to his answer, then jammed the phone in her pocket.

"He says he's busy and he's a long way off."

Dave *was* busy, but he wasn't a long way off. Looking past Allison, I spotted him on the lawn of an office building across the street talking to a couple of deputies. His back was turned to us and Lola sat at his feet, only her haunch and tail showing.

"That's a shame, dear." Mrs. B opened the picnic basket. "Why don't you have a cup of lemonade and a few of those ginger cookies and try again later? It seems to me that this rally will go on for a long time and reporters will be hunting for new people to interview every time they do an update."

89

Distracted, Allison unpacked goodies, and munched away, filling us in on Sam and assuring us she still liked Josh and they were definitely going steady, but if Sam ever asked her out she wasn't sure what she'd do because he was so hot and all the other girls were in love with him and it would make them all totally jealous, and . . .

I refrained from rolling my eyes and concentrated on the next speaker, a man running for an open spot on the court and claiming that had he been on the bench when the Ryder case came up, things would have been different.

Easy to say. Tough to do with no hard evidence.

I yawned and let my eyelids droop.

When I woke up, the shadows were longer, Mrs. B paged through a book on the history of Las Vegas, and Allison played a game on her phone. Iz stood on the table, taking the police to task.

"This is about equality," she roared. "Women don't get fair treatment. Why? Because the men in charge are living in another age. They don't get it. They just don't get it!"

Women leaped to their feet, applauding, taking up the chant. "They just don't get it."

"Not only do they not get it, they don't care," Iz said. "They don't care about justice for women because they don't care about women."

I sat up straight, tapped Mrs. B's arm, and shouted to be heard over deafening applause. "Pudding boy might get his wish."

She flashed me a twinkling smile, slid a silver bookmark between the pages, and tucked the book into her purse. Exchanging glances, we watched Iz point to police around the courthouse. "Their time and talents are being wasted. They should be out patrolling the streets so women are safer, out searching for those who commit crimes against women, out building cases to take to court so the revolving door on the justice system stops spinning. I bet they'd rather be doing that. So why aren't they? Why are they here?"

Iz turned 45 degrees and pointed at the police van. "They're here because their boss, the man hiding in that van, pulled them off their patrols and investigations, ordered them to stay on after their shifts ended, and called them in from their days off."

I blinked. Had Dave talked to Iz while I dozed?

No. Even angry as he was about McBain, he wouldn't do that.

Mrs. B, on the other hand, might spill every bean in the bag. That would explain why she avoided my gaze, and why she was studying the van with an expression of surprise and innocence.

"He wanted an army of police officers here in case things get out of control. And, you know what, he's positive things *will* get out of control," Iz raged. "Why? Because we're women. Because everyone knows women aren't rational. Everyone knows women are emotional and erratic."

The crowd booed and cheered, applauded and stomped.

"And he thinks that because we're women, our demands can be ignored. He thinks we're not logical. We're not organized. We're not disciplined. We don't see things through."

A woman nearby screamed out a string of profanities aimed at every man she had ever encountered, especially a guy named Brent who had testicles the size of gnat's eggs. Eyes wide, Allison put aside her phone and sat up. I doubted she'd hear words that wouldn't enter her ears at CMHS. And I doubted this was less intense than one of the daily dustups in the cafeteria. But I worried this experience would make her see men and women as archenemies with no common ground.

"They think because we're women we'll change our minds," Iz shouted. "Or we'll give up because we're tired or our feet hurt or our mascara ran or our hair got frizzy in the heat."

"Hell no! Let it frizz. We're not leaving." Screams swelled around us.

"They think that if they ignore us we'll give up and go back to the kitchen, back to scrubbing the floors and making dinner, getting those dishes washed, getting that laundry done."

She pointed at the police van. "Well, listen up, Mr. Pinhead. Write this down, Mr. Pencil Pusher. We're not giving up. We're not going home. Not tonight. Not tomorrow. Not next week. Not until we get justice."

"Justice! Justice!" Hundreds of voices cried out.

Iz leveled both forefingers at the van. "We don't care how big your army is. We'll go on breaking your petty rules and regulations as long as it takes to change things in Reckless River from business as usual to liberty and justice for all. For women. For children. For all."

"Justice for all!" the crowd chanted. "Justice for all."

"I hope you're comfortable in that air-conditioned van, Mr. Number Cruncher, because you'll be there a long time. We're digging in. We're declaring ourselves independent. We no longer consent to your government. You're trampling on our lives, our liberties, and our pursuit of happiness."

Definitely the Declaration of Independence, even with Iz's twist.

Mrs. B tapped my hand. "What would Thomas Jefferson think?"

"About being loosely quoted? Or about Iz?"

She smiled. "Imagine her going up against the heavies of history. Wouldn't you love to take her into the past?"

"Would we have to bring her back?" Allison asked.

I laughed. Sometimes I'm wild about that kid.

"I mean, I guess she's good at stuff like this." Allison waved an arm to take in the rally. "But most of the time she's saying stuff I don't understand and criticizing everyone and riding Dad's butt mostly because he's a guy. And he can't help that, so I don't know why she wastes her time."

"You raise interesting points, dear." Mrs. B opened the picnic basket, rooted out a plastic sack filled with foil-wrapped sandwiches, and offered it to me. "I could nibble on a little something. How about you?"

I'm always ready to nibble, nosh, or gnaw. "What are my choices?"

"Cream cheese, cucumber, tomato, and red onion on whole wheat. Turkey with spinach and Swiss cheese on sourdough. Roast beef with sharp cheddar and horseradish on rye."

"Veggie, please."

"Turkey," Allison said. "And chips. You brought chips, didn't you?"

"I never leave home without them." Mrs. B pulled a bag from the basket.

"Ooooh." Allison snatched it and tore the crinkling plastic with a soft explosion of air and a rolling rattle of chips. "You bought the really good kind."

The implication being that Dave and I didn't, thus depriving her. And I suppose that, in an effort to afford things besides that particular brand of chips, we did.

"What's this costing the city? How much overtime will taxpayers have to shell out for?" Iz bellowed in a voice starting to crack. "I'm not faulting any of you in uniform or plainclothes. You were *ordered* to come here. You're doing your job because, in this economy, if you *have* a job you want to hang onto it. I get that. So I'm asking the question Mr. Bean Counter should have asked: If we don't need a show of force, why put on a farce of a show?"

"Good one." Mrs. B unwrapped a turkey sandwich and took a bite.

I raised the top slice of whole wheat bread on my sandwich, pushed aside Allison's grasping fingers long enough to snatch a few of those high-end potato chips, layered them on the cucumber, and munched away while my sister poked the

93

dragon known as Dick McBain. As I chewed my last bite, the rear door of the police van opened and a man stepped out.

Except for the scowl on his face and his clenched fists, he wasn't at all what I expected. He was tall and slender, but had broad shoulders. His brown hair was gelled, his skin tanned. His facial features put him well into the handsome zone. His suit hung as if tailor-made over a crisp shirt and a tie secured with a flawless knot. He could have been a magazine model.

The crowd gave way as he marched toward Iz. Four officers fell in behind him, forming a wedge.

"Uh-oh," Allison said. "Is she gonna get arrested?"

"Probably." I wadded up my foil and tossed it in the basket.

Allison put the chips aside and hugged herself. "Is she scared?"

"Maybe. But she'd never admit it. And it's what she came for." Mrs. B patted her purse. "Do you suppose I'll need to transfer funds from my money market account to bail her out?"

I shrugged. "I don't know how high bail runs. She never asked me to put up the money."

"Probably because you wouldn't," Allison teased.

Mrs. B squeezed my arm. "You would if you had funds to spare, dear."

Would I?

Maybe.

Probably.

But plenty of others always came forward with cash. And when the cases were settled—always without Iz serving time—supporters turned out in droves to help her perform mandated community service. "She probably has a committee standing by to raise funds."

"That's true." Mrs. B patted her purse again. "But if they need a little extra, they can count on me."

A little extra on my planet amounted to ten or twenty bucks. On Mrs. B's, it probably ran to ten or twenty thousand.

Iz planted her fists on her hips and widened her stance as Dick McBain approached. Minus her magenta Mohawk, she wasn't as imposing as she'd been a few months ago, but her billowing shirt, tinged orange and red by the setting sun, created the illusion of imperial power.

Seeming not in the least intimidated, McBain strode to her table, jabbing a forefinger. The officers trailing him remained stone-faced as they spread out to hold back the crowd.

"What's he saying?" Allison folded the chip bag closed and got to her feet.

Mrs. B also rose and stood on tiptoe. "I expect he's telling her to disband the rally or he'll take her into custody."

Lady Justice pushed through the crowd and handed Iz her scales. My sister held them aloft. "We answer to a higher law than yours."

His face blotched with purple patches, McBain jabbed his finger again and shouted something.

Allison dropped the bag of chips. "I'm gonna get closer."

A hand shot out and gripped the back of her shirt. "Forget that," Dave said. "Stay right here."

"Dad!" Allison turned and glared. "You told me you were a long way off."

"And now I'm not."

Allison thrust her lower lip out and glanced at the crowd. Correction, make that the *seething* crowd. Most of the protesters were on their feet and surging toward Iz and Dick McBain. Dave told Lola to sit and handed me her leash. Mrs. B got busy pouring water and digging the sandwich packet from the basket.

"Paulette and Penelope are up there," Allison said. "And lots of other women. Girls, too."

"Paulette and Penelope are adults." Dave accepted a roast beef sandwich and pulled a dog biscuit from his pocket for Lola. "And no one up there is related to me."

95

"Your father's right, Allison." Mrs. B plucked the bag of chips from the grass and handed it to Dave. "I have a feeling we're about to see something worth the price of admission."

"But we didn't pay anything." Flip-flops flapping, Allison stomped her feet. "And it's not even worth nothing if I can't hear. And now that it's not boring, everybody's standing and I can't even see."

"Get up on that." I pointed to a thick root jutting from the base of the tree and, when she was perched, leaned close to Dave. "If it's not safe for us to be up front, isn't that where *you* should be?"

"Yup." He bit off a chunk of sandwich and followed it with a chip the size of my hand. Lola, her eyes filled with longing, watched.

"And yet you're here."

"I'm here to hand off Lola so you can take her home. She isn't used to crowd situations like this." He turned his gaze toward Mrs. B and raised his voice to be heard over the swelling shouts of the crowd and the whump-whump-whump of a TV news helicopter. "But mostly I'm here establishing that I was nowhere near Dick McBain when things went south. A direction they started heading rapidly when Iz launched her attacks on Mr. Pencil Pusher."

Mrs. B ducked her head and rearranged the contents of the picnic basket.

"Did I say attacks?" Dave put a hand to his chest. "I meant to say surgical strikes to McBain's soft underbelly. Jabs so precise and personal it seemed almost as if Iz had insider information. It seemed almost as if someone might have phoned Iz and—"

"Pudding cup?" Mrs. B thrust one at him. "I'm out of chocolate. Try tapioca."

"I'll get to it as soon as I finish this." Dave chomped another huge bite of his sandwich and chased it with a swallow of water. "It must be coincidence that Iz used the word 'army' and mentioned all the officers pulled in on their days off."

"Definitely coincidence," I said. "Lucky shots in the dark. Iz has been involved in a lot of rallies. She has major experience enraging people."

"And of course Mr. McBain was on the radio," Mrs. B said. "He talked about extra security to prevent injuries and destruction of property."

"Something's happening," Allison yelped. "That angry guy in the suit is pulling Iz off the table."

A roar of protest billowed from the crowd. More women shoved their way past us.

"Hold that pudding cup." Dave kissed me in a way that made my toes tingle. "Gotta go help control a riot. If you love me, you'll take my dog and my daughter home and watch this on the news."

"Aw, Dad," Allison moaned. "It's just getting good."

"Well my bones are more fragile than they used to be." Mrs. B pointed to the news chopper. "And that photographer has a much better view than we do. We can see what he's seeing on TV."

"I want to stay," Allison wailed.

"And I want to be in Hawaii on vacation." Dave kissed her forehead. "Don't give Barbara more grief than usual."

Allison stuck her tongue out at his retreating back and stomped her feet again, but in a few seconds she was over it. Thirty minutes later she parked herself on the sofa in Mrs. B's condo with a bowl of ice cream covered in chocolate sauce, whipped cream, and sprinkles. My fat cells clamored for the same, but I settled for a couple of naked strawberries and, in the interest of being able to function in the morning, passed on the frothy beverage Mrs. B offered.

For a while we watched helicopter shots of groups of angry women slowly giving ground to police at the urging of organizers in white blouses with black armbands and ball caps.

Those shots were interspersed with video of Dick McBain strapped to a gurney and loaded into an ambulance, and shots of Iz, her white shirt grass stained and streaked with dirt, handcuffed and stuffed into a police car. Paulette, every hair in place, and only a little flushed despite the chaos, told a reporter that dozens of witnesses would testify Iz did nothing except exercise the rights guaranteed under the Constitution. She went on to say that she and hundreds of others would be in court to make sure justice wasn't subverted, inverted, or perverted.

Mrs. B made a note and called a few female members of the Committee while Allison flipped channels, hunting for a video clip that showed her in the background. Again and again I watched a replay of McBain jerking Iz from the table and a crowd of women knocking him to the ground before officers came to his aid. Yawning, Allison changed the channel yet again, then leaned closer to the screen, and yelped, "Watch!"

"Watch what?" Mrs. B set her olive-packed martini aside.

"Watch Iz fall off the table."

"Again?" I finished my last strawberry and let Cheese Puff lick my fingers. "Why?"

"I think she faked the fall."

Chapter 13

Allison channel surfed and found the video again, this time shot from another angle. "Watch. It's hard to tell because her pants are so baggy, but she bends her knees. Just a little. And see? She leans forward. But not much. When he grabs at her, she kind of dives."

"Find it again." Mrs. B moved to the carpet in front of the TV. I followed suit.

Allison found the video from still another angle and we studied it. "You're right," Mrs. B said. "If she was trying to stay on that table, she would have stepped back and leaned away from him."

"If anyone calls her on it, she could say the table wobbled and she got thrown off balance." I tapped Allison on the shoulder. "She's pretty convincing, don't you think? Maybe you should have taken her up on those acting lessons she offered to give you."

"I don't need lessons." With an expression chilly enough to lower the temperature in Death Valley, Allison turned off the TV, tossed the remote on the sofa, and stalked out, calling over her shoulder. "Especially not from Iz."

At 3:00 AM Dave slid between the sheets and nuzzled my neck. "If I didn't think she'd break my jaw, I'd give your sister a big kiss on the lips."

99

"I'll take it on her behalf," I murmured, snuggling against him.

"Not right now," he said. "My kisses have been known to make hearts race and pulses pound and women stay up all night doing my bidding."

"And the problem with that is?"

"You have to work in the morning. You need your rest."

I hate it when he's right.

"By the way," he said. "It's a kettle."

"Huh? What's a kettle?"

"Hawks," he mumbled, and dropped into sleep.

I tossed for a good twenty minutes before I recalled our discussion about what to call a group of hawks. I tossed another ten considering whether to wake Dave up and say, "Ask me if I care?"

Satisfying as that would have been, I decided to act like an adult, and drifted off to sleep.

Aston was still out on his one-man protest, so it was up to me to continue to guide his students through the thick packet Tremaine Scott came up with. It was designed to acquaint them with Washington's state government, but one quick riffle through it yesterday told me there was no danger it might spark interest in the political system. It was the equivalent of a mashed potato sandwich on white bread—a sandwich without salt, pepper, or condiments.

Even though I opened the windows the moment I arrived, the pungent odor in Aston's room swelled. As the day warmed to a record temperature for late May, even propping the corridor door ajar to get a cross-draft from the windows didn't help.

By the very nature of my job, I often went into the classrooms of teachers taken ill overnight, teachers who hadn't intended to be absent and therefore hadn't cleaned and straightened before leaving at the end of the previous day. To keep my name off the subbing blacklist, my policy is to try to ignore clutter, disarray, disorganization, and the odd half-eaten muffin or bag of chips. But this odor was more powerful than my ability to ignore it. So, while the kids worked—a process involving much sighing and groaning and relatively little scratching of pens on paper because, after all, this *was* Friday— I donned a pair of thin rubber gloves issued by the health staff, and hunted for the source of the smell.

Earlier I'd searched the huge wooden desk in pursuit of that illusive movie, but I'd been focused only on that. Today I went for anything that might create a stink. Before long I uncovered a stained paper sack containing a slimy carrot and what might have been the chunk of the salami I saw Aston gnawing on a few days ago. I popped the sack into a plastic bag retrieved from the bottom of my briefcase, tied it closed, and carried it to a trash can in the hallway.

Within a few minutes, the icky sweet tang riding on top of the odor faded, but the dense, rancid underbody remained. Worse, it ballooned to fill the gap.

Keeping one eye on the kids—who each kept one eye on me—I opened cabinets and sniffed in short, quick breaths. I smelled moss and leather and glue, dust and dried herbs. I found a petrified orange, several dead bugs, and a host of markers missing their caps. I left the bugs, but tossed the orange and the markers. That eliminated a sharp chemical edge of the odor.

During the next period, in between helping kids tackle questions on the division of power between the governor and the legislature, I inched along the bookcases, refining my sniffing technique. I spotted dozens of wads of gum stuck to scale models of log cabins, canoes, and sailing ships. I found two packets of moldy grape jelly, a heap of desiccated fries standing in for a miniature campfire, and a small crock of something that might once have been sourdough batter but seemed to have risen to the point of no return and collapsed.

101

Toward the end of the final period I hauled over a chair and inspected the tops of the cabinets and bookshelves. More dust. More dead bugs. Paper wads. Paper airplanes. Paper clips. A couple of textbooks that had probably been marked "lost" years ago. One moccasin. A grungy T-shirt. Three packs of sticky notes.

Nothing—with the exception of the moccasin—that I might not find in almost any other classroom. And nothing that could be creating the stench.

All eyes were now on me. No one displayed a bit of interest in the assignment, or in education in general. With ten minutes left before the final bell, I gave them something else to think about. "How many of you have noticed an odor in here?"

Every kid raised a hand. A few raised two.

"How many of you noticed it yesterday?"

Every hand except that belonging to a boy with wavy blond hair. "I was absent. But I might have smelled it the day before."

"That was Luke's gym gear," a girl said.

"Okay, how many of you think it's worse today than yesterday?"

Hands shot high, accompanied by gag-me comments and the kind of rude noises high-school-age boys revel in making.

"As you must have figured out, I've been hunting for the source. I haven't found anything."

"Did you look in the file cabinets?" a girl in a spangled T-shirt asked.

"No." I climbed down from my chair. "I didn't smell anything over there. And besides, they're locked."

"We could break them open," a male voice called from the middle of the room.

(For the record, if some form of destruction is likely to be an outcome of a project, most high school kids find that project more interesting than one where nothing could shatter, spill, smash, or splash.)

"No breaking," I said in my I-mean-it voice. "Let's put the books where they belong, put your packets away, and get the chairs up. Then you can walk around the room and see if you can sniff out the source."

Groaning their displeasure about pursuing an option not involving breakage, they packed their gear and set the chairs on the tables. Only one clattered to the carpeted floor, but my back was turned at the time and students in the vicinity manufactured phony expressions of surprise and/or smug innocence. Talk about needing acting lessons!

"Clockwise." The girl in the spangled T-shirt circled her hand in the air. "We all have to walk the same way or it will be a disaster."

A disaster was, naturally, what most preferred, but she carped and badgered until she organized a human whirlpool. I saw a future for her teaching the youth of America. Or perhaps herding cats.

With much sniffing, sneezing, sweating, shoving, and a little low-level swearing, the whirlpool spun. After a minute, spangled shirt pulled aside two girls wearing excessive perfume and one boy with cologne powerful enough to fumigate a chicken coop. She sent them to the center of the room where their fragrances wouldn't interfere with the experiment.

The whirlpool spun on, spawning two smaller eddies, one revolving around Aston's desk and the other forming a vortex in the corner where built-in shelves above a cabinet held that long-unused TV and hundreds of rolled-up posters from projects of yesteryear. Faded posters with fraying edges were piled like logs on the shelf below and more, bundled like sheaves of wheat, stood upright on the floor, blocking the cabinet doors beneath the TV shelf.

A boy with a lip ring dropped to his knees and peered into the two-inch space between the bottom of Aston's desk and the floor.

"Don't touch anything," I warned. "Just tell me what you see."

"Old socks. A potato. Major toenail clippings."

My involuntary cry of "Eeewwww" was echoed by most of the students.

The boy turned his head to the side and rested his cheek on the carpet for a better view. "And a dead mouse. In a trap."

Eeewwww wasn't strong enough for several of the girls. They resorted to screaming and running to the door. Only by reminding myself I was the adult in charge did I refrain from doing the same. And not for a second did I blame the custodial staff. They couldn't move furniture in the few minutes allotted to clean each classroom—especially heavy furniture piled high with papers.

"The mouse is all dried out and shriveled up," the boy said. "I don't think it's what reeks."

A mouse didn't turn into a mummy overnight. I bet myself that Aston—self-sufficient mountain man—set that trap. Months ago.

The boy stood and dusted off his jeans. "Do I get extra credit?"

"I'll see what I can arrange. Write your name on the white board."

"What about me?" the girl in the spangled shirt asked.

"Put your name up there with his." I pointed at the board and turned my attention to the corner where kids had formed a bucket brigade and were ferrying sheaves of posters to the center of the room and tossing them in a heap between two tables. The process shook loose broken rubber bands, bits of glue and paper, and dust, lots of dust. That brought on more sneezing.

I dreaded what we might have to deal with when the last posters were removed and the cabinet doors opened. But if we discovered the source of the stench, it could be worth it—

especially if Aston extended his sit-out until the end of the year and I got tapped to finish the term in this room.

I shuddered. Finishing the term meant I'd be in charge of straightening the classroom to end-of-year standards— standards Aston apparently had ignored for years.

Eeewww. Eeewww. Eeewww.

The last sheaves went along the line, exposing the cabinet doors.

"I don't think we should open those." A girl with long braids blocked the cabinet. "The smell is really bad now that those posters are out of the way."

True. A miasma seemed to slither from between the cabinet doors and raise its head like a cobra. With a crowd of kids gathered around, no way did I want to open those doors and reveal— What? A carcass? A toxic waste spill?

No way did I want to open those doors at all.

"Come on, don't be a wuss." A boy in a yellow tank top confronted the girl with braids. "It's probably a rat's nest or a dead squirrel."

His lips talked tough, but his feet inched away from the cabinet.

Unfortunately—dang it!—my job called for inching forward.

No, not *inching*. Stepping. Stepping confidently.

My brain ordered my feet to get to the cabinet.

My nose ordered my brain to order my feet to get to the door.

My heaving stomach seconded that order.

"You're the wuss." The boy with the lip ring who scouted the area beneath the desk shoved in front of me, slid around tank-top boy, and issued an order to the girl with braids. "Get out of the way and let me—"

The bell sounded.

Finding the source of the stench lost its appeal. Kids surged into the hallway.

"Have a nice weekend," I shouted above the din. "Drive carefully. Party safely. Don't get sunburned."

As if ever I listened to advice like that when I was a teen. I learned from mistakes, not advice or warnings.

Lip-ring boy lingered for a second, bending, stretching, reaching around the girl with braids, grasping for the handles on the cabinet doors. She sidestepped to block him. The miasma coiled around me, squeezing my chest.

"School's out," I wheezed. "And so are you."

"Come on," he said in a voice that implied I was a waste of oxygen. "I want to see what's in there. Let's open it real quick."

"No one's opening anything until I get Mr. Scott and the head custodian up here. There could be dangerous substances inside."

He grinned. "That would be awesome."

"No, it would be the extreme opposite of awesome." I straightened my spine, rocked to my toes, and used my deadly serious voice. "If you open that cabinet, I see a visit to Mr. Scott's office in your future."

He scuffed the carpet with a worn running shoe, then sprinted to catch his buddies.

"Thanks for your help," I told the girl with braids. "You better hurry or you'll miss your bus."

"If I move," she whispered, "I might puke."

A feeling I knew all too well. "That might improve the smell in here."

She gave me a wisp of a smile and tottered a few steps, coughed, then broke into a jog. "Bye."

"Find me Monday and I'll tell you all about it."

"I'm not sure I want to know," she called from the corridor.

Ditto.

As it turned out, Tremaine Scott let me off the hook. "Lock the classroom and go on home," he told me when I phoned from the teachers' room to clue him in about the cache beneath the desk and the smell from hell emanating from the cabinet. "Carl and I will handle it."

"You smell icky," Allison said when she met me at my car.
"I feel icky."

Her eyes narrowed. "You're not trying to get out of coming to my play tonight, are you?"

"I would never do that," I said, meaning I'd never use such a half-baked excuse as feeling icky. Stabbing my foot with an ice pick, however, remained a definite option.

When we got home—after stopping to pick up a booklet on rules of the road—the state of the lawn indicated that Jake had been at work. Long and short patches of grass fitted together like pieces of a quilt, and scrapes on the curbing indicated failure to lift the mower so the blades didn't strike the concrete. Apparently, though, they connected once too often. The mower lay on its side, the blades nicked and bent.

Jake was nowhere in sight. But as we rolled past the manager's office, I heard the far-from-dulcet tones of Bernina Burke and caught the words "simple chores" and "not paying attention."

Booklet in hand, Allison went upstairs to practice her lines and decide what to wear to the opening night party. I went into the shower for a complete scrub and a three-lather shampoo. Holding the clothes I'd worn at arm's-length, I put them in the washer with half a cup of baking soda and sprinkled more of that on my sandals before I set them on the deck on my way next door.

I found Cheese Puff asleep on the sofa with one of the many designer dog toys he mostly ignored—this one a platypus wearing a red beanie—and Mrs. B in her favorite chair. She was watching TV, listening to the Reckless River radio station, and surfing the net.

"They're having a field day with Dick McBain's debacle," she said with a bright smile. "The mayor announced the

107

formation of a commission to look into the way police handled the rally. And here's your friend from the pool."

She popped up a video of Paulette in a fresh white blouse and black armband. Speaking for Iz and for all the women who attended the rally, Paulette made it clear police were not at fault. She maintained they showed remarkable restraint—restraint not demonstrated by the man in charge. Questioning the cost of such an enormous response to the rally, she wondered if money might have been better spent on shelter for the homeless, senior meals programs, or recreational opportunities for children.

"Paulette's a natural," Mrs. B gloated. "She handled every question they threw at her without getting flustered for even a second. And the best part is they can't call her an outsider. Or a rabble-rouser. Or a hothead."

I laughed. "They'd call her a hothead for sure if they saw her last month at the mall when the sheets she wanted were sold out and her coupon didn't apply to new shipments. I heard the store manager resigned later that day to take a job processing fish in Ketchikan."

"Well, I say Iz made a savvy move claiming exhaustion and making only a brief statement after she bonded out. Paulette was born for this. And the camera loves her."

I dropped to the sofa beside Cheese Puff. He sniffed my hand and wrinkled his nose as if to say I needed another shower. "Has McBain issued a statement?"

"He's recovering from his injuries and reviewing tapes and witness statements from the rally. Reporters say he's not available for interviews."

"If he's smart he'll stay that way for a couple of months."

"Apparently he left the hospital in secret and reporters can't track him down, although they managed to get pictures of his wife going into a hair salon. I'm not at all sure she's a natural blond." Mrs. B patted her silvery hair. "And such sharp features. Anyway, the out-going police chief is at a fishing camp hundreds of miles from the nearest phone service and the only one talking is Ron Weador." She tapped a few keys. "Watch."

Weador popped up wearing a white shirt, red tie, and dark blue suit. Mrs. B tapped the pause button. "With his skin tone, he should wear brown and sage."

"Brown and sage don't say 'I'm all about being patriotic.'"

"Clothes don't make the man. Or the patriot. Neither does having a trophy wife hanging on your every word."

His wife—younger, tanner, and in possession of very blond hair—wore a sleeveless red dress and a radiant smile.

"She has beautiful cheekbones," Mrs. B said. "And that hair color isn't out of a box."

I leaned closer to the screen. "I wonder what she's thinking."

"Now or when she agreed to marry him? He's not rich. And he doesn't have much in the looks department."

"Maybe she loves him. Or believes in what he stands for."

Mrs. B tapped the control and Weador launched into a defense of McBain's "strong stance against those who break the laws of this city, county, and state" and then railed against "riffraff coming in and disrupting the peace and tranquility of Reckless River."

"I hardly think a town known for a war between rival fur companies, the massacre of its first settlers, a gas explosion that leveled half of downtown during the 30s, and the flood in the 90s could be called tranquil," Mrs. B said.

"Well, he can't say it's a hell hole if he wants to be elected mayor. Besides, the last few years have been relatively calm."

"With the exceptions of *your* little adventures." She patted my arm. "Before you moved in my life was far too dull and now—"

"My life is ruined! Ruined!"

Chapter 14

Allison hurtled in from the deck. "I don't have anything to wear to the party. All my clothes suck. They're old and boring and they make me look fat and they suck, suck, suck, suck, suck."

"I thought the drama wasn't due to begin until 7:00." Mrs. B held her diamond-studded watch to her ear. "Is it later than I think?"

"You're not funny." Allison wheeled on me. "And you're not, either, so don't say anything."

I pinched my lips closed. It would be like pulling the pin on a grenade to mention that the party wouldn't include dinner and dancing at a five-star resort. And it would be like throwing myself on said grenade to suggest school clothes were fine for a punch-and-cookies gathering in the cafeteria attended mainly by parents and friends.

Mrs. B rolled her eyes and turned off the TV. "What kind of an impression do you want to create? Sophisticated? Sultry? Serious?"

"Hot." Allison stomped her feet. "I want to look hot."

I kept my lips pinched so I wouldn't ask how much skin had to be revealed to achieve "hot," and how she planned to explain the outfit to her father, or get out of being grounded if she wore it without approval. Like a lot of fathers, Dave didn't want his 15-year-old daughter to look "hot."

"When you say 'hot,' I assume you're not referring to body temp and perspiration. I've been told the high school theater has no air conditioning so I fear we shall *all* be hot this evening." Mrs. B stood and headed for the stairs. "Perhaps we should see what's in my closets?"

"Yessss!" Allison raced ahead and in a moment I heard the scrape of hangers and the thud of what I suspected were shoes tossed from their racks to be tried on.

I feared the worst. Mrs. B's closets contained outfits she wore as a showgirl in Las Vegas. Those would definitely qualify as "hot." They would also qualify as not appropriate for a high school function. Which would give them total appeal.

Cheese Puff grunted and rolled over so I could scratch his tummy. When I didn't get right on that, he waved his legs and escalated to a growling yip.

"What am I? Your servant? Allison's chauffeur? Not to mention the nutritious food coordinator?"

Crap.

I hadn't been to the grocery store for days and we were running out of leftovers and sandwich makings—unless you counted frostbitten English muffins, canned parmesan cheese, and barbecue sauce. If I pleaded being overcome by the heat and stench in Aston's classroom, would Mrs. B let me off the meal-planning hook for another day and allow me to run for takeout?

"I hope Dad remembers the flowers," Allison called. "He has to hand them to me when we do the curtain call. That's what all the other girls' fathers and boyfriends are going to do."

"Add secretary/social director to that list of my duties," I told Cheese Puff.

"I told him to get roses. Two dozen. I want more than anybody else."

Of course.

With everything else going on, I'd bet my smelly sandals that Dave hadn't remembered to order flowers. In fact, I was willing to bet the play itself, although not yet slipping his mind, might be one nerve synapse away.

I yanked my phone from the pocket of my shorts and punched in his number. The call went to voice mail immediately, a sign he was in the middle of something. That usually meant interrupting the social networking of local drug dealers, and thus disrupting financial schemes based on making, acquiring, and distributing illegal substances. Drug dealers tended not to like that, and tended to display their displeasure by pulling weapons ranging from knives sharp enough to quarter a baseball, to guns normally seen in war zones.

That tended to cinch my nerves into more knots than in the average hand-tied carpet.

I tried to take my mind off what Dave might be doing by considering the cost of a dozen roses and the few dollars of slack left on my credit card. Did you get a price break if you ordered two dozen? Would supermarket roses pass muster?

I glanced out across the deck. There were plenty of roses in the gardens abutting the river trail. With a little ribbon they—

"Roses with long stems," Allison called. "And really big blooms. Josh is bringing pink ones. I told Dad his have to be blue."

Rats!

Apparently this was a competition. The girls in the cast might be packing tape measures to settle stem-length and bloom-width disputes.

"And not violet or purply blue. Blue blue."

Refraining from asking if the leaves should be encrusted with diamonds, I pulled Mrs. B's phone book from a shelf in the end table beside the sofa and flipped to the ads for florists. A woman at the first one I called—the shop closest to the condo complex—gave me a lesson in rose genetics. I learned roses the shade Allison wanted didn't occur in nature. Growers had tinkered with nature, but that raised the price, required special ordering, and still didn't produce a color to meet Allison's expectations.

"I could dye a dozen," the florist offered, "but the petals wouldn't take up the color by this evening. How about yellow or pink roses instead?"

How about watching Allison sulk for the next month?

I thanked her and moved on to the next closest florist. A man there expanded on the genetics lesson and suggested I make do with deep red and buy an extra dozen.

That would work about as well as presenting three dozen lumps of coal.

But now I knew Dave hadn't ordered flowers—at least not blue roses. If he got a genetics lesson from a florist, he would have gloated about knowing something I didn't "in spite of that advanced degree."

We were up a creek without a paddle, a life jacket, or even a pair of leaky wading boots.

Like a pinball with spikes, pain rolled from one side of my skull to the other, slowed, and settled behind my eyes. Not that I believed we should cater to every one of Allison's whims, but this was a special night, and a girl with only one parent in her life needed a little extra.

As I considered whether high-gloss blue spray paint would adhere to rose petals, Mrs. B came downstairs and glanced at the phone book open on my lap. "The Committee is all over those roses," she whispered.

My headache receded, then flared again. "Blue ones? With long stems?"

"Trust me."

"Trust you with what?" Clutching the banister, Allison teetered downstairs on a pair of sequined heels tall enough to make a foot doctor smile at the prospect of future business.

"Trust me with making sure we have good seats for the play." Mrs. B shot me a wink. "Jim is going early to hold a block of chairs. Now show Barbara your LBD."

"That stands for little black dress," Allison informed me as she twirled in a sleeveless number with a scoop neck that wasn't too deep and a flaring skirt that stopped close to her knees. "And check this." She shook out a gauzy black scarf laced with silver threads and tossed it across her shoulders. "Mrs. B says this makes me mysterious. Mysterious is hot."

Allison was about as mysterious as the recipe for boiling water, but I applauded and, when she turned her back, raised a thumb to Mrs. B. Unless Allison fell off of those heels and required major surgery not covered by his insurance, Dave would approve of her outfit.

Time passed, but Dave didn't turn up to do that—or anything else.

Worse, he didn't answer his phone and didn't return messages.

Allison went from fretful to frantic to frenzied.

The only thing that kept me from doing likewise was the necessity of appearing calm and in control. In the name of distraction, I had her go through my closet and decide what I should wear.

(For the record, you have no idea how outdated, outmoded, and outclassed your wardrobe is until you ask advice from a fashion-conscious teen.)

"This is ugly. This makes you look fat. This would be okay if it wasn't the color of puke."

I winced with each pronouncement, but Allison didn't seem to notice—or care. She tossed tops and slacks from their hangers and into a heap on the floor. Teeth bared, Cheese Puff raced to escape a blizzard of blouses and took refuge beneath the pillows on my bed. I wished I could do the same.

"This is too young for you. This has too many stripes. And this, "Allison waved a skirt with huge side pockets, "is something Bernina Burke would wear."

Ouch. That *really* hurt.

"You should get Paulette to take you shopping. Over in Portland."

A great idea.

And one that would require money. Lots of money.

A few articles of clothing wouldn't be enough. I'd be required to buy shoes and scarves and sweaters and hats. Not to mention jewelry. Paulette was all about accessorizing. Some of her accessories had accessories.

Don't get me wrong, I have nothing against accessories. I just don't have much experience with them. When my parents abandoned their nurturing roles, they left my upbringing to Iz whose idea of an accessory is a can of pepper spray. I never got more than basic grooming tips, never tried on clothing and jewelry, and never got help solving the mysteries of how to apply lipstick and pluck eyebrows. Iz, even then, had no use for anything "girly." I had to make do with what I gleaned from friends who were less helpful than they were amused by my lack of knowledge.

"It's too late now to go shopping," I told Allison. "Even in Reckless River."

"I guess." Allison sighed the way only a teenage girl can, riffled through the remaining clothes, and pulled out a pair of white slacks and a long plum-colored top. "This might be a little warm, but it should make you look thinner."

The tiny part of my brain where self-esteem resided noted the words "should" and "thinner." Not "will" and "thin."

White sandals," she ordered. "And be sure to put on makeup. And fresh polish on your toenails. And gold earrings. Not studs or those little hoops. Dangly ones."

Sheesh.

I pulled on the white slacks, sucking in my stomach and triumphing—just barely—in the battle with the zipper. "Heat bloat," I told myself.

I didn't believe me.

That blouse had a job ahead of it.

115

Having left only eight articles still hanging, Allison considered her task done and resumed freaking out about Dave's failure to appear. While I slapped fresh polish on my toenails, she paced the hallway downstairs, opening the door to peer out each time she reached it. "He knows I have to be there by 6:00. I told him a hundred times."

"I'm sure you did." Probably more like two hundred. "If he isn't here by 5:45, I'll drive you to the school."

"In *your* car?" Her tone was frigid enough to make penguins shiver.

"I'll borrow Mrs. Ballantine's."

Allison considered that.

"When we pull in, I'll hang back until there are a lot of people in the lot. Then I'll blow the horn so they all notice you."

"Okay. But I really wanted Dad to drive me. Where is he?"

A question I'd love to have the answer to. The headache returned with a vengeance, my stomach started digesting itself, and my fingers and toes felt like lumps of steel. I told myself that if he was hurt, someone would have called or come over. Even if Dave forgot to register his change of address, these were cops he worked with. I met a few when Tony Montgomery dognapped Cheese Puff. And Detective Chuck Atwell knew me well from many hours of interrogation after the murder of Henry Stoddard. If Dave was hurt, Atwell would call.

Unless Atwell didn't know.

What if Dave had been stabbed or shot and dumped in the river? What if he'd been knocked out, tied up, and left in a filthy drug house? What if Lola—?

"Stop it," the little voice in my brain ordered. "Lola's fine. Dave's fine."

The little voice almost always carped, criticized, and cast a pall over situations. This show of optimism was so disconcerting it derailed my train of thought and took the edge off my anxiety.

"Maybe he left his phone in his locker," I said as the hands on the kitchen clock jerked past 5:00. "He's probably getting to the police station now. I'm sure he'll call in a few minutes."

"Okay, I bet he saw how late it is and grabbed his phone and ran to his car and he's driving home right now," I said at 5:10 while handing Allison a tin of bandages for the blisters on her heels. Mrs. B's shoes were half a size too small, but apparently if shoes are "hot," a little pain is acceptable.

"He probably stopped for gas," I told her at 5:17.

"Picking up the flowers he ordered," I claimed at 5:26.

"Having them put the flowers in a prettier vase," I speculated at 5:31.

"I don't care what he's doing. He's ruining my entire life."

Allison tromped along the hall to confront me. I refrained from mentioning that tromping didn't seem to be a "hot" move, even in stiletto heels. "I know he wanted to drive you and I'm positive he's not late on purpose. Why don't you go comb your hair and I'll go see about borrowing Mrs. B's car?"

Snuffling, Allison wobbled up the stairs and Cheese Puff and I went next door to plead the case for a classier car for the star. That pleading didn't involve mentioning Dave's status for fear Mrs. B would take extreme action like calling 911.

She tossed me the keys. "The little prince and I will ride with Verna."

"Cheese Puff is going?"

"Of course."

"That theater will be broiling."

"I have a plan to keep him cool." She pointed at a capacious straw purse. "He'll be quite comfortable in there. I expect he'll nap through most of the play."

"Right. I can see how a play might be boring for a dog. All that talking and no one saying anything like, 'How about a treat?' or 'Let me scratch your ears.'"

"Don't be silly, dear. He'll be bored because he already saw it. Sybil took him to a performance in Portland in January." She bent and patted Cheese Puff's head. "Overall he prefers serious dramas. And musicals."

For all I knew, that was true. Thanks to the Committee, my dog had a richer and more varied social life than I did. Ignoring Mrs. B's question about which outfit Cheese Puff would prefer to wear, I headed for the door.

Allison remained quiet on the short drive, checking her phone every minute, fingering the diamond pendant and stud earrings Mrs. B loaned her, and putting a bandage on a fresh blister on her right big toe. I burped the horn as I glided to a stop, and she got out, twitching the scarf across her shoulders and waving to a couple of girls wearing shorts and skimpy tops. Words like "thank you," and "see you later" weren't uttered.

I found a spot in the shade and headed for the school offices and the soft drink machine. Assistant Principal Tremaine Scott was ahead of me, feeding in quarters. "Buy you some bubbly? Or a serving of what I'm having for dinner?"

He rattled a bag of cheesy snacks. Tremaine, a former football player, was a large unit. In his hands the bag appeared the size of a postage stamp.

(For the record, I've never passed on a bag of free cheesy snacks yet, not even a generic brand.)

"Sure," I said, trying to ignore the faint scent of Aston's room clinging to the assistant principal's pale blue shirt and gold tie. "Either. Or both."

"Both it is." He fed coins, then blotted sweat from his glistening forehead. "Want to know what caused the smell?"

"Not really." I punched the number and letter keys for those little orange bits of additives, preservatives, cholesterol, fat, and—for me—culinary bliss. "But, yes."

He took a long swallow of his cola. "Bear fat."

Eeewww.

The cheesy snacks dropped into the bin at the bottom of the machine. I couldn't bring myself to reach for them.

"I know that *not* because I'm an Alabama country boy from the wrong side of the tracks, but because Aston labeled the jar."

"Naturally." I punched the code for a cola. "Because you wouldn't want to confuse bear fat with possum fat or raccoon renderings."

"We Alabama country boys don't joke about raccoon renderings." He used the deep and menacing voice that once weakened the resolve of opposing linemen but now was reserved for freshmen having difficulty breaking middle-school behavior patterns.

"I don't joke about such things either." I pressed my icy cola against my forehead and took a long swallow. My headache sent needles of pain into my sinuses, then started to fade. "In fact, until just now, I doubt I ever used the words 'raccoon renderings.'"

"Well, see that you continue on that course." He laughed, a low rumbling sound like thunder miles off. "But this fat hadn't been rendered—at least not like it should have been. Mice chewed through the plastic jar and the heat didn't help matters. The custodians are using heavy-duty stench suppressor and leaving the door and windows open."

I drank again, feeling caffeine kick the headache down another notch. "Let's hope it works."

He nodded. "I notice you haven't asked *why* Aston had a jar of bear fat in his classroom."

"Assuming it has something to do with his penchant for recreating the past, I can think of lots of reasons, starting with using it to waterproof his boots, slick his hair, or spread on a sandwich."

Tremaine Scott went pale around the lips. "Seriously? A condiment?"

"I eat lunch with the man. And with Brenda Waring. Those guys who travel the world eating weird foods would reassess their careers if they saw even *a few* of the things I have."

119

"Thanks in advance for *not* sharing." He rattled his bag of snacks. "Gotta go knock out a couple of e-mails before our thespians take the stage."

Neither of us added, "If only that stage was leaving town," and he departed for his office, abandoning me to my cola, my cheesy snacks, and a machine filled with other goodies. Normally I would have stood there for a few moments communing with malted milk balls and salted nut rolls, but concern about Dave trumped that. I tucked the unopened snacks in my purse, walked two sides of a lopsided square of hallways—noting the orange cones around Aston's door and a lingering stench still in residence—and made my way to the theater.

(For the record, if the word "theater" conjures visions of Broadway, summer stock in Minneapolis, or a college production, wipe your mind. Now picture this: A windowless box of a room with a floor the color of dead leaves, rows of folding chairs without a shred of padding, a splintered plywood stage, and sets painted by enthusiastic students with brushes that should have been retired before Allison started kindergarten.)

Someone had propped the door open and set fans in the back of the room. With much sound and fury they slapped steamy air. That made the room seem like a convection oven, and I suspected their motors—one making a noise like a peppermill filled with gravel—were actually increasing the temperature.

Jim riffled through a stack of beautifully lettered place cards. "I figured parents and grandparents should have the first few rows." He patted the pocket of a salmon-colored shirt that brought out the color in his cheeks—or what I could see of his cheeks given his flowing white beard and mustache. "I bought half a dozen extra tickets to show support. But if they sell out, I told the kids at the box office they can have my spares to sell again."

120

The odds of all 120 seats selling, even on opening night, were right up there with the odds of Congress agreeing on . . . well, much of anything. "I'll see that Allison thanks you later. Right now she's pretty wrapped up in herself."

"So were we all at that age." Jim smiled, centered a place card on a chair, and glanced toward the door. "Where's Dave?"

I hadn't wanted to worry Mrs. B, but Jim was made of sterner stuff. Despite his Father-Christmas appearance and nature, Jim had done time—time for the kinds of crimes Dave investigated. "I wish I knew. He's not answering his phone."

Jim assured me Dave was cautious, not prone to taking chances, and had Lola with him, but the twinkle left his eyes. He flipped through his place cards, found the one with Dave's name, and set it on a seat at the end of the aisle, then set my card on the next chair. "So he won't have to climb over anyone if he comes in late. I'll tip the kids at the box office to watch for him."

The tapping of heels and the swishing of pastel silks alerted us to the arrival of Mrs. B and the rest of the Committee. With much clucking at Jim and commentary among themselves, they rearranged all the place cards except mine and Dave's and then swirled out to the tiny refreshment stand to stock up on bottled water and provender.

While Jim wheeled in a huge camping cooler, I moved his card to the seat beside mine. I might need to lean on someone with strength and good sense—attributes other members of the Committee were lacking.

"These aren't for me." Verna swished by with a clutch of soft-drink cans, set them on the edge of the stage, and brushed at a spot on her flowered frock. Tall, tan, and willowy, she carried the busy pattern with style. I would have looked like an upholstered footstool. "They're for the kids. It's important to stay hydrated."

And dosed up with caffeine and sugar?

Sybil, petite and pink with pudgy cheeks, set a stack of chocolate bars on an empty chair, and opened a tote bag the size of a small refrigerator. With a flourish, she removed a selection of folding paper fans in bright colors, many with lace and others with pictures of Japanese gardens.

Even Josh got one—black with a picture of a tiger. In a pale blue shirt and tan slacks, he appeared both older and younger. He kept a florist's box tied with gold ribbon between his feet when he took a seat up front.

As if they were social directors on a cruise, Committee members introduced themselves to actors' arriving relatives and friends and handed out soft drinks and candy bars. Mrs. B took the seat behind the one marked for Dave, slid her purse to the floor beneath my chair, and folded the sides back to reveal Cheese Puff wearing a black velvet vest but otherwise appearing cool and comfortable. "I tucked a few of those blue icy things in the bottom of the bag and put a towel over them."

Naturally my dog had the best seat in the house.

Not caring about my makeup, I used the underside of my sleeve to mop sweat from my forehead. Sybil handed me a fan with a picture of Mt. Hood. "And here's one for Dave. I didn't think he'd want flowers or birds."

I flipped it open to reveal a picture of Bigfoot. "Works for me."

She rummaged in the bag. "Only three fans left and those are spoken for. I wish I had enough for everyone."

"I'll see what I can do." Calling over a couple of juniors I recognized, I sent them to scavenge cardboard from the recycling bins and construct makeshift fans. By the time Iz, Penelope, and Paulette arrived, the room felt like Los Angeles under the assault of a Santa Ana wind.

"This makes jail seem like a four-star hotel." Iz went on to complain about paying to sit in a sweatbox.

Paulette shushed her with a manicured fingernail pressed against lips coated with a summery shade of apricot that I knew wouldn't dare smudge or run even if the temperature rose another twenty degrees.

The lights flickered.

I glanced at the door, hoping to see Dave.

Jim laid a hand on my arm.

The lights dimmed.

I glanced at the door again.

The lights went out.

Chapter 15

Stomach knotting, I gripped the back of Dave's empty chair.

Spotlights came up. The boy playing the butler inched onstage wearing a black jacket already soaked with sweat under his arms and along his spine. As he uttered his first words, fingers touched mine.

I swallowed a squeak of fright.

"Paperwork," Dave whispered. "You wouldn't believe how much paperwork a pissed off supervisor can lay on someone."

He settled into his seat and I passed the Bigfoot fan. "Tell me at intermission."

"Trust me, I will."

A few minutes later, Allison flounced on stage as Gwendolen. Attempting a British accent so hideous it hurt my ears, she delivered her first lines with much giggling, twirling of hair, and fluttering of false lashes. Dave leaned closer and whispered, "Correction, I'll tell you at intermission if I don't die of embarrassment *before* then."

He didn't.

Outside where the air was marginally cooler and less humid, Dave gobbled a candy bar and filled me in on the basics. "McBain has a special team reviewing the video from the rally, trying to identify the women who beat on him after he pulled Iz off the table. He wants every one of them arrested for assault.

But they all wore hats and white blouses, and they kept their heads lowered and their backs to the cameras. And, despite a plea for anyone who took cell phone video to send it in, not a single frame has turned up."

I smiled, but kept mum about Allison's theory that Iz leaped from the table.

"Someone finked that I have a 'relationship' with your rabble-rousing sister." Dave wiped chocolate from the corner of his mouth. "Chuck Atwell's making it clear that the 'relationship' isn't of the warm and fuzzy variety and I would never feed her information, but meanwhile I have to follow orders to the letter and act like I'm trying to be named cop of the year."

He wadded the wrapper, tossed it in a dented trash can, swilled water, and ripped open a packet of peanuts. "That means no personal calls. One of McBain's toadies—fortunately he has only two brown-nosing minions—camped out at the next desk all day. I didn't take lunch and worked late to make him suffer. Left with just enough time to drop Lola and get here."

He choked on a peanut and I patted him between the shoulder blades. "How long will this go on?"

"Until the chief returns from vacation or a miracle happens. This weekend Lola and I have to revisit every house where anyone was ever arrested for making or dealing drugs, was suspected of possessing drugs, or is related to someone who can spell the word 'drugs.' Our mission is to show a police presence."

"With one of his toadies tagging along?"

"No. But you can bet they'll keep tabs on where I am and swing by often to observe. And they'll nitpick every report I turn in."

I pointed to the parking lot and Iz, her face two inches from the air conditioning vents in Penelope's pickup truck. "I hope they're not checking on you this evening while you're consorting with the enemy."

125

Dave laughed for the first time since he arrived. "I doubt even McBain himself would follow me to a high school play. Especially one as—"

I clamped a hand over his mouth. "Don't say it. If it got back to Allison, she'd be devastated. Besides, it *is* a high school play. Once she dumped the accent and the primping, she did a good job."

Dave peeled my hand away and kissed me. "You're right. As always."

He said that last bit not like he meant it but like he read it in an article on how to be a good boyfriend. I gave him points for the attempt.

He finished the peanuts and water and, walking like a man facing a root canal without anesthetic, returned to the theater.

When the final lines were spoken, the audience applauded squishily and the actors—boys already unbuttoning their collars—took their bows. Then the houselights went up and Josh and others approached the stage bearing botanical gifts.

"Uh-oh." Dave slumped in his seat. "I forgot all about—"

Two dozen roses landed in his lap. They were as blue as mountain lakes. They had enormous blooms. Their stems were as long as my arms.

Dave gathered them and stood. "How did you do that?"

"Not me. The Committee. Get up there."

He did, to Allison's squeals of triumph and delight, squeals that increased in volume as Committee members plucked a rainbow of bouquets from that giant cooler and came forward with them. When Allison's arms were full, they handed roses to the rest of the cast while Jim snapped photos.

And when I thought it was over, it wasn't.

Mrs. B clapped her hands, commanded everyone's attention, and directed them to walk to the lawn in front of the school and share in an opening-night supper. Instead of cookies and punch served from a cafeteria table, she presented us with a genuine buffet, complete with shrimp cocktail, imported cheeses and meats, salads, vegetables cut to resemble flowers, tiny tarts and cheesecakes, and sparkling cider served in champagne flutes.

Dave loaded a plate—a large china plate handed to him by a young man in a white jacket—with roast beef and macaroni salad. "Did you know about this?"

"How often do I know about *anything* Mrs. Ballantine gets up to?"

"Good point." He picked up a fork and a cloth napkin and strolled to one of the many tables decked out with crisp white tablecloths, flickering candles, and tall vases to hold the bouquets. "This is pretty cool."

"You like it?" Mrs. B trotted over with Cheese Puff in her arms. In addition to the vest, he now wore a tiny top hat, a miniscule white bow tie, and an expression of disgust that made me grin.

"It's amazing," Dave said. "Allison will never forget it. But you didn't need—"

She waved that off. "It's when you don't need to do something that it's the most fun. Besides, I'm testing this catering company for your wedding."

While we gaped, she spun on the heel of one glittery sandal and trotted off, calling, "Be sure to sample everything and let me know if there's something you especially like or that needs improvement."

"Close your mouth," I told Dave after a long moment.

Dave obeyed, blinked, and swallowed. "I . . . uh . . . we . . . our . . ."

"It's okay." I patted his arm. "Breathe."

"It's not that I don't . . . that I haven't . . . that we . . ."

"I know. Me, too."

Dave gulped in a breath "But if . . . I mean when . . . I mean shouldn't we be the ones who . . . you know . . . plan things?"

"In theory, yes. But let's be realistic. Unless we sneak off, we're in for hours deciding on colors, talking to caterers, and meeting with florists. Does that appeal to you?"

"Only if the other choice is being dragged naked behind a team of horses through a cactus-studded desert. But can we let her—?"

"You were the one who called her a force of nature," I reminded him. "You said we couldn't change her, we could only reckon with her. Remember?"

Wincing, Dave poked his fork into the mound of macaroni salad and stuffed his mouth. When he spoke, he did an impersonation of John Wayne that made Allison's attempt at a British accent seem first-rate. "Well, then, little lady, I *reckon* we should stop pulling on the reins and enjoy the ride."

Dave drove Allison home and I chauffeured Mrs. Ballantine who announced she felt "just a wee bit tipsy" thanks to the contents of the silver flasks several Committee members brought along to "give the sparkling cider a little spark." Cheese Puff, minus the top hat and with the bow tie askew, crawled into my lap, burped twice, and fell asleep.

It was nearly midnight when I pulled into Mrs. B's parking spot beneath the canopy that shielded vehicles owned by residents of the large condos that faced the river. The headlights swept across the uncovered second spaces allocated to each large unit and the single spaces for owners of one-bedroom rear units. Just before I killed the lights, they illuminated Winton James and a slender woman in a red dress.

"How nice," Mrs. B said. "Winton has a girlfriend."

Winton lived in the tiny condo that had been mine until Mrs. B's financial wheeling and dealing resulted in me moving to a larger unit. I referred to him as Ghost Neighbor because he was thin, pale, and seldom seen. He worked long hours for a high tech firm with offices on the east side of Reckless River, and Mrs. B worried that his lifestyle isolated him and deprived him of a "real life." She often invited him to events, but Winton pleaded off due to work.

"I only saw that woman's back and blond hair." Mrs. B leaned forward and peered through the windshield. "I don't suppose we could turn the headlights on again?"

"And let Winton know exactly how nosy we are?"

She thought that over for the count of four. "Well, I'll invite him for dinner on Sunday and insist that he bring her."

I didn't argue with her plan. But something about the way the woman kept her chin tucked and drew Winton deeper into the shadows made me doubt that dinner with neighbors was her idea of relationship quality time.

The weekend unfurled with drama onstage and at home.

With much grunting and groaning, Dave hauled himself out of bed before 7:00 on Saturday morning, ate the toasted muffin and peanut butter I set before him, took a second cup of coffee to go, and left with Lola. When he was out of sight, Cheese Puff and I retreated to the bedroom and logged a few more hours of sleep.

When Allison wandered downstairs for a breakfast of potato chips and onion dip at 11:45, she was devastated to learn that her posse/entourage/fan club for the matinee and evening performances would consist only of Josh. Interrogated about why I couldn't attend at least one of the shows, I offered into evidence a list of household chores. With a smirk, I suggested she sign on for a few of them in order to free audience-hours for me. As I suspected, she announced she had to do her hair and post pictures from last night on social networking sites. "And I have to study that lame book on driving. I don't have time for stupid chore stuff that we do for no reason."

After making a note that we needed a family conference to establish basic standards for healthy meals and a fair division of scutwork—perhaps with Mrs. B serving as a referee and backing me up on minimum levels of sanitation required—I dropped Allison at school. On the way home I hit the supermarket and bought what seemed like enough groceries to feed the immediate world. Then I got down to cleaning bathrooms and vacuuming up dog hair. In other words, living the dream.

The local news stations continued to report no news as far as arrests for the assault on Dick McBain, and no comments from the assaultee. Ron Weador, however, commented on everything. He expressed concerns about the decline of the family unit, restated his belief in strong values, and touted his support of the justice system. He also shared his fear that society was in a distinct decline because of those quick to complain and confront instead of gathering facts and participating in the political process. On the plus side, his pontificating created the ideal soundtrack for scrubbing toilets.

I was cooling off with a cola when Mrs. B tap danced in from the deck. "Have you seen the paint job Jake did on those white posts marking the edges of the driveway? Lola could have done better with her tail."

I grinned. "By the time he goes to trial and gets tossed in jail again, this place will make the city dump seem like a destination resort."

"Unless Bernina sees the light and gets over her teenage infatuation."

"Is there a light bright enough?"

"Good point." Mrs. B shook out green-and-blue woven placemats, wet a sponge, and wiped the dining room table. "I know our ingénue is off chewing the scenery, but where's Dave?"

"He and Lola are on a tour of previously busted or identified drug houses. They're showing a police presence and doing penance for McBain's embarrassment."

"Well, I'm sure that's a benefit to the community, but . . ." She slapped the placemats into position. "Isn't there anyone Dave can appeal to? Or file a complaint with?"

130

"Yes, but he doesn't want to do that until there's a clear pattern of . . . well, I guess you could call it abuse of power."

She paced to the sofa, plumped a couple of cushions, then paced to the door and wiped at a smudge with the tail of her crisp turquoise linen blouse. "That man should be dealt with."

I got the same kind of chill I always did when she used the words "dealt with." I was 99.7% sure rumors about her late husband having mob connections were false, but that 0.3% worth of doubt set off shrill alarms in my mind.

"Well, Dave will handle it." Mrs. B plucked a few strands of dog hair from the drapes. "I have confidence in him."

She tapped out the door, Cheese Puff trotting right behind, leaving me trying to remember if she'd ever expressed confidence in me.

"Grow up," I told myself. "Get back to work."

Dave limped home around 10:00 and we waited up for Allison and listened to her gloat over her theatrical success and mourn the lack of dozens of roses and a catered buffet. Dave left before 7:00 on Sunday morning and Allison was still asleep when Paulette turned up with two flotation belts and a mission. "The community pool is closed today, but your condo pool isn't. Let's get a workout in."

I shuddered. The condo pool, at the upriver end of the complex by the visitors' parking lot, was surrounded by a tall chainlink fence and a line of squatty azaleas. That did little to obstruct the sightlines of residents as well as those on the riverfront trail. Not only would they see my pale thighs and flabby upper arms, they might recognize me as a water-aerobics novice, prone to slip sideways or tilt several degrees from the vertical posture necessary for optimum muscle development.

Paulette seemed to read my mind. "Get over it, get out those old glasses you wear at the rec center, and let's get in the water."

I did, dragging my feet on the way to the pool but moving like the wind—a sluggish and uncoordinated wind—after I shed my long T-shirt on a lounge chair and headed for the water.

To my delight, no one else shared the pool area. Only a few people were walking and running on the trail and they seemed intent on completing their workouts before the heat clamped down. While we snapped on our belts, a robin hopped across the patio at the shallow end of the pool, searching for bugs in the spaces between paving stones. Another robin landed beside it.

"Denise is doing better," Paulette told me as we warmed up with a cross-country maneuver. "She and her girls will stay with one of our volunteers in a house with an alarm system in a gated community. And we've got an attorney working on getting her full custody of the kids. Maybe Brendon didn't throw that bomb, but smart money says it was his idea. And he's never paid a lick of child support."

"How is that possible?" I huffed out the question.

A leaf blower fired up with a roar. Both robins took off.

Paulette raised her voice. "No money, no payments. He's had nine jobs since they divorced. Amazingly, it's never his fault when he's fired after a couple of weeks."

"Reminds me of Jake." I sucked air into my lungs. "Except for the physical violence part."

The leaf blower noise swelled. Paulette did a quarter turn and raised her voice even more. "Let's do V-kicks in circles."

I followed suit, turning in the opposite direction. My old glasses didn't correct my vision to 20/20, but they sharpened the edges enough that I saw the swirling cloud of bark dust rising from the landscaping around the azaleas outside the fence. By squinting, I made out the face of the person wielding the blower. Who else but Jake?

"Speak of the devil," I said.

Paulette spun and sized up my ex the way a dog-show judge might scrutinize a mutt trying to pass as pedigreed.

132

Equipped with a new set of goggles and a pair of ear protectors, Jake swung the leaf blower with the same wild abandon he demonstrated with the hedge trimmer. The bark dust tornado swirled higher and higher, then toppled, raining bark and grit onto the patio and into the pool.

Paulette brushed at her hair. "Hey! Turn that thing off!"

Oblivious to her shouts, Jake blew up another funnel cloud.

"Turn it off," I yelled in the give-me-your-attention-or-else voice that occasionally managed to draw the focus of high school freshmen for seven or eight entire seconds. "Turn it off now!"

The cloud sailed over the pool and delivered a payload of chips, splinters, and shredded leaves guaranteed to clog the filter.

Paulette came out of the water like a sleek seal and raced for the gate.

I came out of the water like a geriatric walrus with one flipper in a sling and followed, grabbing my T-shirt and the key to the condo. Dust and grit stuck to my wet skin and by the time I reached the parking lot, my eyes were watering and I felt like a strip of sandpaper.

But I could hear fine. And what I heard was Paulette teeing off on Jake while Bernina teed off on Paulette for "coming in here and harassing a condo employee doing his job."

"You call this doing a job?" Paulette pointed to mess in the pool. "I could do better with a low-flying helicopter."

Jake set the leaf blower down, pulled off his goggles, hung his head, and backed away mumbling, "I thought I had the hang of it."

"You couldn't get the hang of it if you were strung up on a gallows," Paulette shot back.

Good one!

I stuffed my damp body into my T-shirt while making a mental note to steal that remark. I made a second note not to use it in the classroom.

Bernina opened her mouth for a comeback, but Paulette poked a finger at her nose and got in the last words. "You better hope I don't have lung damage or get an infection from these splinters. I'll sue your pants off."

Bernina without pants. Now *that* was a mental image I could have lived the rest of my life without conjuring up.

Paulette steamed my way. "I'm done talking to that woman. I need a shower."

"Who *are* you?" Bernina shouted. "What are you doing on my property? Why is this any of your business?"

I tossed Paulette the key as she strode past. "I'll bring your flip-flops and towel."

Her face blotched red and purple, Bernina spoke with a hiss. "Who is that woman? She's not a resident. Why is she here?"

"She's my guest." I pointed to the sign above the pool saying that each resident was allowed one (1) guest in the pool and said guest must be accompanied by the resident. "Otherwise known as the woman who might sue your pants off."

Wondering what Paulette would do with a pair of large purple stretch pants, I collected our gear. Bernina, always one to get in the last words, especially if they were part of a threat, said nothing. I took that as an apology.

As Jake's whining excuses and her succinct and unsympathetic replies faded behind me, I caught myself humming "The Thrill Is Gone."

One thing you could say about Jake—he had an effect on those around him. Either they embraced his gimme-gimme lifestyle, or they rose—usually in self-defense—to a higher level of maturity.

Chapter 16

At 11:17 Dave slid into bed, kissed my shoulder, muttered "paperwork," and fell asleep. Lola leaped to the foot of the bed between us, nuzzled Cheese Puff, turned around once, and dropped. They were up again before 6:00 and out the door when Allison and I left for school.

"Aston's back," Big Chill told me when I entered her office.

"In his room?"

"Yes. The custodians worked wonders, but it helped that the heat wave broke overnight. I'm putting you in French."

"The only French I know is *déjà vu*. Oh, and the names of a few pastries."

"*C'est la vie.* They're watching a movie. With subtitles." She shot me the evil eye over the rims of a pair of glasses with bright green frames. "You *can* show a movie, can't you?"

"You bet." Although figuring out how to display the subtitles might necessitate throwing myself on the mercy of a student who logged more hours pushing buttons on a remote than I do.

I scrawled my name on the sub form. "What kind of a mood is Aston in?"

"Silent." Big Chill smiled. "It's a refreshing change."

That change was a thing of the past when lunch rolled around. Aston glanced up when I entered the teachers' room and pointed at me with a knife dripping juice from an eviscerated tomato. "Why didn't you show the movie?"

I raised my hands defensively. "I searched everywhere. I couldn't find it."

"You must have searched with your eyes closed. I left it in the mail sack." He aimed a thumb over his shoulder, indicating his desk.

Doug studied the clutter I'd scrabbled through on Wednesday. "Where's the mail sack?"

"On the hook." Aston aimed his thumb again. "Where it belongs."

That's when I spotted the ripped and rumpled canvas sack hanging by a length of frayed rope pinned to the bulletin board beside the desk.

"You should have put 'in the mail sack' on the note," Doug said. "It wouldn't have killed you to add four more words to the shortest lesson plan in the history of public education."

Aston scowled and aimed the knife at me again. "What gave you the right to snoop in my cabinets?"

"Local health and sanitation rules?" Gertrude guessed. "Concern for the safety of our students? The will to survive?"

Aston turned the knife on her. "I wasn't talking to you."

Gertrude drew herself up in her chair. "And a good thing, too. I won't allow anyone to talk to me in that tone. And neither should Barbara."

Doug and Brenda nodded their agreement. I inched to the refrigerator and retrieved my lunch—a Swiss cheese and cucumber sandwich on rye with a packet of jalapeno potato chips on the side. I would not, I vowed, be intimidated into losing my appetite.

Wait. Make that, I would not be intimidated. Period.

"I apologize for disturbing your classroom projects, Aston, but that cabinet is school property, and the stench was unbelievable."

"Atrocious," Brenda added.

"It made last week's chemistry lab disaster seem like an interlude at a perfume counter," Doug said.

Aston stabbed the tomato, sending a spray of seeds and slime across the table. "It was only bear fat."

We exchanged glances that indicated none of us knew how to respond. Finally Gertrude cleared her throat. "Why did you have it in the cabinet?"

"Why did you have it at all?" Doug asked.

"You weren't planning to eat it, were you?" Brenda grimaced. "Or put it on your hair?"

"Not this batch."

We exchanged OMG glances.

Aston stabbed the tomato again. "Haven't you ever heard of forecasting the weather with bear grease?"

Doug shook his head.

Gertrude snorted.

Brenda sighed.

"No," I said.

"People used to do it all the time. It's a dying art."

"And I know why," Gertrude said. "Most people don't like art that stinks."

"You wouldn't have smelled a thing if the damned mice hadn't chewed the container."

"The mice didn't bring it to school," Gertrude insisted. "How long was it there?"

"A couple of . . ." Aston flushed and smeared tomato guts with the edge of his knife. "Six or seven years. Maybe more. I intended to render it, then partner with a science teacher for a joint unit. Never got to that. Now it's too late. The custodians trashed it."

No one said anything for a long moment, and then Doug bowed his head and intoned in a deep voice. "Let's have a moment of silence for our loss. Most of us never knew that Mr. Grease lived among us. He kept to himself. You might say he was contained, bottled up."

Aston glowered, but Gertrude laughed and tossed a carrot stick at Doug. "If Mr. Grease had come out of the closet, things might have been different."

"He might have found a role lubricating the skids to success," I said.

"He could have had a career in the automotive industry," Brenda added, "taking care of squeaky wheels."

"But alas," Doug finished, "Mr. Grease was no slick talker. He never waxed eloquent. And now he is little more than a smear on the pages of the history of Captain Meriwether High School."

"We could hear you laughing all over the school," Allison told me with a pout when we met at the car.

"And that's a bad thing because . . .?"

"Everyone knows it's you. You have a screechy laugh."

Talk about words you don't want etched on your tombstone.

Allison tossed her backpack into the footwell. "It's embarrassing."

Swallowing at least six sarcastic comebacks, I crossed my fingers, hoped the mechanical meltdown of March wouldn't be repeated, and turned the key. The engine fired up and, with Allison listing other ways in which Dave and I humiliated her, we drove home.

I told myself teenage girls complained about allowances, curfews, chores, and dozens of other things. It was normal for a teenager to be self-centered, feel entitled, and have little regard for the adults who fed, clothed, and sheltered her. I told myself I'd been exactly that way at Allison's age. Still, by the time she headed upstairs, texting as she went, I was choking on bottled-up comments.

The door to the deck stood open and I found Mrs. B stretching on a yoga mat and Cheese Puff lounging on the glider. Mrs. B wore black ballet shoes, black tights, and a pink sweatshirt. Cheese Puff wore a white bandage on his right front foot.

"Quilting accident," Mrs. B said.

Cheese Puff raised the paw and gave me a damp-eyed stare implying much pain and suffering.

"He was on Sybil's lap and one of the other ladies set a plate of cookies—peanut butter with coconut—on the table and . . ."

"And what?"

"And thank goodness Sybil was doing that quilt piece by hand and not on the machine."

She stopped stretching and patted Cheese Puff's head. "It could have been a lot worse for his little footsie."

Little footsie? Sheesh.

"Sybil called me in tears. She wanted to rush him to the emergency vet, but one of the other ladies is a nurse and she disinfected the wound."

Wound?

"And I went into your office—I hope you don't mind—and found the file and checked his shot records and they're all current, so I think he'll be fine. But the ladies thought he should have a bandage to keep the laceration clean."

Laceration?

I sat, strove to contain my disbelief, and said in a voice I hoped sounded rational and free of sarcasm. "It was just a needle stick, right?"

"Well, yes, but Sybil says he whimpered a good long while. She feels dreadful and hopes you won't deny her visitation."

I waved that aside. "Isn't it remotely possible that he whimpered to get the maximum attention because he knew this was his fault?"

Cheese Puff raised his upper lip in a silent snarl.

Mrs. B's jaw dropped. "The little prince?"

"No, the little *dog* I attempted to train to stay off the table—apparently to a grand total of exactly *no* avail thanks to the efforts of everyone else. As long as the Committee allows him to do whatever he wants and takes the blame and makes excuses for his behavior, things like this will happen."

Cheese Puff ramped up his snarl. He sounded like a kinkajou gargling olive oil.

Since no one else was being an adult, I gave up my attempt at maturity and stuck my tongue out at him.

Raising his bandaged foot, Cheese Puff whimpered.

"No sympathy. It's a needle prick. And you got it doing something you shouldn't have." I put my thumbs in my ears and wiggled my fingers.

Mrs. B gave him another pat on the head and stood. "I'll make you a frothy drink, Barbara. Apparently you had a terrible day at school and you brought your frustrations home with you."

I sighed, but didn't decline the offer. A frothy drink wouldn't resolve the dog-training issue, and it wouldn't inject Allison with empathy, but it would take the kinks out of my shoulders. And really, with graduate school finished and a desire to put off the next round of chores, why not indulge?

I was sipping the second frothy drink and nibbling on a cracker loaded with an olive and tomato mixture when Lola stuck her head out of the open door to my condo, barked once, and raced to Cheese Puff. The little con artist raised his bandaged foot for her inspection. She licked his neck and made comforting noises. Mrs. B made aren't-they-adorable noises, moved to the edge of the glider, pulled Cheese Puff onto her lap, and patted the seat.

Whites of her eyes showing, Lola considered the swaying bench, then gathered herself and leaped. The glider jerked. Lola pawed at the seat and whined. Mrs. B squeaked and clutched the back of the glider with one hand and Lola's collar with the other. Cheese Puff yipped.

"Sit, Lola," I said.

Lola sat. The glider settled to a gentle sway.

"Lie down, Lola," I commanded.

"She's so well behaved," Mrs. B said as Lola obeyed.

"Yes. Unlike other dogs I know. Dogs that seem to be getting less well behaved every day."

Cheese Puff snuffled and Mrs. B patted his head. "If the little prince had a job with Lola's responsibilities, I'm sure he'd be the very model of obedience."

I shot Lola a life-isn't-fair glance and made a mental note to give her an extra biscuit later on.

Looking like he'd barely survived something on the scale of a volcanic eruption, Dave limped to the chair beside mine, flopped into it, grabbed my drink, and drained it. "Brendon Ryder was shot and killed," he said.

Mrs. B gasped. "When?"

My question was, "Where?"

"Over the weekend. In a foreclosed house on the long list of places where I'm supposed to show a police presence."

"You found him?" I asked.

"Yeah. But I didn't know it was him until Chuck Atwell told me. And it didn't take any great skill to find him. The windows were open."

"And it's been so hot," I said.

Mrs. B put a hand over her mouth and swallowed twice. "We need another round," she said in a choked voice.

"I'll take a double," Dave agreed. "Light on the fruit juice."

Mrs. B hurried off and I patted Dave's arm, trying not to think about what heat would do to a corpse, what a horrible word "corpse" was, and who might have turned Brendon Ryder into one. An hour seemed to pass before Mrs. B returned with a tray and a trio of drinks. We dedicated ourselves to them in silence for at least a minute.

"Surely they don't think Denise killed him. She has those little girls and she just doesn't seem like . . ." Mrs. B's voice trailed off.

141

Dave shook his head and fixed his gaze on me. "They're searching for your sister."

Chapter 17

"Iz?"

Mrs. B bolted to her feet, joggling the glider. Lola squirmed and eyed the deck the way an astronaut riding a rocket to the moon might gaze at earth. "They think Iz killed him?"

"Because of what she said about him at the rally?" I asked.

Dave nodded.

"Pure rhetoric," Mrs. B insisted. "Fiery talk. Iz has strong feelings about women's rights and the failure of men to meet their parental responsibilities. No one would believe she'd go from talking to killing."

"No one except Dick McBain. He ordered Chuck Atwell to bring her in for questioning."

"Bring her in," Mrs. B sputtered. "What does that mean? Slap on handcuffs? Put her in chains?"

Dave shrugged. "That depends on Iz."

Mrs. B cocked her head and frowned.

"It also depends on witnesses and photographers," I elaborated. "Being hauled into jail in chains creates a golden media moment. And it could kick off a backlash to make the sit-in seem like a book club meeting."

Mrs. B thought about that for a moment. "I see. And if Iz knew that would happen, she'd have the media standing by." She clapped her hands. "Wouldn't it be delightful if Mr. McBain walked into *that* trap?"

"It would," Dave said with a kid-on-Christmas-morning expression. "But Chuck's smart enough not to get trapped with McBain, so he won't use cuffs or coercion."

I turned so I could see Dave's eyes straight-on. "Did Chuck ask you if you knew where Iz might be?"

"Yeah."

"Did you tell him?"

"Technically, I don't know where she is at any given moment. She could be at Penelope's or she could be shopping for a clean shirt. But I covered my butt and gave Chuck Penelope's address and Iz's cell number so McBain couldn't come back on me later."

And accuse Dave of withholding information? Or protecting a suspect?

"Well, whatever they do, I'm sure Iz will have a photo opportunity all arranged." Mrs. B turned a pirouette and trotted for her door. "But I'll call and see if she needs more legal firepower to blow McBain out of the water." She halted and pointed at me. "Bring over that chicken from your freezer, the box of bow-tie pasta, and that can of artichoke hearts from the pantry. I'll toss together dinner."

"Music to my ears," Dave said, then lowered his voice as she disappeared inside. "I won't ask how she knows what's in the pantry. And I won't think about how many people traipse through every day providing day care for your dog. And I refuse to wonder if they snoop in my bureau drawers."

"You'll know they snoop if you find your underwear folded and your socks matched up."

"Verna?"

"Or Sybil. They both have straightening and organizing streaks." I trailed my fingers along his arm, wove them with his, and squeezed. "You don't think Iz killed Brendon Ryder, do you?"

"No way." Dave leaned over and kissed me. "He was good for more political mileage alive."

True, but Iz had been worked up over his release. Worked up in a way that wasn't all show. Maybe because she knew Denise Ryder and her girls. But wait— "You said Brendon Ryder was shot. Iz doesn't have a gun."

"Right." Dave kissed me again.

For two seconds I rode a wave of optimism. Then it broke.

"She probably knows people with guns. Penelope might have one." Heck, for all I knew, Paulette had a gun. A cute little derringer complete with grip panels in assorted colors to coordinate with her outfits.

Dave laid his lips on mine, leaning hard into the kiss for a few seconds. "We all know people with guns."

I knew he meant it was a long haul between having access to a gun and using that gun to kill someone, but that didn't scratch away the tickle of doubt in my mind.

Paulette wasn't in the locker room at the Reckless River Community Center when I arrived for the 7:00 PM water aerobics class, so I couldn't ask if she was packing heat. The instructor had it in for us, and the woman who usually kept up a verbal feud with Paulette got me in her sights and unloaded with snide comments about my posture—or lack of it. On the positive side, counting drive and shower time, I logged more than 90 minutes on my own.

Before Dave moved in, I would have ranked "time for myself" far down the list of things I wanted in a relationship. Now it was moving up—and fast. Even if we worked out all the issues surrounding meals and chores and the general confusion, chaos, and crowding created by three people and two dogs sharing a not-quite-big-enough space, I knew I'd want at least my two evenings of water aerobics. Ideally, I could set aside several more hours for activities that didn't include Dave, Allison, Lola, Cheese Puff, or even Mrs. Ballantine. More ideally, I could do that without feeling selfish and guilty.

Taking advantage of my new knowledge of self, I lingered in the shower an extra twenty seconds. Empowered by that, I spent a full minute slathering lotion on my arms and legs, and questioned two women about where they bought sandals. Then, even though I wasn't remotely interested, I talked with another about growing and preserving rhubarb.

I didn't feel guilty and I didn't feel selfish.

I also didn't feel the need to plant rhubarb.

Accompanied by dozens of women in white blouses with black armbands, and backed up by a dark-suited, briefcase-toting woman who had "attorney" written all over her, Iz held a news conference at 10:00 PM on the lawn outside the jail. As Dave ascertained by punching buttons on Mrs. B's remote, every area TV station carried it live after quick lead-ins recapping Brendon Ryder's release, the protest rally, and his murder.

In a few pithy sentences Iz proclaimed her innocence, acknowledged her disgust with a system she claimed provided mild penalties for domestic abuse in all forms, and affirmed her belief that violence was never the way to handle disagreements or promote social and legal change. She expressed confidence that Reckless River police would find the person responsible for Ryder's murder, and announced her intention not to seek bail if they arrested her.

Allison, sprawled on the carpet, glanced up from texting. "Huh? She won't try to get out of jail?"

Mrs. B reached for the popcorn bowl. "It makes a stronger statement about her cause if she doesn't. A lot of great protest leaders spent time in jail. Years sometimes."

"But jail's worse than school. Jake says the beds are hard and the food sucks."

Great. Allison had been talking to Jake.

The last person an impressionable teenage girl should be interacting with was my ex, president of the bad example club.

146

NO SUBSTITUTE FOR MATURITY

But bad examples were often way more interesting than good ones, and my experience with teenagers taught me that the best way to get them to go right was to hint that left was the correct and/or approved direction.

I shot Dave an I-don't-like-this-one-bit glance.

He parried with a don't-worry-I'll-handle-it set to his jaw.

I came back with the ever-popular tight squint conveying that he better get on it or I would, and slid my gaze to Mrs. Ballantine. If anyone could persuade Allison that Jake wasn't worth even waving to in passing, it was Mrs. B.

"Maybe Iz will lose weight in jail." Allison squirmed closer to the TV. "Is she wearing makeup? OMG, she is. She's wearing makeup!"

We all crowded closer.

Sure enough, Iz's lips were glossy, her cheekbones were defined with a touch of blush, her eyelashes were longer and thicker, and her brows weren't one long tangle.

Allison touched the screen. "Her brows are plucked. Her hair's lighter. And there's gel in it."

"I believe you're right," Mrs. B agreed.

"I bet Paulette did a makeover on her," Allison said.

"And a wardrobe overhaul," I said. "That's a woman's blouse she's wearing, not a man's shirt."

"It is," Mrs. B agreed. "It's fitted. You can tell by the darts."

Allison touched the screen again. "And the buttons are all different colors."

"And listen to her tone," Dave said. "She's not being confrontational."

"That's a first," I said.

Mrs. B shot me a give-your-sister-more-credit glance and I shrugged. "Well, it is. But I'll give her points for being flexible enough to change her image to court the male audience."

Allison turned her head to gaze at me. "Huh?"

"Iz knows this is about how men view women and how they treat them based on those perceptions," Dave told her.

147

"Huhhhhhh?"

"Many men stereotype women," Mrs. B explained. "Not your father, of course. But many others think of women only as mothers or princesses or damsels in distress or—"

"But not as real people," I said, jumping in before Mrs. B got wound up and starting inserting words like "prostitutes" or "sex slaves." "Iz is a tough woman and lots of men are put off by that. So she's softening her image to get them to listen."

"You catch more flies with honey than with vinegar," Mrs. B translated.

"That's just stupid." Allison stood. "I don't like vinegar and I don't know why anyone would want to catch flies."

With that, the future of our nation stalked off, leaving us to watch Iz walk up the steps to the jail, hands raised in surrender. A tall police officer with a big grin came out, escorted her to a patrol car, helped her in, and drove to the police station a block away.

"Darn it," Mrs. B said. "I hoped that Mr. McBain would try to get another few minutes of fame."

Dave stood and held out a hand to help me escape the gravitational pull of the puffy cushions on the sofa. I dusted cheesy popcorn salt from my jeans and recalled the hours I'd spent last fall being interrogated by Detective Atwell. I still hadn't managed to put that behind me, but I found myself feeling sorry for him. I knew Iz. So I knew what Chuck Atwell was in for.

"Is your sister in jail?" Doug asked the next day.

I shrugged and popped open a plastic bowl of tuna salad with plenty of green onion, pickles, and celery. I had junior English classes today and except for taking roll and announcing that I'd start *The Great Gatsby* from where they left off yesterday, I didn't plan on opening my mouth much. Yes, I had breath mints, but few mints were up to the challenge of tuna breath. "I haven't heard."

"There's nothing on the local paper's website," Gertrude said, "so I guess she's still being questioned."

Or doing the questioning.

Smiling, I dumped tuna salad onto a slice of sour rye with caraway seeds, added a few tomato slices and a lettuce leaf, and popped on another slice of bread. It was thing of beauty.

"I want to talk to her when they kick her loose," Aston said.

Brenda raised her eyebrows. "About what?"

"About organization. Logistics." Aston thumped the table with a heel of dark bread. "Ways to get the administration to leave well enough alone."

"You mean leave *you* alone." Gertrude forked the tip off a wedge of quiche.

"And you mean *your* definition of 'well enough'," Brenda added. "Apparently that means a curriculum that's a carbon copy of the past decade, and a classroom filled with toxic waste."

Doug rubbed his arms as if he had a chill. I grinned and pretended to blow on frozen fingertips. Talk about the thrill being gone. The romance between Aston and Brenda had cooled off and the mercury was dropping fast.

During fifth period I gave in, checked my phone, and found a message from Dave. "Your sister's still at the cop shop. Refuses to cooperate with the investigation, refuses to tell Chuck where she was when Brendon Ryder died—which the medical examiner puts at late Friday night or early Saturday morning. Chuck's spitting nails and McBain is spitting fire. As for me, I've been assigned drug education duty in the elementary schools. Then more paperwork. See you late, late, later."

Later turned out to be 9:52 PM.

Allison was in her room learning "all those dumb driving rules" and I was scavenging for the next day's lunch and straightening the kitchen when Dave dragged himself through the door. He had the wild eyes and trembling hands of a man swimming in shark-infested waters without benefit of a protective cage. The hair on Lola's head was greasy and matted, a wad of blue gum stuck to her collar, and a green lollipop hung in the feathery hair of her tail.

"I need a beer and a shower." Dave sagged onto the sofa and fused with the cushions, bones and muscles done for the day.

Lola dropped to the carpet, emitting a long hwwufff of air that emptied her lungs. Cheese Puff leaped from his favorite chair, licked her muzzle, then nosed beneath the sofa, retrieved a dog biscuit, and offered it to her. She sniffed it, nuzzled his neck, and fell asleep.

Dave glanced hopefully at me, then transferred his gaze to the refrigerator. "Did I mention that I need a beer?"

"Yes." I plucked one from a small cluster behind the milk and orange juice and waved it in front of him. "Shall I twist off the top for you? Hold it to your lips? Massage your neck while you swallow?"

"Go ahead, poke fun at me while I lack the strength to defend myself." He seized my wrist, captured the bottle, and poured half of it down his throat. "You don't know what it was like at that school."

"Hellooooo. Substitute teacher here."

"You deal with kids you don't have to squint to see. These were tiny. Almost invisible. They had no boundaries." He glanced at Lola, sound asleep and snuffling while Cheese Puff snuggled against her stomach. "Their little hands are like claws. They got in my pockets. I thought they'd steal my keys or lift my wallet."

"And you without a weapon."

"You're still poking fun."

"You're still whining."

"Did I mention the wallet has a picture of you inside?"

"If it's the one where I'm about to eat that chunk of German chocolate cake and my mouth is open so wide you can see my molars and it looks like I have three chins, I'd kiss the kid who made off with it."

"If you did, you'd be wiping your lips for the rest of your life. Those kids were sticky." He drained the rest of the beer. "Speaking of sticky, your sister is still hanging out at the police station."

"She's not in jail?"

"They haven't charged her with anything, but I don't know who wants the DA to come up with charges more—Iz or McBain. That fool is ripping through city and state laws in search of anything to put her behind bars. Meanwhile, she's insisting that's where she ought to be while they conduct their investigation so they can be certain she's not interfering or attempting to flee. Chuck is tearing out his hair."

Again, I found myself feeling sorry for Detective Atwell. And again I reminded myself of what he put me through last fall.

Dave finished the beer and rolled the bottle against his forehead. "Chuck wants to cut her loose and pick her up again if they find any evidence, but McBain wants to hold her as long as they can. He thinks that makes him the king of law and order instead of the duke of dumb decisions. The cop shop is surrounded by women and the crowd is growing."

"It is?"

Snatching up the remote, I aimed it at the TV. There they were, live on the 10:00 PM news, hundreds and hundreds of women with white blouses, black armbands, and determined expressions. Each one held a tall white candle.

I peered at the screen, searching for Paulette, wondering why she hadn't called to let me know about the vigil. Was it because she knew my history with Iz and thought I'd make up cheesy excuses for not coming?

Perching on the arm of the sofa, I mulled that over. Yes, I had issues with Iz that probably would be resolved around the time the sun flamed out. But, had I known about the vigil, I would be there.

"You know about it *now*," the little voice in my head pointed out. The implication was that I should pull on a white blouse, dig a candle from the catch-all drawer in the kitchen, hop in my car, and join the crowd.

As I've mentioned before, I hate that little voice. Especially when it makes a valid point.

While Dave dozed and reporters reported, I worked through my feelings about not being "invited" to take part in the vigil—feelings rooted in humiliating grade-school left-out-of-it-all experiences. When I set aside emotional baggage, I lined up my reasons for staying right here. There was that keep-a-low-profile-so-Dave-keeps-his-job thing, the I-need-tomorrow's-subbing-money thing, the I-require-sleep-so-I-can-function-tomorrow thing, and the ever-popular there-are-plenty-of-women-down-there-already philosophy.

And there was another reason—the question that kept surfacing in my mind: Was Iz innocent?

NO SUBSTITUTE FOR MATURITY

Chapter 18

In an attempt to dispel doubt, I tugged on Dave's ankle. "Do they have any leads? A neighbor who saw someone? Someone who wasn't Iz?"

"Neighbors around there are in the habit of *not* seeing who comes and goes. They're also in the habit of not talking to police."

"Well, maybe someone heard the shot. If we knew the exact time he was killed we'd know if Iz—"

"That neighborhood's in the airport flight path. And Ryder was shot with a small caliber handgun."

Dave stood and stretched. "I'm going up to take a shower. Sure would be nice if someone came along to scrub my back." He leered. "If you get my drift."

I got a full-body tingle. Then I remembered the chore I'd been about to tackle when he came through the door. If he had enough energy for an amorous interlude, surely he had the strength to take out the trash. "I get it, but the kitchen wastebasket is overflowing. And it stinks. I can't scrub your back until someone takes out the garbage."

I emphasized the last five words, hoping Dave would man up and carry the sack to the trash bins at the end of the parking lot.

He didn't.

Turning a thumb up, he headed upstairs, grunting with the effort of lifting each foot, and calling for Lola to follow.

153

She didn't.

Only a single thump of her tail and the twitch of an eyelid indicated there was life in her body.

"I'll sponge her off in the morning," Dave called. "Unless we're on school duty again."

Grumbling, I yanked the garbage pail out from under the sink and hoisted out the plastic bag inside—no easy task because it was wedged tight. Since Dave moved in, the unwritten household policy endorsed using brute force to stuff as much in the bag as possible, rather than emptying it at more frequent intervals.

What is it about some men? Why is the thought of making more than one trip so horrifying?

I braced a foot against the plastic pail and gave the bag a vicious jerk. Something sloshed inside as it popped free. *Ick.* Probably a to-go container with the dregs of a soft drink. I made a mental note to talk with Allison about dumping before tossing.

Holding the bag to the side in the fond hope that I could avoid splatter if it broke, I scuttled out the door. The cool, damp air created a halo around each of the old-fashioned globe lamps illuminating the parking lot. A line of young trees and the canopy over the prime parking spaces lot created plenty of shadows and pools of darkness. On my way back I noticed one of those pools was occupied by Winton James and a woman who appeared to be the one I saw him with Friday night.

Curious, I slowed my pace and changed course, navigating off the sidewalk and into a puddle of murk close to the building.

Thanks to a light-colored T-shirt and his pale skin, Winton almost glowed. The woman had her back to me, but the way she hunched inside a long sweater told me she wasn't happy. Winton's body language—palms thrust out, head shaking—said the same thing.

Dropping my chin so my hair swung forward to obscure my face, I skulked to another puddle of gloom. Being curious, I told myself, wasn't the same as being nosy. Well, not exactly. Being curious meant being inquisitive. Being nosy meant snooping. Snooping could lead to meddling with malicious intent.

Having cleared that up, I gave myself permission to edge closer, trying to make out their words. Unfortunately, Winton and the woman spoke in hissing whispers. More unfortunately, those whispers were swept up by a light breeze blowing away from me. By holding my breath, I made out the words "didn't know," "my needs," "not fair to," "could be months," and "No. I can't."

That last bit came from Winton right before he shook his head a final time, turned his back on the woman, and headed for his condo. The blond hesitated, then straightened her shoulders, tossed her hair, and stalked toward the visitors' parking lot.

Connecting the dots, I took a mental leap and concluded the woman was married, Winton found out, and tonight called things off. I awarded him points for being a stand-up guy. I gave her points for reaching for the gold ring of happiness even if she did it while riding the merry-go-round of marriage. Killing time until I could emerge from the shadows, I gave myself points for never cheating—not even on Jake, not even after he cheated on me.

The woman reached the corner, paused in a cone of light, and glanced behind her for a fraction of a second. I saw the thrust of her jaw, the jut of her cheekbone, the flash of an earring. And then she disappeared from sight with a swirl of that long sweater and a swish of blond hair. She looked like—

Penelope?

Penelope and Winton?

No. No way.

But, maybe.

No. Definitely not. Penelope was at the vigil.

Or had she slipped away from the group? Tossed on that sweater to cover her white blouse and armband?

She could drive here in five minutes. And she could easily slip back into the crowd of women and, if anyone questioned her absence, claim she went to get coffee or find a restroom.

I wanted to share what I saw with Dave, but when I got to the bedroom he was sprawled across the bed diagonally, still dressed, and snoring like a moose with a sinus infection. I tossed a blanket over him, got one for myself, and retreated to the sofa. For hours I laid awake, staring up at the ceiling in the direction of Winton James' bedroom, trying to jam together pieces of a puzzle that didn't quite fit.

Penelope could have met Winton any of the times she and Iz dropped by, when they came to dinner at Mrs. B's, or helped Dave move in. That part was easy, even factoring in that Winton seldom emerged from his apartment. Anyone who saw Penelope with Iz would know they were a couple, but what if Winton bumped into her when Iz wasn't by her side. Penelope could have gone to her truck to get something or taken out a sack of garbage.

What wasn't easy was figuring out how they went from passing in the parking lot to doing a heck of a lot more. And then there was the issue of sexual preference.

Tossing, I reran the snippets of conversation. The woman— maybe Penelope and maybe not—had said "my needs." As in "My needs aren't being met"? Or as in "She doesn't care about my needs"? If Iz wasn't giving Penelope what she needed, she might look elsewhere. But would she look to a man?

I trailed my hand across Cheese Puff and Lola, tight against each other. With the seasonal construction boom and her volunteer activities, Penelope had little spare time. And Iz shared her house. Whatever she had going with Winton had to be of the stolen-moments variety.

I tossed again. If Penelope needed more, surely that would show in the way she acted toward Iz. And what I saw was the opposite. Penelope seemed devoted to my sister.

156

And wait! If the woman with Winton was Penelope, how did she get here on Friday night?

I cast my mind to the late supper on the lawn after Allison's play, trying to remember when Iz and Penelope left. Dinner hadn't gone on for much more than an hour, and I was almost positive I saw Iz going for second helpings of the macaroni salad and thirds of the mini cheesecakes. They left before Mrs. B and I did, but how much before? Half an hour? Would that be enough to deliver Iz to her house on the northwest side of the city, make an excuse to leave, change out of the slacks she wore to the play, dash over here, and make time with Winton?

Hardly.

Unless someone else drove Iz home while Penelope came here.

And if Penelope was here, that meant Iz didn't have an alibi for a slice of Friday night—possibly the slice during which Brendon Ryder caught a bullet.

Maybe that's why Iz wasn't talking. Maybe her silence wasn't just about making a point.

I went cold and hot and cold again. Was my sister a killer?

"Gym." With a malicious grin, Big Chill held out a set of keys.

"What did I do to make you hate me?"

"It's the only job open today." She jingled the keys. "Take it or leave it."

"Maybe I could fill in for a custodian," I offered in a hopeful voice.

"You're not qualified. Besides, you'd have to unclog toilets or mow grass, not drive the machine they use to clean the cafeteria floor."

Dang it! I loved that machine. It made a satisfying roar and turned on a dime. I fantasized about driving it to my condo and cleaning the kitchen. Early this morning someone had dribbled a trail of blueberry syrup from the refrigerator to the counter where that same someone—or perhaps an accomplice—created a puddle of syrup that fed a trickle that dripped into the silverware drawer.

Both suspects denied committing the crime. Each blamed the other. Neither made a move to mop up the mess until I ramped up my I'm-not-kidding-around-here voice.

Mounting a camera on the ceiling became more appealing every day. So did going on strike. When school was out and Dave's situation stabilized, changes *would* be made.

Big Chill swung the keys from side to side and spoke in a monotone. "You will go to the gym. You will be happy to have a job while other subs wait by the phone or sit at the computer refreshing the job website."

"You can't hypnotize a woman who's asleep on her feet." I snatched the keys. "Which is a shame because I'd so much rather come out of a trance at 2:05 and find today's torture is over and I have no memory of it."

"At least the smell in the gym is better than in Aston's classroom."

"Marginally." I signed the sub form. "Five to seven percent."

Which wasn't much of an exaggeration. The gym had a pungent odor all its own. Years of sweat and body odor had permeated the walls and floors and bleachers. Factor in fresh sweat, perfume, cologne, and BO, and by the time the final bell rang my sinuses had swelled to the size of jumbo kumquats.

Allison had no sympathy. "Drive faster." She tapped my arm with her phone. "Mrs. B says Dario is ready to go when I am."

"I can't drive faster." Snatching a tissue from the box in the console, I blew my nose. "My eyes are watering so much I can barely see."

"But this is important. My whole future depends on it." She gripped the wheel. "Go faster. I'll steer."

I batted at her hand. "No."

"Come on. I'll tell you when there's a light or a stop sign."

I let up on the gas. "That's wrong in so many ways."

"You're no fun."

"Being in the hospital or the cemetery is no fun either."

Pouting, Allison resorted to texting in silence—undoubtedly telling her friends what a waste of space I was.

Big deal. I'd been subbing for almost a year now; dozens of students had already said that—or worse. Since I gave up worrying about not being loved, liked, or even barely tolerated by anyone without a high school diploma, my skin was getting thicker by the day.

With the expression of a man sentenced to walk barefooted across a field of fire ants, Dario waited in the condo parking lot. Decked out in gray slacks, a pink shirt, and a purple and silver tie, he leaned against an enormous SUV the color of the contents of a well-used litter box. It had crumpled fenders, dented doors, and more scratches and dings than furniture given a distressed look by escapees from a chain gang.

"Do the detailing yourself?" I asked when he released me from a rib-cracking hug.

He smoothed his tie and grinned. The flexing of facial muscles transformed his usual expression of intimidating menace into one of lighthearted threat. "Picked it up at an auction this morning. Figured a few more gouges might be an improvement."

Allison's lower lip assumed pout position, yet somehow she managed to speak. "It's gross. It's worse than Barbara's car."

"That's the point."

"But I don't want to drive a wreck. I want to drive something hot."

"This will be hot all right." Dario shot me a wink. "The air conditioning's busted."

"Nooooo," Allison wailed. "I'll get all sticky. And my hair will droop. And someone from school might see me."

Dario pooched his lips in and out as if considering her complaint. "In that case, your other choice is to . . ." With a wolfish smile he drew himself up, loomed over Allison, and spoke in a rough gangsteresque whisper, "Fuhgeddaboudit."

She flinched, but managed another sixteenth of an inch of pout.

Dario raised his eyebrows.

Allison climbed into the passenger seat, and began another string of texting.

"OMG." I mimed texting a message. "IMHO you are so not her BFF."

"IDC." He climbed behind the wheel. "See you later. I hope."

The door to the deck was open and I found Cheese Puff flopped on the glider watching Mrs. Ballantine. Wearing a long turquoise T-shirt and gray tights, she was contorted into a yoga position I couldn't have managed when I was ten. I fell into the embrace of my usual chair, took off my glasses, and massaged the area around my eyes. "Is the vigil still going on?"

"Last I checked. If it doesn't rain, I'm going after dinner." She changed to a new position, one I might be able to master with a strong dose of muscle relaxer and incentive in the form of not less than $1000. "Dario and I have reservations at a restaurant up the river."

Cheese Puff lifted his head and thumped his tail.

"Sorry," she told him. "They have a strict no-pets policy."

Cheese Puff sneezed as if to remind her she usually flaunted such rules.

"I know we got away with it in the past, but the hostess recognized my voice and made quite the point of saying if I bring you they won't serve us."

Cheese Puff yipped his annoyance.

"She was snippy about it, too. That was totally uncalled for. I plan to tell her so after we dine this evening."

Another yip.

"I'll make it up to you tomorrow. We'll do lunch."

Sheesh. The person who coined the expression "a dog's life" never met this entitled canine.

"I'm sure you want to go to the vigil, dear," Mrs. B told me, "but it might not be the best thing for Dave's career if you were seen there."

"I agree. But do *you* want to be the one to tell Iz I stayed away because of concern about a man's job?"

Mrs. B's sapphire eyes darkened. "I'd rather not."

"Coward."

"Let's call it self-preservation, not cowardice. Iz likes Dave as much as she'll allow herself, but she doesn't view him as your partner the way she views Penelope as hers."

"Speaking of Penelope . . ."

Mrs. B's eyes darkened another shade when I finished telling her about last night. "It couldn't be Penelope." She stood, dusted the knees of her tights, and adjusted her T-shirt. "I don't believe it for a single minute."

"Well, I don't want to believe it either, but Winton was with *somebody,* and that somebody looks a lot like Penelope."

"At night," Mrs. B pointed out. "From a distance."

Good points.

Mrs. B fidgeted, plumping the cushions on the glider, moving a patio table a few inches to the left, then to the right, and using the hem of her T-shirt to scrub at a smudge on the door to her condo. "I didn't call and ask Winton to dinner like I intended. When I see that he's home I'll drop by and issue an invitation to both of them. Then I'll inquire about her name."

"Good luck finding Winton at home. When it comes to describing his work schedule, the word 'inhumane' leaps to mind." I pried myself out of my chair. "And on that topic, I don't know when Dave will be home or when Allison will return, so I better see what I can scrounge for dinner that will keep in the fridge."

"Slice that ham and make cornbread to go with it."

Not a bad idea. As long as I didn't take off a finger, slicing was easy. And I had a mix for corn muffins.

"You'll want to use that cabbage soon. The outside leaves are drying out. And the carrots are getting a little limp but they'll work fine for slaw and you can use the red onion you have on the windowsill."

I picked up Cheese Puff, warm and languid from the sun, while she weighed the merits of mayonnaise-based dressings over others and announced she would whip something up and bring it over.

(For the record, you might feel this is intrusive. You might even call it culinary bullying. But in an odd way I found it reassuring and calming because A) I needed all the help I could get in the kitchen and B) I'd come to think of Mrs. B as family. I took more crap from family than I did from strangers. Not that Mrs. B handed out a lot of crap. At least not compared to Iz.)

Raging in a shrill voice, Allison stormed in while the cornbread baked. The gist of her tirade involved ridiculous questions concerning heights, distances, and miles per hour. Through it all, I concentrated on carving the ham into slices that were kind of, sort of, almost the same width. At the same time, I charted her rise in acting out compared to the amount of time Dave hadn't been home. When her bedroom door slammed, Dario called from the hallway, "Is it safe?"

"Yes," I called, "this act in the latest drama appears to be over. You sound like a man who needs a beer."

"A beer won't cut it." He lumbered into view, his shirt limp and streaked with sweat. "Got any of the hard stuff?"

I opened the cabinet where the rum resided and handed him the bottle. He twisted off the cap, tipped his head, poured about four shots worth into his mouth, and swallowed. Eyes watering, he hammered his fist against his sternum and gasped, "Smooth. Real smooth."

I got a can of cola from the refrigerator as a chaser. "I surmise things didn't go well."

He raised the rum and poured a little more down his throat, then set the bottle on the counter, popped the top on the cola, and swallowed a prodigious quantity. "Yeah, it didn't go well in the way that Dillinger's night at the movies didn't go well. Or Valentine's Day didn't go well for the Moran gang. Or Al Capone's tax audit—"

He drank the rest of the cola, cast a wistful glance at the rum, and slouched to the sofa. "They let you miss 5 questions out of 25. She missed 13."

"Let me guess—it wasn't her fault, right?"

"Right. The test wasn't fair, people were standing too close, somebody's 'yucky' cologne made her head hurt, the room was too hot, and the air conditioning blew on her neck." He cast another longing glance at the rum. "I worked with a psychotic enforcer in Miami who had more patience and self-control."

"Probably better if we skip the details of *that* employment interlude."

He held the empty can to the side of his head. "After she washed out, I let her drive around the development they put on hold until the economy improves. I had less fear on that job in Indianapolis when the wheelman had a seizure."

"Another incident best kept buried in your checkered past." I handed him a second cola and made a mental note to tell Mrs. B she should drive this evening. Even with his bulk, six shots of rum in two minutes might make Dario as dangerous behind the wheel as Allison. "You gave it a try. Dave created this monster, he can teach—"

"Dario O'Brien is no quitter." He popped the cola. "When Dario O'Brien agrees to do a job, he doesn't walk away until it's finished."

(For the record, I find it weird and a little unbalanced when people refer to themselves in the third person, but I made allowances for Dario. Working for guys—fictional or not—with

163

nicknames like "Cement Shoes," "Rabid Weasel," or "Belching Barracuda," hadn't prepared him for Allison.)

"It's your funeral, but no one will think less of you if you back out."

"I'm not backing out." He lurched to his feet and headed for the door to the deck. "But let's hope she learns before I need a casket. Black isn't Muriel's best color."

Chapter 19

Perhaps because of the vigil, there were only three of us in the deep area of the pool during aerobics class. In Paulette's absence, her nemesis took a run at being the bane of *my* existence. "Apparently you don't care enough about the cause of justice to take part in the vigil," she sniped.

"Apparently you don't, either." Panting, I tried to do the cross-country move without leaning so far forward I did a face-plant in the water.

She flushed, but then waded in (pun intended) for round two. "Don't you think your sister needs your support?"

"You met her. Did she give you the impression she needed anything from anyone? Especially from me?"

"Hmmpphh." The nemesis snorted and, with a burst of speed, crossed to the far side of the pool for the rest of the class.

It was a pleasant change.

At 8:30, I drove by the police station. A sea of women in white blouses surrounded it and, despite a damp breeze and a forecast calling for thunderstorms, rivers of white fed into that sea as more women joined the vigil. Many carried umbrellas or raincoats or folded tarps. Parked cars lined every street and filled every lot for blocks around. Traffic moved in a rolling snarl.

I didn't mind. Thanks to the modern marvel known as the voice message, I wasn't in a hurry to go home.

While I was at the pool, Allison left three messages on my cell phone, all in varying degrees of disturbing.

The gist of the first was that she didn't like anything I made for dinner and intended to cook something that would be "much better."

The second message consisted of questions. "How come nobody ever told me spaghetti gets fatter when it cooks? What should I do if there's no room for more water in the pot? Can I use the pancake turner to get burnt cheese off the bottom of the oven or should I use a knife? A big knife or a little one?"

The third message, delivered in a confrontational tone, indicated that she called Jim when I didn't answer and he got the sink unclogged and opened all the windows so maybe the smoke wouldn't be so bad and the curtains on the window over the sink were only burned a little and if it rained soon that spot on the deck would probably wash away and this wasn't her fault and she was going to call and tell Dave so he wouldn't yell at her and she didn't have time to clean everything up right now because she had homework.

Sheesh.

Apparently Allison needed as much help cooking as she did driving. Maybe a few members of the Committee would sign on to teach culinary skills. Although cooking had its hazards, it didn't usually involve the risk of high-speed collisions or breakdowns miles from anywhere. In the meantime, a question loomed in my mind—did I want to go home tonight?

Or ever?

Allison was out of control, and I couldn't help but wonder if Dave was milking his in-trouble-with-the-boss situation. Could he be using it as an excuse to avoid dealing with fallout from the move and his daughter's issues? To avoid me? To avoid confronting second thoughts about our relationship? Second thoughts like the ones I was having?

Yikes!

I pulled over at a convenience store and tried to reverse the course of my thinking with a small bag of cheesy snacks and, because it was too late for caffeine, a child-size root beer with plenty of ice. Everyone knows a stomach full of cheesy snacks and sugar slows the brain and keeps it from leaping to conclusions. Or maybe the combination helps the brain leap to so many conclusions they cancel each other out.

Nibbling and sipping, I slumped in my car at the far end of the lot. A steady stream of customers came and went making dietary choices not unlike my own—ice cream bars, beer, jerky, nuts, cookies, potato chips, and soft drinks.

Air smelling like hot metal gusted through the spaces at the top of the windows. A few dozen raindrops spattered the windshield but dried in minutes, leaving dusty splotches. More customers came and went, then a familiar car pulled in and parked at the other end of the lot. After a long moment, a man got out and limped into the store.

Dave.

I scooched lower in the seat and peered over the steering wheel. He shuffled along the aisles, settling on a bag of sweet and salty cashews and a drooping rose from a display by the cash register. Eyes half closed, he stumbled to his car and fell inside. With a series of starts and stops, he reversed, then drove toward the condo in a line that would be described as straight only by someone severely under the influence.

Part of me wanted to rush home and wrap him in my arms and poor-baby him. A larger part wanted him to suffer for saddling me with Allison, additional chores, and a raft of worry about his job and our future.

I gobbled the remainder of the cheesy snacks, stuffed the evidence under the seat, gave him a two-minute head start, and followed.

Lola at his heels, he was unlocking the condo door when I eased into my parking spot. He never glanced around, and I took my sweet time gathering up my swim gear. On the way to the door, I paused to watch a long line of lightning-laced clouds rolling in from the south. Unless those clouds veered off, Reckless River would get hammered.

Inside I found Lola stretched out in the hallway, not flinching, whining, or growling as Cheese Puff chewed at a blue glob on one of her ears. Neither of them gave me a glance or a wag as I passed. The kitchen smelled like a burning landfill, the once crisp white curtains hung in scorched tatters, dirty pots and pans crowded the counter, and the floor resembled an abstract painting.

Dave stood at the stove, sponge in hand, and an expression on his face that asked the question, "Where do I begin?"

"I'm sorry," he said. "I'm sorry about this mess, sorry about the mess I made of my job, and sorry about the mess I'm making of your home and your life."

He set the sponge aside and reached for the cashews and the dried-out rose. "These are for now. I'm going up to tell Allison the princess act is over. Then we'll divide up the chores and you'll show me how to do them right. And when I can get some time off from this demolition derby I call a job, you and I will go to the coast and I'll be your slave for as long as it takes to make up for everything."

I pretended to ponder that. "Would the slavery thing involve a back rub?"

"Definitely."

"A foot rub?"

"Certainly."

"Ear nibbling?"

"No doubt about it."

"Hmm." I rubbed my chin.

He dropped to his knees.

I stretched out a hand to cover his mouth if I heard the start of a marriage proposal. No way were we ready for that. We had a pile of baggage to sort out, set aside, or repack. And right now that pile loomed like Mount Rushmore.

"Please don't toss me out," Dave said. "I love you. Please don't give up on me. On us."

I'd heard a man plead before, but that was Jake begging me to turn on the cash spigot. This was different. This had deep emotional content. I allowed myself a few seconds to enjoy it, then dropped beside Dave and rubbed my cheek against his stubble. He smelled of burnt coffee and bubble gum and onions. I planted my lips against his. He sighed.

"I won't say the thought of booting you and Allison out hasn't crossed my mind," I said after a long moment. "But since you came home bringing gifts—such as they are—I'll hold the idea in abeyance for a time."

He nuzzled my neck. "How long a time?"

"Until you cease to satisfy my carnal desires."

He pulled at the neck of my T-shirt and nuzzled lower. "I'll be here for years. Decades."

"Maybe for the rest of your life." I sucked back a moan of pleasure. "But let's put this on hold until after you talk with Allison and take a shower."

Dave kissed the point of my collar bone. "A more macho man would pull off your clothes right here." He got to his feet and offered me a hand. "And a lesser man would put off talking with his daughter until tomorrow."

I got up as gracefully as a gazelle wearing a hobble skirt. Should have stuck with those ballet lessons in second grade. "But *you're* the ideal man?"

"If you believe your sister, there *is* no ideal man." He rubbed his knees. "And speaking of that particular devil, Chuck escorted her out of the cop shop an hour ago, but she's calling for the protest to continue indefinitely."

"She talked?"

"Not a peep, but they have evidence pointing to someone else. Two people saw a slender blond woman in the neighborhood around the time Ryder died." Dave started up the

169

stairs. "Iz may be a lot of things, but she's not blond and she's not slender."

Penelope, however, was both.

Fighting a wave of dizziness, I gripped the counter and told myself she wasn't the only slender, blond woman in Reckless River.

And why would Penelope kill Brendon Ryder? Because she was enraged by what happened to Denise? Or was it more personal? Maybe jealousy? Did she want him out of the way so the protest would end and she could get her life with Iz back the way it was?

But wait! If Penelope was the woman I saw with Winton James, then she wasn't totally focused on a life with Iz. So why would she be jealous?

"Jealousy isn't logical," the voice in my brain reminded me.

True. There were embarrassing incidents in my past that were proof of that—one involving mayonnaise funneled into a bottle of hair conditioner belonging to a girl in the next dorm room.

Obviously not my most mature moment.

So as not to dwell on that, or on doubts about my sister's innocence, I walked to the staircase and eavesdropped on the discussion between Dave and Allison. That discussion was characterized by high-pitched squeals of protest and a deep, rolling river of words I couldn't quite make out.

Sensing it could be a while before that river wore down the peaks of Allison's defensive outrage, I opened the door to the deck to clear the air. Listening to thunder rumbling closer, I climbed on a chair, removed the remains of the curtains, put them in the trash, and carried the bag out to the bins at the end of the parking lot.

Wind gusts were intensifying, powering dust and bits of litter along the asphalt. Tree branches thrashed and leaves fluttered loose and spiraled upward. The storm hovered close to the river. Jagged bolts of lightning arced from cloud to cloud and jabbed at the ground. Thunder growled and cracked. Cold rain slapped me and I raced for the shelter of the condo.

Watching the storm through the smoke-filmed window, I filled the sink with hot water and dumped in the pots and pans for Allison to wash. That cleared the counter so I could wipe it with a vinegar solution. I used more vinegar on the greasy smoke on the windowpane and walls, and went over the cabinet doors with lemony wood cleaner.

That gave me the courage to open the oven door a crack and assess the burned cheese issue.

Ugh!

Not just a few drips. A lava flow of cheese. And clearly not my job. Neither was the floor. Or the soot-smudged ceiling.

Feeling virtuous for doing more than many other women would have—and probably more than I should have—I stood at the door to the deck for a few moments and gazed off to the south. Air currents coming down the Columbia Gorge seemed to be slowing the storm's northward progress. The clouds, illuminated from within by chains of lightning, mounded higher.

I took a pad of paper to the dining room table and made a list of what needed to be done to restore order in the kitchen, the steps in the process, and the cleaning products to be used. As I finished, Allison plodded down the stairs and stood beside me. I awarded points to her drama teacher for the eyes glimmering with tears, the crease of worry between her brows, and the upper teeth caught on the quivering lower lip. But her body language—feet eighteen inches apart and arms crossed over her chest—didn't mesh with the please-forgive-me expression on her face.

"Dad says I'm acting self-centered and entitled and you do a ton of stuff that I never thank you for and I have to apologize and clean up my mess."

Her tone implied Dave's conclusion was not only false but absurd.

I jabbed my finger against the point of my chin as if contemplating.

Allison's lip ceased its quiver and thrust into a pout.

I was pretty darn tired of that particular brand of lip service, so I didn't mince words. "Your father is right on all three counts. There are evil dictators who work and play better with others than you have lately."

I set my pen aside and folded my hands on the edge of the table. "Now let's get to the apology."

Allison's eyes widened. "I already did that."

"No, you didn't."

"I did too!"

"No, you told me your father said you had to apologize. That's not the same as actually telling me you're sorry."

Her lower lip slid out once again.

"You won't win this argument and skate off without apologizing." I stood and stared into her eyes. "And if you keep pouting, a short and simple apology won't be enough."

"What does that mean?"

"It could mean I'll demand you knee-walk across the room with your hands in prayer position, then kiss my toes before you scrub the deck with a toothbrush."

Allison's gaze slid toward the deck. She drew in her lip and swallowed. "I'm sorry, Barbara. I'm really, really, really sorry I was such a drama queen and didn't help out and made a lot of work for you. I promise I'll stop complaining all the time and appreciate what you do and clean up my mess."

Keeping my face still, I waited a few seconds, enjoying what I suspected would be a fleeting moment of power.

"Really. I will."

I waited another five seconds. "Okay. I forgive you. But I think you should also apologize to Dario and Mrs. Ballantine."

She sighed. "I guess."

I handed her the sheet of instructions. "Here's how to make things right. Lucky for you I put the pots in to soak. Luckier for you, that's a self-cleaning oven. You can turn it on tonight and it will burn up the gunk, but you'll have to remove the ash and sponge it out tomorrow."

Her lower lip twitched, but she pulled it in and got busy. Dave joined us in a few minutes, hauled out the step stool, and went to work on the ceiling. I got a scissors and, much to Cheese Puff's dismay, cut the glops of gum and candy out of Lola's hair and cleaned her up with a wet washcloth.

Then, braving a wind now snapping decorative flags and rocking patio furniture, I ordered both dogs to follow me out through bursts of chilly rain to the tiny rose garden at the far edge of the deck. Cheese Puff yipped his annoyance, then dashed ahead. Lola plodded, squatted, and trudged inside, raindrops glistening on her ears.

Shaking the rain from my hair, I thought of the women at the protest. Iz, for so many reasons, would never call a halt to the demonstration, no matter how hard rain fell or how close lightning struck. But if Paulette was there—

I laughed.

Paulette would have a designer umbrella and a pair of adorable rain boots that matched a stylish water-repellent hooded coat. But even given such preparations, she would insist they suspend the protest and take shelter until the storm passed.

At 10:05 we voted unanimously to leave the rest of the cleanup for tomorrow.

At 10:21 Dave and I were in bed, drifting to sleep to the rolling boom of thunder in the distance and the sound of rain drumming on the roof and gurgling in the gutters.

At 12:07 the phone rang.

Chapter 20

Heart pounding, I scooped it up.

A siren wailed and then Penelope gasped. "Somebody shot your sister. We're on the way to the hospital."

I sat up, clutching the phone with one hand and Dave's arm with the other. "How bad is it?"

"They don't know." Her voice rose and broke into a sob. "Her blood pressure's dropping."

"I'm on the way."

"I'll drive." Dave hurtled from bed and pulled on a pair of jeans, going commando. "Where?"

"The hospital." I struggled into a pair of shorts. "Somebody shot Iz."

"How bad?"

"They don't know." My T-shirt went on backwards and I tossed a bra in my purse to wrestle with later. "Or they won't tell Penelope."

Cheese Puff leaped off the bed as I toed into a pair of flip-flops. "You're not going."

He yipped an objection.

Dave tossed him beside Lola. "Stay," he ordered.

Cheese Puff gathered himself to jump, but Lola stretched out a paw and pulled him against her chest. "Good girl," Dave called over his shoulder.

In a minute we were in his car—a vehicle even older and in worse shape than mine—and headed for the Reckless River

Hospital at speeds double the limit. Tires skidded on leaves, twigs, and small branches brought down by the storm. The back end fishtailed at every turn.

I braced my hands against the dashboard and flashed on the mean things I'd said and thought about Iz since childhood. It was a heck of a long list. But it was also characterized by repetition and similarity. And, given that my brain speeds up in times of crisis, I finished within a minute and moved on to reviewing kind things Iz had said and done. That list was far shorter, but anchored by the fact that she stepped in to raise me when my parents lost the will to nurture.

Dave joggled my arm. "Iz will be okay. She's tough."

But tough might not be enough.

I retrieved the bra from my purse and tried to wiggle into it without unsnapping the seat belt.

"Stressing about it won't help. Call Mrs. Ballantine and tell her what's up. Ask her to see that Allison gets to school if we're not home by morning."

Allison!

I'd forgotten about Allison. Some potential stepmother I was.

I abandoned the bra project and dug in my purse for my phone. Mrs. B answered on the second ring and got with the program within seconds. "Don't worry. Dario and I will take care of everything."

I thanked her, wondered for a second if I should tell her about the new and improved Allison, wondered for another second about the shelf life of that version, then disconnected.

With a screech of brakes and an acrid cloud of burnt rubber, Dave cornered into the hospital lot and skidded to a stop at the emergency entrance. Penelope, her blond hair wet and matted, long rain jacket open to reveal a white blouse splotched with blood, broke from a clutch of police officers and fell into my arms. "She's unconscious. They took her to surgery. They won't . . ."

The rest got lost in a series of racking sobs and she sagged against me. My knees buckled. Dave slipped his arms around her and took the strain. "I've got her," he said. "I'll get coffee. You check on Iz. Meet me in the waiting room."

I strode toward the door and the desk beyond. They'd tell me her condition. They had to. I was her sister.

But wait! How would I prove that? Iz and I didn't share a name. She had hers legally changed years ago. And my friends, unless they were lying through their teeth, said we looked nothing alike.

My steps faltered. Then a hand gripped my arm, a hand belonging to Detective Charles Atwell.

I recoiled reflexively. Memories of being viewed as a murder suspect took time to erase. Dave called him "Chuck." I called him as "Atwell," or sometimes, as Big Chill did, "Atweird" or "Atweed."

"Let me go," I said. "I have to check on my sister."

"That's why I'm here." He towed me past the cluster of officers and through glass doors that slid open at our approach. Inside he flashed his shield at everyone in scrubs or white coats, fixed them with glares from beneath his jutting brows, and got promises to update him. The expressions on their faces indicated her condition was somewhere below stable.

"You can release me now," I said as he half dragged me to the waiting area. "Unless you think I'm a suspect."

"Sorry." He shook his hand to work out the kinks. Thin lips twitching at the corners, he gave me what passed for a smile in his galaxy. "You'll have bruises. Why didn't you say something?"

"I didn't want to interrupt while you were on a roll." I crossed my arms over my braless chest. "I figured you'd get more information than I would."

"Hmm." He tugged at the thick lobe of one ear. "With a gunshot wound it could be hours before she's out of surgery."

Not what I wanted to hear. And not what I intended to pass on to Penelope who clutched a cup of coffee as she huddled against Dave on an institutional faux leather sofa the color of dead moss. Easing in beside her, I drew her against me and stroked her damp hair, leaving Dave free for cop talk with Atwell. "They'll let us know as soon as she's out of surgery."

"When? When will that be?"

"Soon." I guided the coffee to her lips. "They're experts. This is what they train for. And she's strong and healthy. And determined. You know how determined she is."

Penelope nodded in that automatic way you do when you're too numb to really listen or think.

"Or should I say she's tenacious? Unwavering? Stubborn? Fixated? Especially when she's angry," I went on. "And imagine how angry she is right now. Odds are there's at least one *man* in there messing with her insides."

I aimed a finger at Dave and Atwell who were conferring in the corner. "And there are *other men* trying to find the person who shot her."

Penelope's lips quivered into a smile that lasted a fraction of a second. "They kept asking me, but I didn't see who did it. It was dark. And we were all wearing white shirts and rain coats." She twisted her hands in the tails of her bloodstained blouse and sobbed. "No one noticed her, so she must have dressed like us."

"She?" Atwell broke from the huddle with Dave. "A woman shot Iz?"

"I . . . I don't know." Penelope's eyes widened in surprise. "But I remember thinking that the only men I saw were police officers. And they were wearing dark slickers and stayed around the edges. They didn't come into the crowd."

"Are you sure?" Dave asked.

"After what happened when that man pulled Iz off the table, someone would have yelled or argued if a man got close. And everyone would have turned to see what was going on."

"So it had to be a woman," I said.

"Or a man dressed like a woman," Atwell said.

Dave raised one eyebrow.

"Just covering all the bases. But for now, let's assume it would take a woman to get that close. A woman with a small handgun she could conceal easily." Atwell touched his side. "Iz got hit here. The trajectory of the bullet was slightly upward. The shooter had to be close."

As close as Penelope must have been?

I shook off what that implied. Unless Penelope was an amazing actress, this was real. She was wrecked by the shooting and the possibility of losing Iz.

"How close?" I asked.

"Two or three yards," Atwell said. "Close enough to have a clear shot." He leaned over Penelope. "You're sure you didn't see or hear anything?"

"We were huddled together because of the storm. Everyone had their umbrellas up or tarps held over their heads. We knew we shouldn't stay out there, but no one wanted to leave." Penelope drew in a shuddering breath. "Women were screaming and rain was falling so hard and there was hail, too. Iz was on the curb that borders the sidewalk telling everyone to stay calm. I was in front of her hunched over with my hood up and I was counting the seconds between lightning and thunder and it was one, one, one, and then two and three, so the numbers were going up and that meant the storm was moving off and—"

"Slow it down," Dave said. "Replay this in your mind second by second, sound by sound. Did you hear anything besides thunder and rain and hail? Do you remember anything else?"

"No. There was so much noise. But maybe. I don't know. Somebody on my left nudged me." Penelope patted the jut of her hip and leaned to her right. "I lost my balance for a second and took a step to the side. And I thought someone must have shoved Iz, too, because she staggered off the curb and fell. She didn't try to catch herself. And I wondered why. And then—"

I snatched two tissues from the box on the table beside the sofa and pressed them into her hands. "That's when you realized she was hit?"

"No. Not for a few seconds. Not until she didn't get up." Penelope covered her face with the tissues. "She didn't get up."

To his credit, Atwell gave her a moment. "I know you didn't see the person who pushed you, but did you get any kind of impression? Maybe a sense of that person's size?"

"Close your eyes," Dave advised. "Slow it down again. Take your time."

Penelope wiped her face, blew her nose, and took in several deep breaths. Then she touched her hip again. "Her hip bumped mine. She was about my height. And maybe close to my weight."

"Good," Atwell said. "Anything else? Anything at all?"

Penelope closed her eyes tighter, took in a breath, and held it. "I smelled . . . something. Perfume? Maybe soap or lotion? Coconut I think."

I hugged her and watched Atwell. "That's good, right?"

"It's something," Dave answered.

"And nail polish," Penelope said.

"You smelled nail polish?" I asked. "Someone in that driving rainstorm was polishing her nails?"

"I didn't smell it. I saw it. On her toes." Penelope opened her eyes. "It *was* a woman. It was!"

Dave and Atwell leaned forward and I bet they were thinking what I was: this might be the same woman spotted near the drug house where Brendon Ryder took a bullet.

Penelope sucked in a breath. "Lightning flashed. That's why I saw her foot. She had on jeans and a sandal with gold straps. Not a flat sandal, one with a heel. Her foot seemed tipped forward and her toes bent a little. And she had dark pink

179

nail polish. Raspberry or fuchsia." Her eyes filled with tears. "That's all. That's all I saw."

"That's a lot," I assured her. "We know it's a woman. And a woman who wears gold sandals with jeans and polishes her toenails."

"Lots of women polish their toenails," she sniffed.

"Iz doesn't."

Penelope nodded and I thought of something else. "Close your eyes again. Concentrate on those toes. Was the nail polish a smooth professional job? Were her toenails shaped?"

Atwell shot me one of his trademark scowls, but Dave nodded encouragement. I tossed in another question. "Were the jeans old or new?"

Penelope chewed at her lower lip. "New. Faded, but new. They had a crease. A sharp crease. And there was mud on her foot, but her toenails were smooth and curved and the polish wasn't chipped or worn. It was fresh and shiny. It made me think of Paulette."

Atwell snatched a notebook and pen from the pocket of his slacks. "Who's Paulette?"

"The spokesmodel for good grooming," I said.

"How tall is she?"

"About my height," Penelope said. "But it wasn't her. Paulette's husband has four days off and he wanted to go to Seattle for a boat show and she went, even though she'd rather be at the protest. He's a pilot and he's gone a lot, so when he's home she wants to be with him."

Atwell kept his pen poised over the notebook, not ready to give up Paulette as a suspect. "You know where she's staying in Seattle?"

"Near the market," Penelope offered in a tentative voice. "A hotel with a view."

"And probably a pool and a spa and proximity to top restaurants." I dug for my cell phone. "I'll call her."

Atwell and Dave shook their heads, Atwell with a glower, Dave with a hand motion that signaled I should put that idea aside.

"Or not." Seeing their point, I slid the phone inside my purse. If Paulette was the shooter, I'd be tipping her and possibly compromising the investigation. Not that I believed for one minute Paulette could be the shooter, mainly because— murderous intent or not—Paulette wouldn't ruin a pair of gold sandals and a fresh pedicure by crossing a muddy lawn in the pounding rain. If she'd wear gold sandals with jeans. For all I knew that meant courting arrest by the fashion police.

Atwell glared at his notebook, then stuffed it into his pocket and, after a few words with Dave, went out.

"Who was that man?" Penelope asked me.

"Detective Charles Atwell."

"The one who thought you killed that teacher?"

"The very same."

Penelope heaved a sigh.

"He's okay," I assured her. "Maybe he gets a little fixated now and then, but he doesn't quit. And when there's light, he sees it."

"Chuck's good at what he does." Dave settled on the other side of Penelope. "He'll find the person who shot Iz. And every cop in Reckless River will help."

"Because it might be connected to the Brendon Ryder shooting?" I asked. "This might be the same woman neighbors saw around the drug house where he died?"

"We won't know that until they compare bullets," Dave said in a voice that implied I watched too many TV detective shows. "But your sister got shot under the noses of half a dozen officers."

"That's not their fault," Penelope protested. "With the storm—"

"They won't see that as an excuse. They'll tear this town inside out to find the shooter."

Penelope seemed comforted by that and let me help her out of the rain jacket and pull off her sodden shoes and socks. Dave laid the shoes by an air vent in the corner of the room, slung the socks over the back of a chair, then lobbied someone for a blanket and retrieved a T-shirt from his car. It had a faded picture of a pumped-up bodybuilder and was two sizes too large, but Penelope traded it for her bloodstained blouse.

Then, except for updating Mrs. B and making a trip to the ladies' room to strap myself into that bra and turn my shirt right side out, it came down to waiting.

Once Atwell buzzed through to report the bullet was out and on the way to the lab, and a doctor came in to say surgery was going well, I took the advice I'd been giving Penelope, and relaxed enough to do some of that waiting in a light doze.

Dave shook me a few minutes before 5:00 and a second doctor told us Iz was in the intensive care unit and expected to make a full and speedy recovery even though she'd have to live without a slice of her liver and the inflamed gallbladder he removed while he was in there. Knowing she'd hate for me to see her with tubes and wires attached, I left the ICU visit to Penelope.

"You should turn off the phone and sleep for a few hours," Dave said as we rode the elevator to the front lobby.

"Can't. I promised I'd sub in the library. And besides, I wouldn't be able to sleep."

"You were sleeping fine in the waiting room."

A flush burned my cheeks. "That's why I won't be able to sleep now."

"Because you're slept out?"

I flushed again. "Because I feel guilty about napping in the waiting room."

"Don't."

"I can't help it. I mean, I know that staying awake wouldn't have helped Iz. I know that in a rational way. But . . ."

He pulled me close. "I value and appreciate the rational side of you. But it's the not-so-rational side that I love."

His lips met mine.

The world receded in a rush of warm pleasure.

Then the elevator bell pinged and we broke apart.

The door stuttered open revealing Dario O'Brien.

He wore a bulky trench coat and an expression of icy determination. "What room is your sister in?"

Chapter 21

Dave shoved me behind him and blocked the elevator door.

"Relax, kids." Dario patted a bulge beneath his coat. "Muriel sent me to protect Iz in case the shooter tries to finish the job."

Dave slumped. "I should have thought of that."

"It's your boss who isn't thinking."

"Not his strong suit." Dave stepped out of the elevator. "She's in ICU. Penelope's up there."

"Wait a minute." I held my hand against the rubber bumper to keep the elevator doors open. "You think the woman who shot Iz will try again? While she's in the hospital?"

Dario didn't say "I hope so," but his predator's smile conveyed that.

"It's possible," Dave told me. "Depending on the shooter's motive and what's at stake if your sister isn't out of the way permanently."

"Amateurs usually lack patience." Dario didn't add that he considered women to be amateurs at this game, but his tone implied that.

I released the door and stepped to the rear of the elevator. "I'll help keep watch."

"I thought you had to get to school," Dave said.

"I do. I mean, I should, but—"

"Go to school," Dario ordered. "Odds are she won't try anything today."

"Why do you think that? Because *you* wouldn't?"

Dario shrugged.

I wondered again how much of the thug act wasn't an act.

"Night's better," Dave said. "Fewer people around." He took my hand. "Let's get breakfast. If you want to come back after that, I won't argue. I'll even call Big Chill and tell her she'll have to find another sub."

If I needed more proof that he loved me, taking on the Chillster was it.

"I got it covered, Barbara. I'll update Muriel every hour and she'll pass it along." Dario patted another bulge beneath his coat. "Don't worry about your sister. Nobody's getting by me."

Dave eyed the bulge. "Out of curiosity, what is it I'm going to pretend I didn't see? What are you packing?"

"Salami on rye, a jar of pickles, two cans of diet cherry cola, a sack of oatmeal cookies, and a crossword puzzle book." Dario opened the coat, revealing a polyester Hawaiian shirt that would get an R-rating in most circles, and peered into an inside pocket. "Oh, and chocolate covered pretzels, a wedge of cheddar, beef jerky, celery, and an apple. No, three apples. Muriel says I need more fiber."

I laughed. "What *aren't* you packing?"

"Heat." Dario flexed the fingers of his enormous hands. "I won't need it."

Dave didn't laugh. I took that to mean he agreed. Realizing I would only be in the way if I hung around, I followed him outside.

Getting to the car was easy. Getting to the street wasn't. A fleet of news vans blocked several aisles of the parking lot thanks to the media event on the oval lawn in front of the hospital. Ron Weador. Who else?

As Dave squeezed past a van with the logo of the Reckless River radio station, I snapped on the radio and twirled the knob to that frequency. ". . . every confidence in Dick McBain," Ron Weador stated. "This incident does not constitute a failure on his part. Every agent who protects the President will tell you that if someone is intent on assassination, that person will find a way. And when the target of an assassination demands that police keep their distance, like Indigo Zephyr did, it makes an assassin's work that much easier."

Nothing I could argue with there, except for Weador's sly intonations. He uttered the word "target" the way I might say toxic waste.

Dave turned the radio off. "They don't pay me enough to listen to him."

"He has a point."

"Yeah." Dave muttered expletives best left deleted as we rolled by the news conference. Weador jabbed a forefinger at the hospital, obviously saying more about my sister's pursuit of an agenda of confrontation that bought her a bullet. Wearing a red suit, his wife stood by, adoring smile firmly in place, head nodding, blond hair swinging like a hypnotist's gold watch.

Mesmerized, I wondered whether she shared his views and to what degree. Was she the driving force behind his political agenda, an equal partner in his campaign and career? Or was she arm candy? And if that was the case—

"Breakfast in the car." Dave spun us out onto the road and gunned the engine. "Otherwise you won't make it to school halfway close to on time."

My train of thought derailed by the word "breakfast," I focused on the road ahead and concentrated on sorting possibilities by location, the speed at which orders were filled, and how closely the food in the sack matched the order given. That last part narrowed it down to my favorite Mexican restaurant, a breakfast burrito, and a tall cup of coffee. With that sloshing in my stomach, I took a fast shower, jumped into white jeans and a striped blouse, collected Allison, and headed for Captain Meriwether High for a relaxing day in the library.

Not.

When I promised to fill in, I neglected to ask if the routine would be as usual—helping students locate books and reference materials, checking out their choices, shelving returns, and straightening displays. Consequently, I'd remained ignorant of that torturous process to be completed before the end of the school year—that horror known as taking inventory. It involved not merely accounting for every book on the library shelves, but scanning every magazine and pamphlet, every textbook assigned to every classroom, and every piece of equipment labeled with a barcode.

Deciding to pace myself, and trying not to dwell on the myth of Sisyphus rolling that boulder up a mountain time and again, I got to work.

After lifting the 232nd textbook from a high shelf in the storeroom—a massive chemistry text that weighed more than I did at birth—the tendons in my wrists were in open rebellion and sending shooting pains up my arms. When my lunch break came, I scurried to the nurse's office and begged her to tape me up before I hit the teachers' room for sustenance.

The lunch bunch had departed except for Brenda Waring who was grading papers and sipping a cup of something that smelled like steamed asparagus. "What's with the tape?" she asked. "You look like a boxer before a bout. Are you subbing in PE again?"

"Library inventory." I popped a cola and swigged the caffeine and sugar every exhausted cell in my body cried out for.

"Oooh. Those textbooks weigh a ton. Plus who knows where they've been and who handled them. You should get hazardous-duty pay."

"I wish. If we had such a thing, imagine the bonus I'd get for finding the source of the stench in Aston's classroom."

She laughed, but not in the way people do when they're genuinely amused. I excavated a heat-and-eat meal from the freezer compartment and scraped off a thick layer of ice crystals. Pasta and broccoli. Good enough. I slid it into the microwave and punched in three minutes. "Is he still mad?"

"Deranged. He's applying for a job with that private academy on the east side."

I snorted cola through my nose. "The one where the kids wear those blue and red uniforms?"

Brenda laughed. "Staff members wear uniforms, too. Talk about a bad fit for Aston." She stabbed her pen at the pile of papers. "I told him he's a fool. The pay is less, the pension is a joke, and he'd be leaving his support system. But he said when hunting gets tough and firewood's scarce and water's fouled, it's time to move camp to the other side of the mountains."

Brenda rolled her eyes. "This from a man who last week didn't want to move to the other side of the building. But, of course, *that* wasn't his idea."

True. Even when we come up with a plan for change, most of us hate to move our camps and risk encountering new issues and stresses. Because change was a constant for a substitute teacher—even one who stayed at the same school—I had a more flexible attitude toward change than previously. But I didn't embrace the concept. And I longed for a classroom of my own.

The microwave dinged.

Brenda smacked her forehead. "I can't believe I forgot to ask about your sister. It's all over the news. How's she doing?"

"Better." I retrieved my lunch, set it on the table, and dug my phone from my pocket. "Hang on and I'll check the latest update."

"Her vital signs are improving all the time," Mrs. B's voice said. "She's still asleep. They hope to move her to a room this evening."

I relayed that to Brenda.

"Do they know who shot her? And why? I mean, she's been stirring people up for years, so why now?"

I didn't pass along what Penelope saw and the tenuous connection to the Ryder shooting. Not just because Dave and

Atwell would frown on me blabbing about details of an investigation, but because those details were so flimsy they weren't worth blabbing about. "Nobody saw who shot her."

"That's a shame. All those people around, too."

I nodded, alternated bites of pasta and swigs of caffeine, and reminded myself to get another cola and sip on it through the afternoon to prevent an after-lunch crash.

Brenda gathered her papers, tapped them into a neat stack, and slipped them into a folder. "To tell the truth, I'm surprised something like this hasn't happened before. Your sister certainly incites strong feelings. She puts herself out there."

"And she will again. As soon as she's able, even if they have to roll her in a wheelbarrow and prop her up with rope and tent stakes."

Brenda smiled and patted my shoulder as she passed. "Wouldn't that give Dick McBain fits? And Ron Weador, too." She halted at the door. "Or maybe not. He's building a platform standing for everything she's not. If your sister pulls out of the game, he's left punching air."

Plus he'd be forced to run on issues instead of innuendo.

"And his wife," Brenda mused. "She'd be left . . . well, I don't know what she'd be doing but she'd have more time for it if she didn't have to worship him. I couldn't handle being married to a politician."

She scowled at Aston's chair. "I'm not sure I could handle being married at all. There are too many issues to argue about."

"She's awake," Mrs. B's recorded voice said as Allison and I walked to my car. "They'll move her to a private room this evening. That McBain person promised Penelope he'd order protection, but I don't trust him, so Dario is staying put. You come home and take a long nap." Then she said the three words I longed to hear. "I'll make dinner."

"Iz is doing better," I told Allison. "Mrs. B is making dinner."

189

"I'm not eating anything except carrots," she informed me. "And maybe a teaspoon of peanut butter."

I unlocked the car. "And why is that?"

She put a hand on a stomach that was a centimeter from being concave, and pushed hard enough to shift several internal organs. "I'm too fat." She dug her fingers into nonexistent excess flesh above the waistband of her low-riding jeans. "I've got a muffin top."

(For the record, this was a bald-faced lie. In fact, the lie was so bald it had no eyebrows, no eyelashes, and none of that bristly stuff inside the nose that I have nightmares about.)

Being aware of the contrary nature of the teenage beast, I didn't argue with her statement. I had every confidence that when dinner hit the table, Allison would have a different and healthier attitude. Surreptitiously, I fingered the fold of flesh lapping over my belt. There was less of it than a few months ago but, heredity being what it is, I had no illusions it would disappear entirely unless I starved it into submission. And starvation wouldn't start tonight. Not while Mrs. B was cooking.

Not that she was doing the actual cooking. No, she supervised while Verna and Sybil sautéed and stirred, and while other Committee members moved furniture to make room for a pair of twin beds in the living room.

"For your sister and Penelope," Mrs. B said. "They'll stay here while Iz recovers. Dario and Jim will provide protection and the rest of us will take charge of care. Sybil bought a new thermometer and found the cutest striped pinafores. And Verna will prepare nutritious meals to tempt your sister's appetite."

Iz, as I'm sure you know by now, has the kind of appetite that needs no tempting. But reminding Mrs. B of that would be childish, so I didn't.

"You go on and take a nap, dear." Mrs. B patted my arm. "Dinner will be ready in two hours—roasted vegetable lasagna, salad, and garlic bread. Then Sybil will take Allison to her play and you and I will go to the hospital and see your sister."

Notice the "we" in that sentence. Notice the lack of questions. The Committee juggernaut was in motion. If I got in the way, they'd mow me down like spring grass. So I went to my bedroom, cranked open the windows to bring in the breeze off the river, shucked my shoes and slacks, crawled between the sheets, and fell asleep with Cheese Puff at my side.

Ten minutes later the phone rang.

Cheese Puff snarled.

I did the same, clawed myself to the surface of consciousness, and plucked it from its cradle. Paulette didn't wait for me to say "hello." "Guess what? I'm a suspect. Me. They think I'm the one who shot your sister. Me. It's so exciting."

"It wouldn't be if you didn't have an alibi," I grumbled. "Or if you didn't have money for a lawyer."

"I guess," Paulette admitted after a moment. "Why are you so grouchy?"

"I don't know. Is it because I was up all night at the hospital with my sister? Because I subbed today? Because you woke me up?"

"Sorry. Sorry, sorry, sorry. But having a detective ask me for an alibi was thrilling. I felt like I was on a TV crime show!"

I sighed.

"I'm hanging up now," Paulette said. "Before you tell me to get a life."

"You have a life," I said. "You have more of a life than a lot of people. And you do more with it than most."

"I do, don't I?" She chuckled. "All right, I'm apologizing one more time. Sorry. There, now you can nap. Right after you tell me how your sister is."

"She's doing well. They're moving her to a private room this evening."

"Okay. Bye."

I replaced the phone, tumbled into sleep, and dreamed of lasagna, doctors in white coats, herds of elementary school children chasing Lola, and another storm barreling down on

Reckless River. It came closer and closer. A gusting wind blew rain across the deck. Rain lashed the side of my condo.

"You idiot," someone shouted. "If you don't know how to use that thing, then shut it off before you blow the siding loose."

Chapter 22

"I'm trying," a second voice howled. Water blasted the window. "The switch is stuck."

"Aim it the other way," a third voice shrieked. "You're soaking my carpet."

"I'm trying."

Crap.

I opened my eyes.

I knew all three of those voices: Jim, Jake, and Mrs. Ballantine.

I also knew this wasn't a dream.

This was yet another Jake-infused waking nightmare.

I slid on my glasses and stared at the windows that overlooked the deck. Rivulets of water streamed down the wide central pane. Water showered through the screens of the narrow side windows I'd opened. Drops sparkled in a beam of sunlight as they plopped onto the carpet.

"Back up," Jim shouted. "Aim it the other way. Don't get that connection wet. Don't—"

A flash.

A pop and a sizzle.

Something thumped on the deck.

The clock beside my bed stopped at 3:43.

The deluge ceased.

Someone moaned and grunted like a woman trying to give birth to a baby the size of a phone booth.

Feet pounded on the deck.

"Is he okay?" Mrs. Ballantine called. "Should I call an ambulance?"

"He got a jolt," Jim assured her. "He'll be up in a minute."

"I have a thermometer if you need it," Sybil offered.

"If it's a rectal thermometer bring it out and I'll jam it up his butt all the way to next week," Jim shouted.

That was harsh. If Sybil—a woman who wasn't all that good at identifying sarcasm—brought him the thermometer, I didn't doubt Jim would make good on that threat.

I tossed aside the sheet and went to the window where I stood on squishy carpet and peered at my ex-husband lying in a pool of water, his feet tangled in pressure washer hose and a length of orange electrical cord. Jim yanked at the cord, separating it from a yellow one that snaked across the deck, through the railing, and out of sight.

Cheese Puff stood on his hind legs and tapped his front paws against my leg. I picked him up so he could watch the show.

"What in hell were you thinking when you rigged this up?" Jim waved the plug in Jake's face. "This cord is frayed. The insulation is stripped off."

Jake didn't answer. Drool ran from the corner of his mouth. He blinked and rolled his head back and forth. He reminded me of those cartoon characters that slam into walls and rebound. I could almost see stars twinkling above him and spinning concentric circles in his eyeballs.

Jim threw the cord aside. "You're a menace. And not just to yourself. I ought to report you to . . . to someone in charge of health and safety for the county. Or the state. I ought to call the fire marshal. I ought to get that thermometer and stick it so far—"

"Jake! Are you all right?"

Bernina Burke steamed up the steps from the river trail wearing a billowy blouse made from shiny neon green fabric patterned with brown vines and gigantic orange flowers.

Mrs. Ballantine steamed out to meet her clad in a tangerine silk blouse and two strands of pearls.

I squished closer to the open window.

When Mrs. B put on her pearls, she meant business. A double strand meant serious business. No one could stand up to pearl power. Even Detective Atwell had faltered before it. Bernina didn't have the chance of a baby chick taking a stroll through a reptile house on the night someone left all the cage doors open.

Mrs. B and Bernina met on either side of Jake's twitching body.

"What happened?" Bernina dropped to her knees. Three months ago that would have rattled the glass-topped patio table, but Bernina had shed more than a few pounds. "What happened, Jake?"

Jake moaned and said something that sounded like "Phlltft."

"Jake always had a gift for language," I told Cheese Puff as he wiggled in my arms and pressed his nose against the screen.

"The idiot used a worn cord. Then he soaked it with spray. And that blew out the equipment." Jim pointed at a twist of smoke rising from the pressure washer. "Blew a few breakers, too."

Bernina pursed her lips, then patted Jake's cheeks. "Speak to me, Jake. Are you okay?"

"He got a shock." Jim's voice thickened with disdain. "Not bad enough to stop his heart or fry his brain. Not that he has much of a brain to fry."

Bernina pursed her lips again, but didn't leap into the conversational gap to defend the contents of Jake's skull. "The equipment is old. I should have replaced that cord last year."

She stood and plucked at damp fabric sticking to her knees. "It was an accident. It isn't Jake's—"

"This isn't working, Bernina." Mrs. B fingered her pearls. "We know it. You know it. Even Jake knows it."

"Phttllmph," Jake said.

I hugged Cheese Puff. "He's a wizard with words, isn't he? A linguistic Lothario."

Cheese Puff snorted.

"A lying linguistic Lothario," I qualified.

"But Jake's learning," Bernina protested. "He's getting better."

Mrs. B shook her head. Her pearl and diamond earrings shimmered in the sunlight. "I wish he was, but he's not. There isn't a single chore around this place that he's completed to minimal standards."

She stepped across Jake, grasped Bernina's arm, and led her to the glider. "You did a nice thing by providing a job for him, Bernina. And despite his many shortcomings—all of which I'm sure you now recognize—having him around has been good for you. You've lost weight. And I'm sure you've gained insight into what you want in a man."

They sat and rocked, Mrs. B's voice rising and falling like ripples on a pond. "It's time you got out of these puffy blouses and dumpy slacks and into something more fashionable. Verna's sister runs that consignment shop near the post office. They have lovely things and a nice range of sizes."

Bernina plucked at her blouse. "I don't know. I—"

"I'll give her a call," Mrs. B went on, "and have her set aside a few outfits in flattering colors. Blues and grays and sage greens. No more orange."

Bernina tweaked the hem of the blouse.

"I'll be happy to come along," Mrs. B. said. "Whenever you want. There's no hurry. You let me know when you're ready for a change."

"Maybe . . . tomorrow?"

196

"Tomorrow will be fine. Shall we say 9:00?"

Bernina nodded.

Jim coiled up the hose and electrical cords.

Jake rolled over on his side and wheezed.

Bernina didn't cast even a fleeting glance in his direction.

"And I'll ask Sybil to schedule you with her cousin," Mrs. B said. "She does hair and nails and makeup. You'll need three hours at least."

"I can't af—"

"You can't afford not to make the most of your assets. I'll see that you get a deep discount." Mrs. B patted her knee. "You have lovely skin, but we need to make your eyes appear larger and accentuate your cheekbones."

Three months ago I would have bet Bernina didn't have cheekbones, but Mrs. B was right, Bernina had slimmed down significantly. Jake—for once, and likely in spite of himself—had improved a woman's life.

Mrs. B went on talking about shoes and accessories and night creams.

Bernina went on nodding.

Jake got to his hands and knees, crawled to the edge of the deck, stuck his head through the railing, and barfed into the rose garden.

Cheese Puff growled.

"I know." I patted his head. "He's defiling your bathroom. But we'll give him a pass because it's a fair trade for the entertainment he provided."

Cheese Puff growled again to let me know he didn't agree.

"I'll hose it off when I go downstairs."

He huffed out a sigh, then settled on my pillow while I blotted up the excess water under the window, humming a variation on "Hit The Road Jack." I had a feeling we wouldn't have Jake to kick around much longer.

Three hours later, full of lasagna and having passed the identification and lack-of-weapons tests given by the young officer posted outside the door, I gazed at my sister. She seemed older, smaller, compressed. Her skin was only slightly darker than the bleached white cotton sheets and her voice sounded faint and hoarse. "Don't make a fuss. I'm fine."

Penelope, curled in a chair beside the bed, caught my eye and shook her head a fraction of an inch.

"Okay," Iz admitted, "I'm fine except for when I move. Then it hurts like hell."

"That's normal." Mrs. B fluttered over to the windowsill and rearranged vases of flowers, putting the tallest in the middle. Never let it be said she could resist leaving her stamp on things, especially when she had on one of her many strands of pearls. "You'd hurt worse if you hadn't developed muscle working on those building projects. And if Barbara hadn't taken you to water aerobics."

Iz rolled her eyes as if to indicate I had no influence over the state of her health or much of anything else, but she took my hand and squeezed it. Her fingers were callused and cold. Her grip was strong.

Forcing myself to smile instead of wince, I waited until the pressure slackened and then squeezed quick and hard. Iz covered a wince with the worst pretend cough I ever heard.

Considering our history, this was a greeting-card moment.

"The doctor thinks she can go home tomorrow around noon," Penelope said.

"They kick you out quick if you don't have big bucks or a luxury health plan," Iz groused.

"We have everything ready for you," Mrs. B said.

"We'll be out of your place and back at the sit-in by Sunday," Iz informed her. "Monday at the latest."

Penelope rolled her eyes again. "Thank you so much for offering to put us up," she told Mrs. B. "Dario thought my house would be hard to protect. It has a lot of windows and it backs up to a greenbelt."

"I don't need protection," Iz complained. "And I don't want it. It sends a message that I'm afraid."

"We know you're not the least bit afraid, dear." Mrs. B adjusted blinds that appeared fine to me before she touched them. "This is for the peace of mind of family and friends." She made another tiny adjustment. "And Dario is enjoying it so."

I glanced around. "Where *is* Dario?"

"Here and there," Penelope answered. "I saw him mopping the floor about an hour ago. Before that he walked by carrying a stepladder and a pack of light bulbs. And before that he had a plunger and a wrench."

"No, in between he was pushing the laundry cart," Iz said. "And once I saw him with a clipboard."

"So he's blending in." Mrs. B smoothed the light blanket folded at the foot of the bed.

Penelope giggled. "He blends in like bison at a ballet recital. But knowing he's here makes me less nervous." She lowered her voice to a whisper. "That officer at the door doesn't look old enough to buy booze. I doubt he's been on the force more than two weeks."

Was that intentional? Had McBain seen to it that an inexperienced officer was responsible for my sister's safety? I glanced at Mrs. B who gave me an I-told-you-so nod and smoothed the blanket again. "Well, tomorrow we'll get you settled in my condo and you'll sleep like babies. And eat like royalty."

"You know I don't eat meat," Iz reminded her. "Or processed food. Or wheat. Or sugar."

Mrs. B shot me a wink that said we were all aware that Iz was both omnivorous *and* a liar. "I'm well aware of your dietary needs, Iz, and the Committee is prepared to do all they can."

I stifled a smile. My experience with the Committee told me that doing all they could meant exactly the same as doing what they wanted.

Dave limped in shortly after I got home, Lola plodding at his heels. He pulled a beer from the refrigerator, flopped on the sofa, and stared at the bottle. Lola stood with her head hanging while Cheese Puff danced around her. When he yipped, she licked his head once and collapsed against the sofa.

"I don't see any gum on her ears so I assume you're off school duty."

"Off school duty and on the streets." With a grunt, he twisted the top off the bottle and raised it to his lips with both hands. "*All* the streets. *Every* street. Not to mention every alley."

I sat beside him and rubbed his neck and shoulders. "Doing what?"

"Working sources. Turning over rocks." He drank more beer. "Staying out of Dick McBain's way."

"And how's that last part going?"

"Surprisingly well. Dick's too busy to leave his office."

"Busy doing what?" I kneaded a knotted muscle.

"Being conflicted mostly. He has to pretend shock and outrage that your sister got shot, while hiding his delight that she's off 'his' lawn for the time being. And he has to urge us to bring the shooter to justice, while secretly wanting to congratulate the gal with the gun for taking the shot, and chastise her for not finishing the job."

"Really? You think he's that bad?"

"Nah. I think he's in over his head. Waaayyy over his head. Marv made being chief look easy, so Dick assumed it was." Dave sucked beer. "Now he's afraid of doing or saying anything that isn't scripted. Weador, on the other hand, has a quick mind and a way of spinning straw into publicity gold. He can shoot from the hip without blowing his toes off."

He rolled his shoulders beneath my hands. "That feels great. How about sneaking upstairs for a mutual massage while Allison's at the theater?"

I checked my watch. "They had an early performance tonight and she's coming straight home. Besides, my wrists are killing me from taking inventory in the library. How about a rain check?"

"A rain check with massage oil?"

"Okay, but not that pineapple stuff. And you wash the sheets."

"Done."

Except for those few moments when she used silence like a cudgel, Allison was sarcastic and snippy the next morning, complaining that the bread was the wrong kind, the toast too brown, the peanut butter too sticky, the jam too lumpy, and the milk too milky.

Dave and I did what I suspect most adults would do in this situation—declined every opportunity to get involved in her mini-crisis, tucked our heads, zipped our lips, and tiptoed around like cat burglars.

As we pulled out of my parking spot, Allison pointed at Winton James' condo and said, "If he'd answer his phone, I wouldn't be so tired."

"Hmm."

Allison swiveled in the seat. "What does that mean? I'm *not* being a drama queen. His phone rang all night long. Every ten minutes."

I gripped the wheel, recalling that Winton's condo had once been mine, recalling that the wall between what was his bedroom and the room Allison occupied, was thin—so thin that I'd heard far too many explicit details of Jake's afternoon frolic with a former married neighbor. Okay, so maybe I'd put my ear up against the wall during that frolic, but purely in the interest of accuracy should I be called to testify in her divorce proceedings.

"And like every third or fourth time it rang, the jerky caller didn't hang up in time and his stupid answering machine clicked in. 'This is Winton James.'" Allison adopted a mocking tone. "'I'm not in right now. Leave a message.' But nobody ever left a message. They just called back and called back and called back. All night long."

Allison drummed her heels on the floor mat. "Who does that? Who doesn't leave a message?"

Interesting question.

I thought about possible answers all the way to school.

Right away, I ruled out a boss or co-worker. They were bound to be as dialed-in as Winton was. They'd call his cell phone number or text him before trying a landline. And no doubt they'd leave at least one message.

Family and friends would have his cell number. And they'd certainly leave a message.

That left telemarketers and robocalls.

And lovers.

And stalkers.

Someone who had to hear the sound of Winton's voice, if only on a machine, would call back again and again. So would someone he was avoiding, someone hoping he'd give in and answer, or someone checking to see if he was home.

Winton's love life and phone calls were none of my business, but a ringing phone that kept Allison awake and made her crabbier than usual was. I gave myself a green light to speak with him about turning down the volume on his phone or unplugging it. If Winton had a stalker, and if he or she escalated from phone calls to something more up-close and personal, someone could get hurt.

Who might be stalking Winton?

The blond woman he sent packing Tuesday evening? The one who looked like Penelope? But wasn't. Couldn't be.

Penelope was at my sister's side. In a room with people coming and going, people who would notice her phoning every few minutes.

Or would they?

Chapter 23

When we pulled into the school parking lot, I had exactly no answers.

But questions about Winton's phone stalker drained from my mind at the speed of water over Niagara Falls when Big Chill dangled a set of keys. Flashing a gloating smile, she cackled like that witch with the flying monkeys. "Guess where you're subbing today."

My wrists shot bolts of pain up my arms all the way to my shoulders. My stomach knotted in sympathy with my wrists. "The library?"

"Guess again."

(For the record, the only thing I hate more than a sentence that begins with "Guess" is the two-word sentence "Guess again.")

"Gitmo? Sing Sing? The Gulag? A deep-fried butter stand?"

She cackled again. "Worse than that, my pretty, far worse than that."

"A pig pedicure parlor?"

"Not even close. You're in band!"

I recoiled. "You swore that Phil Benson had no more sick days or personal days or any other days he could take off without losing pay. And you further swore Phil had no desire to lose even a single hour's worth of salary."

"That I did, but all bets are off when a horse steps on your foot at the Memorial Day parade and the wound festers."

Festers.

Ugh.

"More than I wanted to know." I snatched the keys, checked that my earplugs hadn't disappeared from the side pocket of my briefcase, and headed for the band room where the slogan was "Go Loud, Be Proud." After all, it could be worse. I could be shopping with Mrs. B and Bernina Burke. I could be Iz. I could be out on the streets with Dave and Lola.

On the other hand, though, it could be better. I could be headed off to the deli with Verna and Cheese Puff. When I next saw him, he'd smell of salami and garlic.

I could also be home in bed. Or, better yet, home in bed with Dave.

We'd moved in together with the intention of having more time as a couple, but so far we'd had less, a lot less.

Dreaming of a time when life settled down, I took roll, stuffed in my earplugs, and pasted an encouraging smile on my face. Then the band played on—and on and on and on.

By the time lunch arrived, my lips were numb and my head throbbed. Prying the plugs from my ears, I made my way to the teachers' room.

And was greeted only by brief nods and silence.

Or, as close as you can get to silence in a room occupied by four people and situated in the middle of a high school. I heard the scrape of Brenda's fork against her plate, the faint sawing of Aston's knife on a chunk of dried meat, the muffled pop of Doug's jaw as he chewed, and the drip of onion soup from Gertrude's spoon as she lifted it from the bowl.

I held a cardboard container of frozen spinach lasagna to my forehead and studied the group. Aston had his full attention on the surgical removal of a green spot from the meat. Everyone else focused on Aston, although in oblique ways. Doug shot him sidelong glances. Gertrude squinted at his reflection in a shiny metal mug filled with pens and pencils.

Brenda hunched over a plate of something best left unnamed and strained her eyeballs to peer up at him.

The second hand swept around the face of the clock hanging on a nail over the door.

I slid the lasagna into the microwave and punched three minutes on the display. The carousel spun. The seconds passed. The silence continued.

I popped a can of cola and made a game of betting who would crack first. Doug, the youngest of the group? Brenda, the most impatient? Gertrude, the solution-finder? Aston, man of action?

Turns out I did.

"What the hell is going on?" I smacked my hand on the table. "What did I miss?"

Doug, Brenda, and Gertrude exchanged glances. Gertrude nodded and took another sip of soup before she spoke. "Aston got a job at the academy. He's turning in his letter of resignation at the end of the day."

"Ah." The microwave dinged and I retrieved my lunch.

"It's a free country. A man can do what he wants." Aston stuffed a sliver of meat between his lips. "Mostly."

"And a man is free to make a big mistake," Brenda added.

The way she said the word "free" tipped me that her relationship with Aston was off again. Way off.

This issue was, of course, absolutely none of my business, but it seemed that no one was happy with Aston's decision, including Aston himself. And it also seemed that everyone at the table had locked down a position and wouldn't budge. They were like squabbling children, separated to their corners and ordered to apologize, but each unwilling to take the first step toward reconciliation.

Fine.

I sat, forked up lasagna, and stuffed it in. After a morning in the band room, silence was a nice change.

I chewed. I swallowed.

The lasagna went down like a cup of uncooked oatmeal.

I coughed, gulped cola, swallowed again.

Silence gripped my neck like a giant hand, squeezing, squeezing.

The meal in the cardboard serving trough taunted me.

My stomach rumbled.

My salivary glands went into overdrive.

Silence squeezed again.

Dang it!

Someone needed to be the adult in the room.

Unfortunately that someone was me.

Double dang it!

I chopped at lasagna with my fork and considered. Teachers came and went and Aston had every right to depart for pastures he believed were greener—even if we all knew those pastures would be far too confining for his frontier spirit. But he and Brenda and Gertrude had shared this room for many years. Doug had bonded with them. And Susan's arrest brought them all even closer. If Aston left, would they keep his chair empty like Susan's? Would they find reasons to keep others out? Or would they search for new jobs themselves? Would I be sitting here next year with a group of strangers?

Silence gave me another squeeze.

I didn't want this room to change. More than that, I didn't want to adjust to strangers. I wanted to lean on Gertrude to explain the workings of the teen brain. I wanted to joke with Doug, hear about Aston's latest adventure in reenacting, and marvel at the weird mix of ingredients in Brenda's cooking.

Part of my dream about landing a teaching job was that the job would be here at Captain Meriwether and I could continue to be part of this group.

I laid my fork aside, took a long swallow of cola, and cleared my throat. When at Captain Meriwether High School, invoke Meriwether Lewis and William Clark. I'd appeal to

Aston's sense of responsibility and remind him the team depended on him.

First, however, I had to get him to cast aside his baggage— that grudge against the administration for forcing change. I had to get him to, well, man up.

"Aston, I won't argue with you, and I won't tell you this is a mistake. But I will say I'm sorry you're leaving. Your wealth of knowledge about the details of battles and everyday life on the frontier in the 1800s is astounding. I've learned so much during these lunch periods."

Yeah, learned I didn't want to play the role of a camp follower. Learned I preferred a pemmican-free lifestyle. Learned to watch for knives and traps and snakeskin when accepting a ride in Aston's truck. Learned that Aston thought I was as tough as a coyote flank steak.

"I'll miss you. Your departure means a huge loss to the history department and the school."

Aston blushed, color creeping from his beard and across his cheeks. "They should have thought of that before they pushed me too far."

"Yes, they should have. But they didn't. And maybe that's because of who you are."

Four sets of eyes locked on me. "Who *is* he?" Doug mouthed.

Aston cocked his head and frowned.

"You're a man of the caliber of Lewis and Clark and the members of the Corps of Discovery. Strong. Steadfast."

Aston nodded and fingered his beard.

The hook was set.

"Lewis and Clark and the Corps didn't turn back when the trail got rough, not even when they got to the Great Falls of the Missouri, not even when they had to drag their boats over sharp rocks. Not even when those rocks shredded their moccasins and cactus pierced their skin."

Aton nodded again.

I sighed with relief. So far, so good. A subbing assignment in the fall had called for showing a Lewis and Clark documentary to five classes in a row; parts of the video remained embedded in my brain. "They faced bears and snakes and swarms of biting insects."

I was pretty sure about the rocks and cactus, the snakes and bears. The insects, however, not so much.

Aston didn't correct me. "Hell of a portage. The whole journey was amazing."

"Legendary," Doug said, turning a thumb up.

"Incredible," Gertrude added.

"If I could travel in time," Aston mused, "I'd be there with them, eating elk steaks, shooting grizzlies the size of small cars, running the rapids of the Columbia."

"And think of what they came back with," I said. "Knowledge of the terrain and tribes, the flora and fauna. Their drawings and journals are gold mines. And they lost only one man."

"Sergeant Floyd." Aston bowed his head over his lunch. "Probably a ruptured appendix. They did what they could for him."

"They were a team. A great team." I paused and stirred my chopped lasagna. "It must have been difficult when the journey ended and the team broke up. I bet some of them wished it could go on and on—not the really hard parts like the portage or crossing the mountains in the snow or that winter of endless rain after they reached the ocean, but the sense of purpose, of commitment."

Aston nodded and glanced around at Doug, Brenda, and Gertrude. He said nothing, but deep in his eyes sadness smoldered.

My work here was done. I raised the fork and pointed it at Doug.

He blinked, then gripped Aston's shoulder. "If you want help packing up, say the word. I don't have to move to a new

209

room and the only curriculum change they handed me adds a class I taught last year. I kept the lesson plans that worked best so I'm good to go."

"I'm not moving, either," Gertrude said. "There's a new computer system to learn, but there's always a new computer system to learn, so I can help."

"I'll pitch in," Brenda said after a pause. "If only to make sure you really go and don't leave any of that rancid meat behind."

Aston glowered and muttered something under his breath. Brenda glared and did likewise.

Contented with this return to normal, I bolted the rest of my lunch, jammed in my earplugs, and scurried to the band room for an afternoon of aural agony.

Allison dozed on the way home, walked like a zombie to the door, and stumbled to her room for a nap. Well, to be accurate, she went to her room after drinking orange juice and leaving the glass on the counter, sighing because Dave hadn't had time to run cable to her bedroom, complaining that her TV was too small, asking if she could nap in our room, and pouting when I said I might do that very thing myself.

The new and improved Allison was clearly no longer in residence, but I didn't have the fortitude to mention that.

Cheese Puff hadn't moved when we came in. He slept in his favorite chair, lying on his back with his bloated belly up. A note on the bulletin board by the door indicated he had been "a naughty little puppy" and jumped from a chair onto the counter and got into the prosciutto where he ate "just a tiny smidgen" while Verna prepared lunch for Iz.

Great. Ham and salt. And, from the tight skin across his distended gut, way more than a smidgen. Not only would his belches be the stuff of small-dog legend, but his emissions would clear the room.

"You're sleeping down here tonight, buster."

210

He opened one eye and grunted.

The next sound he made was the one I dreaded.

Poot.

I backpedaled and opened the sliding door to bring in a breeze. "I'm having a talk with the Committee. Prosciutto isn't good for you. And neither is most of the other stuff you scarf when you're out of my sight. They're endangering your health. Not to mention the condition of my carpets if you get the squirts."

He raised the edge of one lip.

Poot. Poot.

"You're making my case every time you do that. But if you want to die before you live out your allotted dog years, then go for it. I'm tired of arguing. I'm going next door."

Next door where, with Iz in residence, conflict would have been elevated to an art form right up there with cow tipping.

She didn't disappoint.

"Took you long enough to get over here. I heard your car pull up ten minutes ago."

I paused on the threshold, wishing for the earplugs in my briefcase and coaxing my lips into a smile—a phony one, but a smile nevertheless. "How was the trip from the hospital?"

"Painful." Iz shifted on the sofa, sending a trio of throw pillows tumbling to the floor.

Sybil, wearing a green and pink striped pinafore over a white blouse and slacks, scurried across the kitchen, the soles of her white running shoes squeaking on the linoleum. "Dario insisted on taking side streets and looping around so no one could follow us." She scooped up the pillows, piled them on a chair, and retreated to the sink and a bowl of peas to be shelled. "And the doctor wouldn't give her anything extra for the trip."

"As if I'd sell it on the streets." Iz tossed a green velvet pillow decorated with beads and gold fringe. "As if someone with my strength of character couldn't resist addiction."

Not a good time to mention that she couldn't resist chocolate or pizza or the frothy drinks she criticized me for indulging in. I nodded and changed the subject. "Where's Penelope? And Verna? And Dario and Jim? And Mrs. B?"

"Mrs. Ballantine is out with that obnoxious woman who manages this complex." Iz drew air quotes around the word "manages," wincing as she raised her arms. "She's called twice to say they'll be here soon. Dario said shopaholics with money are the worst kind and went up to take a nap. Jim is outside on the deck standing guard—not that I need protection with the door to the parking lot double locked and people milling around in here like a herd of cattle. I sent that police officer packing before I left the hospital. I told him to tell Dick McBain to find the killer instead of wasting resources."

She hauled in a breath and finished the accounting. "Verna had a meltdown when I pointed out that the soufflé was rubbery and those ham and melon things were as filling as whipped air. And Penelope went to our place for fresh clothing."

She pointed to a glass on the narrow table behind the sofa. "Sybil is doing the best she can, but she's failed to notice that the ice in my drink melted."

"That's dreadful. Let me hop right on it."

I made rabbit ears with my hands and bunny-hopped to the table to retrieve her glass. Sybil watched, her mouth forming an *O* of stunned surprise.

Iz snarled and threw a cushion—red with gold fringe—at me. "You never had any sense of the gravity of situations. Never."

Or perhaps I had so much sense of said gravity that humor became my shield. Still, I had enough sense to stop hopping and carry her glass to the kitchen for a refill. "What were you drinking?"

"Lemonade. But I'd rather have a cola. Regular. Not diet."

Sybil gave a tiny shake of her head.

212

"I thought you avoided caffeine," I said to Iz. "And what about the sugar? And the carbonation? Won't that cause gas pains?"

"I *want* a cola. With three ice cubes. Wounded as I am, is it too much to ask that I get it without an argument? And before the sun sets?"

"One cola, coming up."

Sybil filled a fresh glass and I delivered it with a smile, then plumped a couple of pillows. "Need anything else?"

Iz squinched her face in thought, but I rushed on. "Okay. Then I'll go check on Jim and do a load of laundry and be back in a bit."

"Liar." Iz tucked her chin. "You'll stay away as long as you can. Or at least until Mrs. Ballantine gets home."

Busted!

"I don't blame you. I can be hard to get along with on a good day and when I hurt . . ." Tears welled in her eyes and slid down her cheeks.

I bent to give her a hug, expecting to be pushed away.

But Iz opened her arms and said, "Careful."

Her hair was greasy and she smelled of sweat and disinfectant and potato chips. The aromas of my childhood. I knelt and rested my head on her shoulder.

She stroked my cheek. Then pushed me away and reached for the cola. "Get on with your life. Get that laundry done. Don't worry about me."

I stood and grinned. "Why would I worry? Because you took a bullet? One single bullet no bigger than the end of my little finger?" I waved that aside. "Really, I have better things to be concerned about."

"I should hope so."

Iz raised the glass to her lips. I dashed off before the needle on her mood meter swung back to entitled.

The first leg of my dash took me to the far edge of the deck where Jim, chair tipped, sat with his feet propped on the railing. He wore a safari hat to keep the sun off the bald patch at the crown of his head. The khaki jacket, I suspected, kept prying glances off whatever form of firepower he had strapped beneath it.

"Iz says she doesn't need protection," I reported.

"And I don't need a raincoat in December or that breakdown kit in my trunk."

"Caution isn't her middle name."

"How about annoying? Is that her middle name?"

I snickered. "One of them."

"Overbearing? Hard to take?" Jim raised a hand to shade his eyes and peered at a chunk of wood floating with the current. "Full of herself?"

"All of the above." I patted his shoulder. "Thanks for putting up with her."

"Aw, she's all right."

I didn't concede that. "Nobody argued when she sent her cop guard packing?"

"Isn't much point in arguing with her, is there? But she's safe here. We got this entrance covered. There's a steel door out to the parking lot and anyone who tries to take on the bars across the office window better bring a tank."

Wouldn't Bernina Burke love to see a tank tearing up "her" parking lot?

"Is there—?"

"Quiet!"

Jim stood and shaded his eyes.

Feet pounded on the trail, coming toward us.

Chapter 24

Jim slipped his free hand beneath his jacket. "Get back inside."

I hustled for the door.

"It's okay," he called before I covered half the distance. "Just a kid getting some exercise."

I ambled to the railing and watched the runner, a boy who appeared to be in his early teens. He wore black sneakers, long, loose basketball shorts, an oversized T-shirt with the image of a guitar, mirrored sunglasses, and one of those knitted caps with earflaps and tassels pulled so far forward it covered his eyebrows and cheekbones. Talk about hat hair. He'd have a case for the record books.

Jim snorted. "What's with the hat?"

"Beats me. A lot of kids in high school wear them year-round."

Huffing, arms pumping, heels flicking out behind, the kid ran past, head turned our way. Our reflections slid across his sunglasses.

"Kid needs coaching," Jim observed when he rounded a bend in the trail. "Runs like a girl."

"At least he's getting exercise. He's not indoors with a videogame."

"Yeah. Can't fault him for moving his muscles. But he needs to work on his form."

I sucked in my stomach. When things settled down, I'd work on *my* form.

Ha! Who was I kidding? In my life, things settled down only far enough to provide a lull before the next storm.

"You need anything? Water? A snack?"

Jim pointed to a cooler beside the chair. "I'm good."

"Bathroom break?"

"Not yet. But if you're serious about that, check in an hour."

I promised I would and headed in to round up dirty clothes. While they sloshed in the washer, I changed into a T-shirt, shorts, and sneakers, then forced Cheese Puff out of his chair and into his harness. A walk—even the spraddle-legged one that was all he could manage with a stuffed belly—would get his system moving and clear the air more quickly.

"I'm definitely having a talk with the Committee," I fumed as he waddled along the sidewalk at the edge of the parking lot. "They may think jumping on the counter is cute, but it's a bad habit. And if you keep gorging on rich foods you'll be dead—or on a diet so strict a stalk of celery will be a feast."

Poot.

I took a few quick steps to get upwind. Twice he veered from the concrete path to inspect patches of grass and clover. "No." I tugged him to the sidewalk. "Let's get to the bench."

He closed his eyes, yipped his annoyance, and grunted.

Poot. Poot.

I let out the leash to the limit and towed him along. It appeared the prosciutto would make a run for it soon (pun intended). Would the three plastic bags stuffed in my pockets be enough? Would he make it to the grassy patch off the river trail where he could hunch beneath overgrown shrubs instead of squirting in full view of condo residents or, worse yet, Bernina Burke?

Mrs. B seemed to be taming that beast, but Bernina's loathing of me and Cheese Puff ran deep. Now that her

216

infatuation with Jake was fading, she might realize I used her emotional Achilles' heel to get her to abandon her effort to limit the number of pets per unit. Bernina couldn't toss dogs out, but she could press for restrictions on where they were allowed on the property.

Poooooottt.

Cheese Puff opened his eyes and waddled a bit faster, heading for the tall grass around a lamppost.

"No. Absolutely not. No eating grass until we get to the river trail."

He bared his tiny canine teeth, snarled, and sat.

I bent, scooped him up, laid him over my shoulder and patted his back. "You make me crazy. You're spoiled and willful and your own worst enemy. But I love you."

"I knew you'd admit it someday," a voice said.

Cheese Puff growled.

I turned to see Jake holding a large plastic bucket and a jumble of plumbing gear—wrenches, short lengths of pipe, two washer hoses, a faucet, a sink trap, a shower head, and a toilet repair kit. "I knew you never stopped loving me."

"I was *talking* to my *dog*."

He shot me one of the many smiles he practiced daily in front of a mirror. Each had a distinct purpose—inviting trust, promising pillow talk, exhibiting boyish charm. Not one was genuine. "But you were *thinking* about me."

"Close. Dog poop."

Jake frowned. "Is that supposed to be funny?"

(In case you haven't noticed, most irony and sarcastic humor are lost on Jake.)

"Not to you," I said.

"Oh." He frowned again and shifted the plumbing supplies. A pipe slipped from the bucket and clattered to the sidewalk.

Cheese Puff yipped. I patted him. Not too hard. Wouldn't want to bring up more than a burp. "So, you're doing some plumbing?"

217

He pointed his chin at the unit he'd been hired to rehab. "A few little projects in my place."

The unit belonged to the condo association, but I didn't correct his misuse of a possessive pronoun. Nor did I suggest that with Jake handling the tools, a few little plumbing projects could lead to an urgent call for the National Guard to respond with sandbags. What I did do was make a mental note to tell the gang that if they enjoyed Jake's hedge-trimming and pressure-washing adventures, they should stay tuned.

"I promised Bernina I'd start on this tonight. She's been on my case since the pressure washer malfunctioned and almost killed me. But this project will prove I'm not incompetent. If there's one thing I know—besides investments—it's plumbing."

He juggled the gear, dropped the sink trap with a clang, and kicked it onto the grass. "Once I get a few more parts and a fresh drill bit and finish cutting the grass, I'll have dinner and then get right on this. Should have it done in no time. Remember that garbage disposal I installed for the people who lived next door to us?"

"How could I ever forget?" A geyser of chopped lettuce shot from the sink when they hit the switch for the overhead light. "It was astounding."

Jake beamed, apparently remembering the incident in the same totally incorrect way he recalled the "investments" that wiped out my nest egg.

Cheese Puff lifted his lip in a snarl.

"Your dog doesn't like me much, does he?"

"Surprisingly, no. And you two have so much in common, especially the need to be adored by all around you."

Jake frowned.

Cheese Puff growled.

I made my exit.

When we returned—Cheese Puff at least a pound lighter— Dave and Lola were sprawled on the sofa, Dave drinking orange juice from the carton and Lola chewing on a twist of rawhide. "You're home early."

"Just here long enough to get rehydrated."

"And spread your germs?"

"Huh?"

"The carton."

He studied it. "Huh?"

"You're drinking from it."

"Yeah."

I waited for further realization to sink in. When it didn't, and he put his mouth to the spout again, I added "drinking from the carton" to the ever-growing list for discussion later. Then I removed Cheese Puff's harness, and set him on the floor.

Lola eased off the sofa and sniffed him all over, including his muzzle and a place I wouldn't put *my* nose for a million dollars. Cheese Puff belched, attempted to jump into his favorite chair, missed, executed a half cartwheel, and sprawled on his side. I swear Lola grinned as she slid a paw under him and flipped him upright. I further swear Cheese Puff wore an expression of mortified indignation.

Outside, I found Jim didn't need me to relieve him. Dario, looking like six miles of dirt road after a hard winter, stood by his side. "Couldn't sleep." He scratched the back of his neck. "Got that itchy feeling. Something nasty is coming."

"Like Allison insisting on another driving lesson?"

He shuddered and scratched his neck again—this time with both hands.

"When I get that itchy feeling, it means I need to take a warm shower and then use a double handful of that skin cream Sybil buys in bulk." Jim chuckled. "Smells like gardenias, but it cuts the itch. And women like the feel of my skin."

"I'm not slathering on scented slop," Dario growled. "Give me that man stuff in a tub."

Leaving them to the pros and cons of moisturizers, I returned to the condo and found Dave changing into fresh socks and shoes. "Gotta go. Chuck needs backup. He's hitting a couple of hangouts on the north side. Places where guys trade information. Guys you're better off not knowing—or even knowing *about*."

Now *that* was reassuring.

"Why you? You're exhausted. Aren't there other detectives?"

"McBain commandeered them."

"For what?"

"He's running his own investigation. Wants to bag the shooter and take all the credit."

"Seriously?" Talk about someone who needed to grow up. "Atwell must be livid."

"Actually not." Dave tied knots on top of the bows in the laces. "McBain was getting in his way and wanting a report every hour. Now he's ignoring Chuck and he's off my tail, so Chuck and I are teaming up." He kicked his discarded shoes and socks under the sofa. "If Josh isn't taking her, can you drop Allison at the play? If she needs a ride home, tell her to call me."

I stared at the half-hidden shoes. "Really?"

"Uh, sorry. I forgot Iz needs you. If Josh can't take Allison I guess she'll get a ride with someone else."

"Iz needs me like a snake needs mittens." I pointed at the toe of a shoe peeking from beneath the sofa. "I was commenting on your attempt to hide the evidence."

"Evidence?"

"Those smelly shoes and socks you kicked under the sofa."

"Oh." He nudged the shoe out of sight. "I'll get them later."

"Later when?"

"Tonight? Tomorrow? Chuck's picking me up in two minutes."

"You're a good friend. But not necessarily a good roommate."

"I'll get the hang of it." Dave smiled—a smile that was authentic, from the heart, and bore no resemblance to any of the contrived twitches of Jake's lips. "Come here and let me give you a preview of what I plan to do to make up for everything."

He didn't have to ask twice. He didn't even have to say "please."

"I'm leaving Lola here," he said when we came up for air.

"Maybe I'll take her next door for another layer of protection for Iz."

Dave's gaze shifted to Lola, half under the coffee table and snoring loud enough to rattle cups in the closets. He raised an eyebrow.

"Or maybe not." I rubbed my cheek against his chin. "Ummm. Have I told you I like stubble?"

"Often. When I get home you can show me how much. I'll only call for help if you need it." He kissed me again, then headed for the door. "Later."

I'd heard that word a lot in the past few days. And I'd put a lot of things off until then. By the time the clock ticked around to later, that time period would be severely overbooked. I made a mental note to move activity involving me, Dave, a locked door, and a minimum of clothing to the top of the "later" list.

He hadn't been gone long when Allison stumbled downstairs and spied Lola. "Dad was here?"

"For about five minutes. Did you need to talk with him?"

"Uh . . . I guess not." She pointed at the carton of orange juice on the coffee table. "Was he drinking out of the spout?" She stamped her feet. "I hate when he does that."

"I'm not so wild about it myself."

"Last time I yelled at him he said it made us healthier if we shared germs. And I said, 'How do you know? Are you a doctor?' And he got all, 'It's just a little spit.' And I told him Lola has spit, too, but I don't want to share it."

Lola raised her head. "No offense," I told her.

"We gotta make Dad stop doing that."

The pronoun kicking off that sentence gave me hope that changing Dave's behavior was not only possible but might be accomplished in the next decade. "We'll have to gang up on him. Be a team."

"Deal."

"Okay. Now, do you need me to drive you to the play? And/or pick you up?"

"Josh is driving me there and home again. And he's buying dinner at my favorite burger place." She tugged at the waistband of her low-riding shorts. "But all I can have is a salad without any dressing because I'm so fat."

I made with the sympathetic eyes, but said nothing, especially nothing about the five pieces of garlic bread and two helpings of lasagna she ate last night not long after making a similar statement. If Allison took this concern to the next level and clamped her lips instead of flapping them, then I'd worry. And act. An eating disorder required immediate treatment.

I told her to call Dave and let him know her transportation plans. Then, to test whether worry time loomed, I set a tub of hummus, a fresh bag of pita chips, and a sack of baby carrots on the dining room table. I ate two carrots and got busy moving laundry to the dryer and collecting more dirty clothes for the washer. When I passed the table a few minutes later, a significant crater marred the surface of the hummus and the chip bag gaped open. Allison's appetite had triumphed over unfounded concerns about her weight.

Much as I could do without another dose of my sister, when I heard Mrs. B's voice next door, I hustled over. I found her pulling articles of clothing from bags and holding them up while Verna, Sybil, and Penelope watched and Iz snuffled deeper into a pain-killer induced nap.

Bernina Burke stood at the center of the group like a portly paper doll, a pink flush on her face and a shy smile on her lips.

I rewound the end of that thought. A shy smile. On Bernina Burke's lips? Lips that in the past pressed into a tight line or cited condo regulations and spewed threats?

Yea verily!

And those lips, usually slathered with lipstick that leaned toward purple, were tinted with a faint pink. The eyes normally outlined with bright blue, were shaded in soft browns and greens. The hair was lighter and shorter, layered in a way that made her face seem longer and narrower. The billowy flowered blouse was gone, replaced by a pearl gray number.

My nemesis had been made over.

Mrs. B beamed at me. "Doesn't she look terrific?"

A few weeks ago—heck, even yesterday—I would have found a snarky way to respond to that question as an act of petty vengeance. But, considering the raw material, Bernina looked pretty good.

Too bad that smile she wore would crumple when Jake's knowledge of plumbing reached its limits and he employed that fresh drill bit he mentioned. We had excellent water pressure in the condo complex. Tonight's fiasco could eclipse the pressure-washing debacle.

"Terrific." I echoed Mrs. B. "I love that gray top. Is it silk?"

Bernina flushed a deeper pink, stroked the blouse she wore under a long, loose, royal blue jacket, and turned to Mrs. B. "Is it?"

"Yes. And we picked up the whole outfit for twenty dollars." Mrs. B's gaze slid to my T-shirt and then to my shorts and sandals.

"Don't even think about it," I hissed.

"If you get a teaching job, you'll need outfits that are more professional—dresses and suits and decent shoes with heels."

Spoken like a woman who hadn't seen too many teachers in their natural habitat lately and certainly hadn't glimpsed Aston's wardrobe. But if there was one thing I'd learned since I met her, it was not to refuse Mrs. B outright. It would be safer to strap fried chicken to your head and take a stroll in grizzly country.

"Let's wait until I have a little success before I go broke dressing for it," I said with a hollow laugh. "Show me what else you bought."

The fashion show repeated from the top and I made appropriate noises of awe and disbelief, a few even genuine. If there was one thing Mrs. B had in spades, it was good taste. And her enthusiasm was contagious.

"I have a pair of earrings that would be marvelous with that top and your hairstyle," Sybil said. "I'll dig them out and bring them by the office."

"And I have a scarf that would accentuate the green jacket," Verna added. "And a bracelet you might like."

"I have nothing except advice." Penelope held out her hands. "Keep your nails short and you'll get more done and won't break them as easily. Oh, and take care of your feet and they'll take care of you."

"We got that covered," Mrs. B said.

"I ordered special shoes with extra support. Walking shoes." Bernina gathered up bags and headed for the door to the deck. "I plan to do five miles a day. Every day." She patted the pocket of her jacket. "But don't worry. I'll have my cell phone with me. Call me any time you need me."

Jaw sagging I watched her go. "Who was that woman? It can't be Bernina Burke because she wants to help and she said we could call any time."

Taking credit for the transformation, Mrs. B buffed her nails on her lavender cotton summer sweater.

"And you're not even wearing pearls!"

"Once you believe in your power, dear, you can leave the pearls in the jewelry box."

Uh-oh.

"What if I don't have pearls?"

Chapter 25

"You don't have pearls?" Mrs. B, Verna, and Sybil gaped as if I said I didn't have lungs.

"Not even cultured pearls?" Sybil asked in a whisper.

I shook my head. "Not even glass beads painted like pearls."

Verna clucked her tongue.

Penelope snickered.

Iz rolled over, groaned, and opened her eyes. The next thing she opened was her mouth. "When's dinner?"

"In an hour, Iz," Mrs. B said in voice sweet enough to drizzle on pancakes.

"What are we having?"

Verna, apparently still traumatized by my sister's verbal assault on lunch, gasped and eased toward the door. Mrs. B patted her arm and turned her sapphire gaze on Iz. Syrup gave way to steel. "There will be plenty of choices, Iz. I'm sure you'll find something you like."

Iz scowled, then subsided into her pile of pillows.

"That sounded more like it was powered by a string of ball bearings than a string of pearls," I said with a laugh. "I can *afford* ball bearings."

Mrs. B barely smiled. "The trick is deflecting the argument whenever you can or changing the game. If you can't do that, watch for an opening or a weakness, then try to get your opponent off balance or off rhythm."

"Like you did when you took Bernina aside and told her she knew the experiment with Jake wasn't working?"

"Yes." Mrs. B winced. "But I'm not proud of that. It was hardly fair. Jake already wore her down."

"And if your opponent isn't worn down? If you don't see an opening?"

"Then do what they don't expect. Lay down a bunt or swing for the fences." She mimed a swing with an imaginary baseball bat. "Now run along. Bring over three chairs from your unit. Then you can help Verna with dinner."

Run along?

I fumed for about three seconds, then reminded myself of the age gap between us (at least 30 years), Mrs. B's attitude toward me (honorary daughter), and all she'd done on my behalf from the first days of our relationship (tons). After that I ran along and got the chairs.

Along the way, I realized that I'd handled Aston precisely as Mrs. B recommended. He was expecting me to punch one back at the mound but I came to the plate accompanied by the ghosts of Lewis and Clark and pounded the pitch into the stands.

Aston, however, was more used to recreating physical battles than engaging in the emotional conflicts Iz reveled in. I'd used reverse psychology against her in the past, but she was wising up and not taking the bait. Worse, I felt guilty about resorting to such blatant manipulation. Time for new strategies.

Before I took my seat at dinner, I imagined myself wearing a necklace of pearls alternating with ball bearings. Hey, why not?

When Iz took a bite of creamed peas and new potatoes, curled her upper lip, and opened her mouth to comment, I jumped in and pronounced the dish delicious. "It reminds me of fresh-out-of-the-garden dinners I had as a kid in Nebraska. Isn't it scrumptious, Iz?"

(For the record, those fresh-out-of-the-garden dinners were eaten at the homes of friends. After Iz took over shopping and cooking, meals consisted of cereal, sandwiches, and concoctions dumped from cans. I don't blame Iz one bit. She was young herself and she had her own life to live. She did what she could. And she got us through—at least to *physical* maturity.)

Iz took another bite. I could almost see her searching for something to say that wouldn't be out-and-out critical, but would make it clear she didn't care for this culinary offering, didn't care for being reminded of our childhood or Nebraska, and, at this moment, didn't care for me. "I suppose there's a lot of butter in it."

Having watched Verna, I knew the cream sauce in the bowl making the rounds contained half a cup of genuine butter, and a mix of cream and milk. I speared my sister with smile. "Butter adds flavor. But if you're counting calories or watching your cholesterol, go easier on the sauce."

Iz's eyes blazed.

Mrs. B flashed me a wicked smile and took over. "You're flushed, Iz. Are you in pain? Do you want to lie down?"

"No." Iz frowned at Penelope who had leaped to her feet, ready to assist. "I'm fine." She forked up a tiny red-skinned new potato dripping with sauce and stuffed it in her mouth.

"If you say so." Mrs. B raised one brow a sixteenth of an inch. "But I wouldn't eat too much if I were you, not after that cola you had." She patted her stomach. "An attack of gas can be especially painful after surgery."

Which is why, an hour later, Iz tossed on the sofa, jaw clenched, arms crossed over her gut. Her pain was palpable, but she'd never admit second helpings were a bad idea.

As I brushed my teeth, I pondered the lessons learned. Deflect an argument when you could. Hit the ball where they didn't expect it. Make sure you had what it took to continue if that didn't end the game.

It all sounded good, but what if your opponent wasn't Iz or someone like her who depended on power and aggression? What if your opponent followed the same playbook and practiced the same stealthy—or sneaky—moves?

I vowed to make a closer study of Mrs. B and to keep on wearing my imaginary necklace, then took the dogs out on the deck. Once I got beyond the bright beams of the automatic security lights, I gazed into a clear night. Planes landing and taking off at the Portland airport skimmed a backdrop of stars.

Dario sat in the chair by the gate, wearing a khaki jacket with more pockets than I have excuses for ditching a diet. He was nibbling on a piece of Verna's cheesecake swamped with sliced strawberries and whipped cream. "I need this like Vegas needs more slots, but Muriel said I better get it before your sister did. I'd like to see what that woman could do to a casino buffet."

"You might get your chance. She'll deliver a diatribe against Las Vegas, but I bet she'll be part of the entourage when Mrs. B records *Still Got That Strut*." I opened the gate and ordered the dogs to get with it. "Is there a date for that yet?"

"That's what the producers keep asking me. Muriel won't commit until she works out a routine and practices until it's perfect."

Uh-oh. The P-word. I was living proof of how fast things went down the drain if I used the word "perfect" in connection with my life.

Dario set the plate of cheesecake on the deck railing. "I tell her there's no such thing as perfect in this world."

"I'm with you. We should strike the word from the language."

"She says she'll settle for 99% but not a tenth of a percent less."

"You know what? She'll probably get it."

"She always has," he said in a voice filled with awe and amazement and devotion. "She's one of a kind."

"Dave says she's a force of nature."

"Dave's—"

Cheese Puff growled and Dario stood and slid his right hand beneath his jacket as he scanned the shadows between the lamps lining the river trail. "What do you see, boy?"

If my nerve endings hadn't been on high alert, I might have chuckled. That sentence belonged in a movie with a heroic dog on the level of Rin Tin Tin. Cheese Puff's beady little eyes didn't see far even at noon on a sunny day. Lola, trained sniffer that she was, had great hearing and eyesight. But Lola, busy squatting as I ordered, wasn't growling.

Cheese Puff growled again.

"Get behind me." Dario eased to the first step, unclipped a long flashlight from his belt, held it out to one side, and lit up the ground in front of Cheese Puff.

The light reflected off a pair of eyes. They belonged to a brown toad the size of coffee mug.

Cheese Puff barked.

The toad didn't budge.

"Come," I ordered.

Ever obedient, Cheese Puff eased toward the toad, lowering his head and snarling.

"Cheese Puff, stop." I pushed past Dario. "Don't get near that thing. It's dangerous."

Dario laughed. "What? The toad? Is it packing a grenade?"

"No." I scooped up Cheese Puff. "Venom."

"Really?"

"Maybe." I climbed the steps to the deck with Lola on my heels. "Some toads do. I don't want to find out the hard way that this is one of them."

"Come to think of it, you're right. Knew a guy who used to lick toads to get high. Licked snakes, too. One time he licked a gator." Dario latched the gate behind us and clicked off the flashlight. "That didn't go well. Lost an ear. Didn't get high, either."

I wondered if there was more to the story—like maybe the guy who licked the gator had a gun to his head.

Dario returned to his chair and his cheesecake. "Dave still out?"

"Yes."

"Well, keep your door locked, kid. I still have that itch."

I took his advice, latched the windows and slid the safety bar into place on the sliding door. The blinking answering machine yielded a message from Allison delivered with several eardrum-rending shrieks of excitement. "Mr. Mason's friend from New York City came to see the show! He's all famous on Broadway! Well, kinda right near Broadway. And he's going to tell us about it. I'm soooo excited! And Josh is totally cool about staying and driving me home. Okay? Bye."

"Kinda right near Broadway," I told Cheese Puff and Lola as I gave them each a treat—a large dog biscuit for Lola and a crumb from the corner of another for the piglet of a pooch still letting out an occasional poot. "She'll be so wired she won't sleep until Sunday."

And that reminded me: I'd intended to speak with Winton James about the late-night caller who kept Allison awake. In case he was intentionally not answering his phone, I took a personal approach.

Winton's condo had been mine until a few months ago, so I knew there was only one entrance from outside—a door on a tiny porch set on a miniscule scrap of lawn transected by a narrow walk. The porch, large enough for a two-person swing, was a paltry consolation prize for the lack of a riverfront deck. The lawn, set off by skinny hedges no higher than my knees, lay between the entrances to my present unit and Mrs. Ballantine's. I leaped the hedge and approached the two shallow steps to Winton's porch.

Deep shadow enveloped it. The bulb in the security light above his door had burned out or been "borrowed" by someone from another unit.

230

For a brief second I toyed with the idea of calling Bernina Burke to see if she really meant that part about wanting us to call any time. She was responsible for outside security lighting—a responsibility probably delegated to Jake back when she still believed he had even a vague idea of the definition of "competent."

I sighed. Bernina and I were now in the same club, the club for women who had trusted Jake and been let down—way down. She deserved a night off to enjoy her new clothes. At least she could count on *those* to be there for her.

Besides, I didn't need more light. I knew the steps to this porch like the back of my hand. Maybe even like the front of my hand.

In another three seconds I was rapping on Winton's door and waiting for a shouted "Be right there," approaching footsteps, or light visible through the hairline space between the door and the top of the frame.

Nothing. Not even that faint and distant vibration signaling the movement of someone creeping to the window to check out the visitor.

I hopped from the porch and scanned the lot for Winton's car. The space formerly mine was empty. But that meant nothing. If Winton suspected the all-night caller might come by, he'd create the illusion that he was out by parking on the street and making a stealthy approach to his unit.

I checked the second-floor window above the door, Winton's bedroom window. Not a trace of light, not even the weak glow of a computer screen or a thin slice of brightness at the edge of a curtain.

On the chance that he was skulking, I hopped up on the porch, knocked again, and called out, "It's Barbara. Your neighbor." In an effort to make it clear that I wasn't the stalker, I added, "Mrs. Ballantine asked me to invite you to brunch."

No response.

I pressed my ear against the door and heard only that rush and swish you get when you hold a seashell or a cup against the side of your head.

Either Winton was out or deep in a drugged sleep or playing possum better than I ever had.

So, on to Plan B—leave a note on his door.

Writing the note was easy. Finding tape to attach it wasn't.

Two weeks ago, before Dave started shuttling over boxes and bags and bits of furniture, the tape dispenser had been in plain sight beside the printer in the office. Now a notepad with Allison's doodling and a pile of pistachio shells occupied that space.

I put "don't mess with my stuff" on the mental list of issues that needed to be addressed and searched drawers, bookshelves, the floor, and the row of open but unpacked boxes along the wall. "Get this crap put away" went on my list along with "note contents on boxes headed for storage." Four boxes labeled simply "junk" were three too many.

When I found myself whistling and calling "Here, tape, come on out," I abandoned the search and went for the wide silver stuff stowed in the plastic caddy behind the cleaning products under the sink. Two inches remained. I got out my mental notes and added "If you use something up, put it on the shopping list."

I suspected Dave depleted the tape repairing the toes of his running shoes. I further suspected he'd argue that, since two inches remained, technically he hadn't used it up.

I sighed, spotted the brimming trash can, and sighed again. Dave and Allison generated a lot of trash, trash that apparently remained invisible to them. Might as well take it out before it started to smell like Aston's classroom.

Because the garbage bins stood at the far end of the parking lot, I locked the door as I went out. With the bulky bag slapping my bare leg, and something I didn't want to think about sloshing in the bottom, it was too risky to leap the hedge.

I walked three sides of a square from my door to Winton's, checking his parking space as I went. Still empty.

I tapped on his door again anyway, then tore the scrap of silver tape in two and anchored the note top and bottom.

As I lifted the garbage sack once more, a woman's voice asked, "Who the hell are you? What are you doing here?"

Chapter 26

"I'm Barbara Reed," I blurted, peering into the wedge of shadow from which the voice emerged. "I live here."

"No you don't. Winton lives alone."

Her voice was low but edgy, decisive but with a manic ribbon of uncertainty running through it. If that reflected her mental state, this wasn't a conversation I wanted to prolong.

"Yes, you're right, he does live alone. When I said 'here,' I meant I live in the condo complex. Next door."

"How convenient for you."

Her tone was laced with caustic contempt.

"And how convenient for Winton," she went on. "I should have known he was seeing someone else. Although you're not his type at all. You're too short and plain and dumpy."

Short was a given.

Plain? Okay, I'd accept that.

But dumpy? I refused to own that adjective. I resented being called anything beyond "healthy" or "well-nourished" or even "a little plump."

Sucking in my stomach, I stretched my spine in an attempt to appear taller and thinner. Every response that blasted into my brain seemed not only wrong, but risky as well, so I remained clam. (That's calm, but with silence.)

A shadow moved within the wedge of darkness and a figure emerged onto Winton's lawn.

It was the boy Dario and I saw on the trail.

No. It wasn't.

The tasseled hat was gone, eyebrows were evident, cheekbones stood out, and blond hair whisked against shoulders.

The boy was a woman.

A woman with a gun.

A gun pointing at me.

Raising the sack of garbage as a shield, I backed up against Winton's door.

She stepped closer, hair glowing in the dim light, hair like Penelope's.

But this wasn't Penelope.

She was familiar, though. I'd definitely seen her before.

Where?

Eyes aching, I strained to scan the parking lot. Why was there never anyone around when I needed help? And why did I have the only car in the lot without an alarm I could set off from here?

"What does your little love note say?" the woman asked in a taunting voice.

I wiggled my right foot from my sandal, raised it, and drummed my heel against the base of Winton's door. The impact made almost no noise but perhaps the vibration would annoy him enough so he would at least peek out the window. *If* he was home. "Uh, it says I'd appreciate it if he'd answer his phone or—"

"I bet you would." Her voice rose and sharpened. "I bet you and Winton have a lot to talk about. When you're not involved in other activities."

My first rule of dating was "Don't go out with anyone who weighs less than you do" so I would never give even a passing thought to engaging in "other activities" with Winton. But apparently she had. And, if I read the suspicion and jealousy in her tone correctly, they'd done more than think about those activities.

Which made her the woman I saw with him twice in the past week.

She stepped closer and held out her free hand. "Give me the note."

Clutching the garbage to my chest while drumming with my heel, I groped with my left hand. My fingers touched the paper. I tore it loose.

Gun leveled at the center of the sack of garbage, she snatched the note and squinted at it. Her right hand gripped the gun, knuckles gleaming in the gloom.

It wasn't a big gun, but I doubted my internal organs would say, "Hey, hold back on the blood loss, it's only a small caliber slug." In fact, hadn't I read somewhere that small caliber slugs can bounce around inside the body and do a lot of damage? Not a comforting thought. I hoped I was mistaken.

"What's this about the walls being thin?" She shook the paper. "What does that mean?"

"The builder skimped on insulation. When the phone rings in Winton's bedroom, Allison hears it in hers."

"Who's Allison?"

"My boyfriend's daughter." I raised my voice and drummed harder with my heel. Maybe someone in Mrs. B's condo would feel the vibration.

"Boyfriend? Huh." The gun wobbled, veered to the side, then swung back. "How do you know it's the phone in Winton's bedroom?"

Crap.

The truth would probably *not* set me free.

"I used to live in that condo." I slammed my aching heel into the door one last time. "Winton bought it from me in December."

She crumpled the note and spiked it to the walk. "So, this has been going on since then." The gun came up, aimed at my head. "You've been cheating on your boyfriend and Winton's been cheating on me."

And you've been cheating on someone else.

I bit my tongue so the words couldn't bolt from my brain. This was no time for pointing out flaws in her logic or playing devil's advocate. This was no time to insist Winton wasn't my type. This was the time to run. Actually, this was the *ideal* time to run.

But Ms. Irrational Behavior blocked my escape. And she, I now realized, was Mrs. Ron Weador, Kymberli to her friends.

Holy Traditional Values.

The wife of Mr. Family, Law, and Order was waving a gun because she believed I was sleeping with her lover. If I wrote fiction for a living, I couldn't make this up.

"Admit it!" Her voice ratcheted up another notch, going from creepy to crazy. "Admit you're cheating with Winton!"

I scanned the parking lot again. Still no one in sight. And no sound of an approaching car. Only a dull and distant clanging.

"Admit it or I'll shoot you!"

And if I admitted it, she *wouldn't* shoot me?

I hugged the sack of garbage closer. I had no illusion that it could stop a bullet, but something in the sack might deflect the shot.

Deflect.

Mrs. Ballantine's suggestion. A possible way to control a confrontation.

I chomped on my tongue while I thought. Couldn't say, "Don't shoot me." That put us into head-on conflict. Had to say something to throw her off balance.

"I will. I'll shoot you. Don't think I won't."

Ah. Grounds for agreement. Nothing throws an opponent off balance like agreement.

"I know you will. I don't doubt that. But are you sure you want to do it here? Like this?"

The gun wavered.

"I mean, there's the noise issue. Someone might hear the shot and see you before you get away. You and your husband have been on TV a lot in the past few days."

"That wasn't my idea. I'm trying to stop that. I hate those lights and cameras and endless, boring speeches. And I really hate smiling." She massaged the corners of her mouth with her thumb and forefinger. "I'm getting wrinkles. The minute he's elected, I'm filing for divorce."

That answered the question about what went on in Kymberli Weador's head. Too bad I probably wouldn't be alive to tell Mrs. B and Brenda that I had the scoop. "I don't blame you. I could never be a political wife. But the point is that if people hear the shot, someone might recognize you."

She frowned.

A trio of distant clangs marked time. They came from somewhere at the end of the complex.

"And then there's this sack of garbage. I'll probably fall on it. The plastic is pretty flimsy, so it will break. There's really nasty stuff sloshing around in here."

In a show-and-tell move, I shook the sack. "It will make a mess. Someone walking their dog or coming home from a date will see it or smell it."

More likely they'd smell me. I'd heard muscles let loose when you croak.

Yuck.

"Someone might call the police—maybe before you have time to establish an alibi."

Her frown deepened. The gun didn't waver.

"If I threw the garbage in a trash bin, it would solve that problem." I pointed past the trash containers. "And down that way there's an isolated spot along the river trail. You could shoot me there." I took a deep breath and enumerated the selling points of the area. "It's dark, and if you kick my body under a shrub, it could be days before anyone finds me."

That closed the deal.

She aimed the gun toward the trash containers. "Get moving. Not too fast."

That last bit fit right in with my plan.

Well, it wasn't exactly a plan. It was more of a single idea than a plan, or maybe the first—and so far only—step of a plan. But it was all I had.

One sandal was off already. I left it at Winton's door, hoping she wouldn't notice that or spot my clumsy attempt to walk as if I still had it on.

She didn't.

I lowered the garbage sack to hide my naked foot as I descended the shallow steps, pretended to stumble, and shook off the second sandal. I doubted Allison would look for me when she returned—she'd assume I was asleep or next door and go up to her room. But Dave surely would hunt for me so he could unload about his day. Maybe his cop training and instincts would lead him from the open cabinet doors beneath the sink, to the garbage pail without a fresh liner, to the conclusion that I'd gone to the trash bins. When he came out to see why I was taking so long he'd spot my sandals and . . .

Or maybe he'd slam his knee against the open cabinet on the way to the refrigerator for a beer, curse, and flop on the sofa with the remote in his hand.

My hopes plummeted. My life depended on a guy who drank from the OJ container and kicked his dirty socks under the sofa. My future hung on whether he'd notice that the garbage pail wasn't lined.

I was doomed.

At the pace of a funeral march, I made my way along the sidewalk at the edge of the parking lot. Pebbles and twigs dug into the soles of my feet and clumps of soggy grass squished between my toes. Jake hadn't swept the walk after he mowed. What a surprise.

Kymberli Weador took up a position beside me. "If we see someone, I'll talk about the summer sales at the mall. You

239

better do a good job with your end of the conversation or I'll kill that person, too."

Great. Now I was responsible for another life. Wasn't it bad enough that I'd die barefooted? That she'd kick me under a bush to rot? That my last conversation would be about shopping?

Freaked out by the present, my mind leaped into the past, to my teen years. Back then, my experience with death consisted of my brother's heroic demise while saving women trapped in a burning dormitory, and the deaths of characters in books and on the screen. Women in tear-jerking films like *Love Story*, *Terms of Endearment*, and *Steel Magnolias*, were cherished by friends and family. They went out of this world gracefully.

That was a far cry from listening to a killer prattle about slashed prices on camisoles, then being stuffed under a bush. Possibly the same bush Cheese Puff hunched under earlier today.

Frightened as I was, that hacked me off. And being angry kicked my brain into the present again.

That clanging sounded louder now, but there was still no hint of an approaching car, no footsteps, no doors opening or closing. For a Friday night, this place was a morgue.

Poor choice of words.

I'd end up at the morgue unless help arrived or I got out of this on my own.

The sidewalk made a gentle turn. The clanging grew louder. The trash containers loomed ahead.

On any other night, I would have cut across the parking lot to shorten the journey with a sloshing sack of garbage—a sack growing heavier by the minute. Tonight I kept to the walk, buying time.

Kymberli Weador didn't seem to notice. Perhaps she was the kind of person who walked the short legs of the triangle instead of the hypotenuse. Or perhaps her mind was on other things.

She seemed distant, but not distracted. Edgy, but in control. Like she knew this territory. Like she killed before.

Not that I was an expert on the homicidal mind, although I'd encountered two killers—Hillary Dunne and Susan Mitchell. Hillary had been fueled by steroid-induced rage and Susan by lofty educational goals. What fueled this woman?

We passed beneath a lamppost. Her blond hair shone. The stubby gun barrel glittered.

My brain leaped to a conclusion. My mouth blurted it. "You killed Brendon Ryder."

Crap!

Way to make sure she wouldn't change her mind about killing me.

"I had to," she said in the casual way Paulette might say she had to buy a sweater or a new pair of shoes. I found her tone more frightening than her words. "Ron said the case was an embarrassment to his campaign."

"And Iz? Was she another embarrassment?"

"A big embarrassment. If I find her, I'll finish her."

I clamped my teeth to prevent another blurt. Kymberli Weador had come here hunting Winton. She didn't know Iz was in the condo next door to his, maybe didn't know Iz was my sister. Two tiny positive points.

I hugged the sack of garbage.

Not a good idea. Something poked the soft flesh above my waistband. Something else squished and popped.

I let up the pressure, laced my fingers through the plastic ties, and dragged the bag. If it broke, someone might notice the trail of trash.

"Ron *has* to be elected. If he's not, he'll run for something else and insist I stand by him. He'll fight the divorce. Then I can't be with Winton. I *have* to be with Winton."

241

An especially loud clang rang out and she raised her voice. "Winton is so strong. So fascinating. So passionate. He's the only man I ever loved. The only man I ever *will* love."

Apparently there was a heck of a lot to Winton I never noticed. Or—no offense to Winton—this woman was deranged.

Well, duh.

We were almost to the end of the condo complex. Almost opposite the trash containers. Almost to the right angle in the sidewalk.

I glanced over my shoulder. Not a set of headlights in sight. Not even a stray cat. Not even a—

"Worthless piece of garbage," a male voice shouted.

Glass shattered.

A huge wrench spun from the window above us and struck Kymberli Weador on the shoulder.

Chapter 27

She staggered and stretched out her arms for balance.

"Useless piece of crap."

A drill trailing an electrical cord followed the wrench from the upstairs window.

Kymberli ducked.

I planted my right foot and swung the sack of garbage like it was a bat and her head was a fast ball in the strike zone.

Half an hour later, Detective Charles Atwell surveyed the arc of trash spread out on the lawn of the foreclosed unit. "What the hell was in that sack?"

"What the hell wasn't?" I gave Dave the stink eye and pointed as I enumerated. "A half-full can of cola. A bottle of shampoo. A couple of sprouting potatoes. A jar of pickled corn. Tomorrow we're going to have a loonnnggg talk about emptying cans and containers, the rules of recycling, *and* adjustments in behavior."

Dave tucked his head. "Allison decided she doesn't like lemon shampoo. The cola can slipped when I was aiming for the recycling. The potatoes were spongy. And I thought I'd like that pickled corn, but it tasted weird. Kind of like week-old shrimp."

"See, this is what I'm talking about. The cans should be drained and rinsed and put in the recycling container. Someone at the gym might like lemon shampoo. And *you know* Jim

243

collects organic materials for the community garden compost project."

Dave flashed an apologetic smile and dug the toe of his shoe into the grass. The lawn was soggy from the deluge that burst from the broken window of the foreclosed unit.

I wasn't surprised that Jake hadn't turned off the water in the unit before beginning his plumbing adventure. But for once I was thrilled by his incompetence.

Dazed and drenched, Kymberli didn't realize it was the drill I held against her neck when I ordered her to drop the gun. And she didn't fight when I tied her to a lamppost with the electrical cord.

Thanks to more than a dozen residents who responded to my shrieks and called the police, a patrol car arrived within minutes. Thanks to her husband's many news conferences, three residents recognized Kymberli without even a hint from me. Thanks to the wonder of social media, pictures of her were already on the Internet. And thanks to her insistence that someone call Dick McBain because he would let her go once she explained why she had to kill Brendon Ryder and take a shot at Iz, I doubted the world's greatest spin doctor could salvage McBain's job aspirations or her husband's campaign.

"What do you suppose the captions will say?" Mrs. Ballantine speculated from one of the chairs Dario and Jim had positioned behind the police tape strung across the parking lot. "Killer walloped by waste?"

"Trashed by trash," Penelope suggested.

"Laid low by litter," Iz contributed.

"Cops got a break, thanks to Jake." My ex strutted up to the tape and cocked his finger at me. "Admit it, Barbie, I saved your life."

"Purely by accident," Iz said with a snarl.

"In the process of destroying that unit," Penelope added. "You're lucky I cut the power and Jim shut off the water before the ceiling caved in."

"Hey, I almost had that shower fixed. All I needed was a bigger bit for my drill."

"Like no man ever said that before," Iz muttered.

Penelope giggled, Mrs. B smiled, and Jim and Dario guffawed. Sybil frowned and cocked her head, and Verna blushed and whispered that she'd explain later.

Jake scowled at my sister, then slapped on a smarmy smile as Bernina Burke arrived wearing jeans and a loose sage green T-shirt. She ignored Jake and halted beside Penelope. "Thanks again for helping with damage control."

"Happy to do it," Penelope said.

"I almost had it fixed," Jake insisted. "All I needed—"

"What you need is to find another job and another place to stay." With a deep sigh, Bernina turned to face him. "The condo association has been very patient, but you're not cut out for this job."

"Or any job," Iz said in a hoarse whisper.

"Except a con job," Dave added.

Jake frowned. "But I was trying—"

"Yes, Jake," Mrs. Ballantine said, "you've been very trying. But you'd be much happier in a job that wasn't so demanding, in a situation where you weren't required to work long hours and have so many people reviewing your performance."

"I would," Jake agreed. "This job was hard. Harder than my three days in the Marines."

Dave rolled his eyes. "Three days?"

I shrugged. "First I heard about that. I'm surprised he made it to three."

"I'm stunned they took him at all."

"Well, he talks a good game. And he was probably in good condition."

Dave pulled me against his side and lowered his voice. "You want good condition? Let's leave the rest of this to Chuck and go to our place. I'll show you good condition."

"Get that soggy carpet and pad out of there," Bernina told Jake. "You can think about your future while you're doing it."

Iz opened her mouth to comment, then let it go and grasped Penelope's arm. "Show's over. I'm tired."

With Sybil assisting, my sister stood and flashed me a victory sign. "Nice going." Then she shuffled off with her entourage, Jim lugging a stack of chairs.

"Couldn't have done better myself." Dario piled up the remaining chairs. "You're all right, kid."

Footsteps pounded along the sidewalk and Allison darted into view with Josh right behind. She skidded to a stop at the police tape, eyes wide. "I'm sorry I'm late, but I have a really good reason so you can't ground me and— What's going on? What did I miss? Why does this whole place smell like that icky shampoo I threw away?"

"That," Dave said, "will be part of a long discussion."

"Tonight?" Allison wailed.

"Tomorrow." Dave kissed my neck. "I have other plans for tonight."

Sunday afternoon the Committee held a celebration barbecue on the deck. Iz sat in a lounge chair, holding court as Penelope waited on her. Half a dozen women clustered around, including Denise Ryder wearing a loose cotton shift and bandages on her legs. Paulette was back from Seattle and throwing herself into the Bernina Burke makeover project with a suitcase full of fabric swatches, color wheels, lipstick samples, hairstyle magazines, and an assortment of pots, tubes, and jars.

Denise's twin girls sat cross-legged on either side of the suitcase, sipping from juice boxes, giggling, and painting their toenails—and a good portion of their toes—with glittery polish from tiny bottles. They seemed oblivious to the baleful glares Iz launched at the suitcase and occasionally at Paulette. Iz, of course, seemed oblivious to the fact that she indulged in her own forms of body decoration—the former Mohawk and several tattoos.

You go, girls, I thought. Try it all out. Decide for yourselves what you like and what makes you feel special. Notice that no matter how much she scowls, Iz doesn't tangle with Paulette. Absorb the lesson that you can be tiny and pretty *and* powerful.

Jake, who had ambled up from the river trail and announced he knew he hadn't been invited and would fix a plate and get on his way, watched Paulette as she wielded a brush and a palette of eye shadow. "I'd be good at selling stuff like that," he told me.

I groaned, imagining the lonely women of Reckless River finding Jake on their doorsteps with one of his smarmy smiles and a satchel of perfume samples. They'd be flattered, flirted with, and fleeced.

"I hear it takes a long time to start making enough money to live well," I improvised. "Instead of getting a job, wouldn't it be easier to go back to jail until your trial?"

"Can I do that?" Jake had the expression of a kid promised a pony ride or a trip to the ballpark. "Will they let me?"

"I don't know. But those guys might."

I led him over to Dave and Chuck—I finally thought of him as Chuck—who stood by the grill conferring with Jim and Dario about the correct time to flip a burger and the best height from the burner for marinated chicken breasts. "Jake's wondering if the jail is still full."

Chuck and Dave guffawed. Dario snorted. Jim did an end-zone dance.

I left them to it and watched Sybil and Verna flutter around the tables arranging and rearranging colorful plates and bowls containing summer salads, chips, condiments, fruit, and cookies. Allison and Josh, with only a little prodding, had taken the dogs for a long walk to tire them out and reduce the chances Cheese Puff might repeat that unfortunate prosciutto incident.

That left me free to go to the door when Winton James rang the bell.

He was bent by the weight of his burden—four boxes of chocolates, two bottles of rum, three sacks of cheesy snacks, and an enormous canister of premium cashews. "Mrs. Ballantine invited me. I come bearing gifts and apologies for what Kymberli Weador did."

Salivating like one of Pavlov's pups, I flung the door wide and ushered him along the hallway. "You didn't have to. There's no need. It wasn't your fault."

"Not your fault at all." Mrs. B helped offload his offerings.

"I should have realized how unstable she was. But I was kind of . . ." He paused, a flush spreading across his sallow cheeks and rising to the roots of his pale hair. "It blew me away. Women like her can have their pick. They *never* pick me."

"Then those women are short-sighted." Mrs. B stripped the plastic seal from the canister of nuts, poured half into a blue glass bowl, and handed the canister to me. "You need a different kind of woman, one who shares your interests *outside* of the bedroom."

"I met her nine days ago in the parking lot at the liquor store. We were in the bedroom only once." Winton flushed a deeper shade of pink and lowered his voice. "It was intense and . . . well, a little scary."

Mrs. B patted his arm. "A man likes to feel he has some control."

Winton's cheeks turned the color of borscht. "When she told me she was married, I tried to break it off right away, but she kept calling. So I checked into a hotel." He stooped to peer into my eyes. "I never thought—"

"Why would you?" I popped a giant cashew between my lips. I deserved it. I'd almost been worm food. "Don't beat up on yourself."

"She could have killed you."

"But she didn't."

"And now Barbara has another story to tell," Mrs. B said with a chuckle. "Although it's not quite as dramatic as her sister's."

"I'm to blame for that, too," Winton said. "Iz must hate me."

"I doubt it." Mrs. B shook the bowl of cashews. "That bullet gave her a million dollars worth of free publicity. She should thank you."

"That'll never happen." I popped another cashew. "No matter how much pearl power you generate."

"You're probably right, dear. Even pearl power has its limits." Mrs. B took Winton's arm. "Shall we go outside and get a drink?"

He shook his head. "I can't stay. I have to pack. I'm moving to Texas."

I swallowed. "But you just got here a few months ago!"

"I got an offer that's too good to pass up." He backed toward the door. "And this seems like a good time to get out of town."

"Can't blame you." I saluted him with another cashew. "See you at the trial."

"We'll talk tomorrow," Mrs. B told him. "About your unit."

Winton nodded and left. "What about his unit?" I asked.

"I think I ought to buy it. We'll need the space."

"You and Dario?"

"Oh no, dear. You and Dave and Allison. And the baby."

"What baby?"

I spotted Allison and Josh coming up the steps from the river trail. "If Allison is pregnant, Dave will—"

"Not Allison. You."

"Me?"

I clutched the canister like a life preserver. "I'm not anywhere near ready to have a baby. I don't even have a real job. Besides, Dave drinks out of the orange juice carton and kicks his dirty socks under the sofa. Allison's a drama queen. And you know what a fantastic job I've done training my dog."

Mrs. B waved that aside and headed for the deck. "There's nothing like a baby to make you grow up fast."

I rolled my eyes. Having Allison hadn't made Dave's wife focus on more than her own needs and desires. Having two babies at once hadn't made Brendon Ryder grow up and stop beating his wife. Having kids hadn't given Dick McBain the maturity necessary to be a leader. "You're a wild-eyed optimist."

"About you," she called back, "always."

Chapter 28

Monday morning Big Chill slapped a substitute form on the desk in front of me. "Thanks a heap. You've subjected us to another year of buckskin, BO, and BS."

"Aston is staying?"

"Yes. The administration is thrilled."

She said "thrilled" the way most of us say "infected" or "contaminated."

"But he's a good teacher. He makes history come alive. Kids like him."

"Kids are *amused* by him." She tapped the form. "You'll be seeing a lot of *these* next year. You talked yourself out of a job."

"Huh?"

"Brian has been wanting out of English for years. The administrators planned to shift him to history and hire you."

Dang it!

I felt a sinking sense of loss and then, instead of self-loathing, a buoyant feeling of satisfaction. I did the right thing—for the team, for Aston, and for myself. A job that came my way because he left in a huff would have misgivings attached—more baggage piled on while I was attempting to cast baggage aside. And getting a classroom ready, creating lesson plans, and setting up a grading system would eat into my time with Dave. What with merging households, working at the auto repair shop, and somehow getting Allison to realize the rules of the road were there for a reason, I didn't need that stress as well.

"You never know, someone might pack it in before the end of the summer." Big Chill tapped the signature line on the form. "I'll give you a call if something opens up."

I bent to sign the form and saw my assignment. "Band? Again? Isn't that cruel and unusual punishment?"

"I prefer to call it an average day of subbing at Captain Meriwether High." Big Chill laughed. "Let's face it. You thrive on a mix of drudgery, distress, and danger."

She had a point. I was far stronger—in many ways—than a year ago. "I may thrive on it, but that doesn't mean I'm wild about it."

"You'd be certifiably crazy if you were." She ripped off the bottom copy of the form and handed it to me. "If nothing opens up, shall I expect to see you right here when school starts in September?"

I stuffed the form into my briefcase and nodded.

Her eyes twinkled.

"Shall I expect you to be on time?"

I shrugged. "Within a few minutes."

She smiled. "Shall I expect you to accept your assignments without whining?"

Laughing, I dug for my earplugs. "Oh, grow up."

Carolyn J. Rose grew up in New York's Catskill Mountains, graduated from the University of Arizona, logged two years in Arkansas with Volunteers in Service to America, and spent 25 years as a television news researcher, writer, producer, and assignment editor in Arkansas, New Mexico, Oregon, and Washington. She founded the Vancouver Writers' Mixers and is an active supporter of her local bookstore, Cover to Cover. Her interests are reading, gardening, and NOT cooking.

Website: www.deadlyduomysteries.com

Blog: http://deadlyduoduhblog.blogspot.com/

Also by Carolyn J. Rose

No Substitute for Murder
No Substitute for Money
Hemlock Lake
Through a Yellow Wood
An Uncertain Refuge
Sea of Regret
A Place of Forgetting

With Mike Nettleton
Drum Warrior
Death at Devil's Harbor
Deception at Devil's Harbor
The Paladin mysteries to be re-released in 2014

8372943R00140

Made in the USA
San Bernardino, CA
06 February 2014